SCARLETT M. HONEY

BENEATH THE FAE MOON'S FIRE

AN EPIC ROMANTIC FANTASY

CROWN OF EVERGUARD
BOOK 2

Copyright © 2025 by Scarlett M. Honey

www.scarlettmhoney.com

Scarlett M. Honey asserts the moral right to be identified as the author of this work.

All rights reserved.

No part of this publication may be reproduced, distributed, or transmitted in any form or by any means, including photocopying, recording, or other electronic or mechanical methods, without the prior written permission of the publisher, except as permitted by U.S. copyright law. For permission requests, contact Scarlett M. Honey via Dragon in a Teacup Publishing.

The story, all names, characters, and incidents portrayed in this production are fictitious. No identification with actual persons (living or deceased), places, buildings, and products is intended or should be inferred.

First printing, 2025

Print paperback ISBN 979-8-9922964-3-3

Print hardcover ISBN 979-8-9922964-4-0

EBOOK ISBN 979-8-9922964-5-7

Cover design by INK Designs

Edited by Claire Bradshaw

For all my sisters—by birth and by choice. The ones I've known forever, and the ones I've yet to meet—you make me whole.

For Sloane, whose endless confidence makes my heart sing.

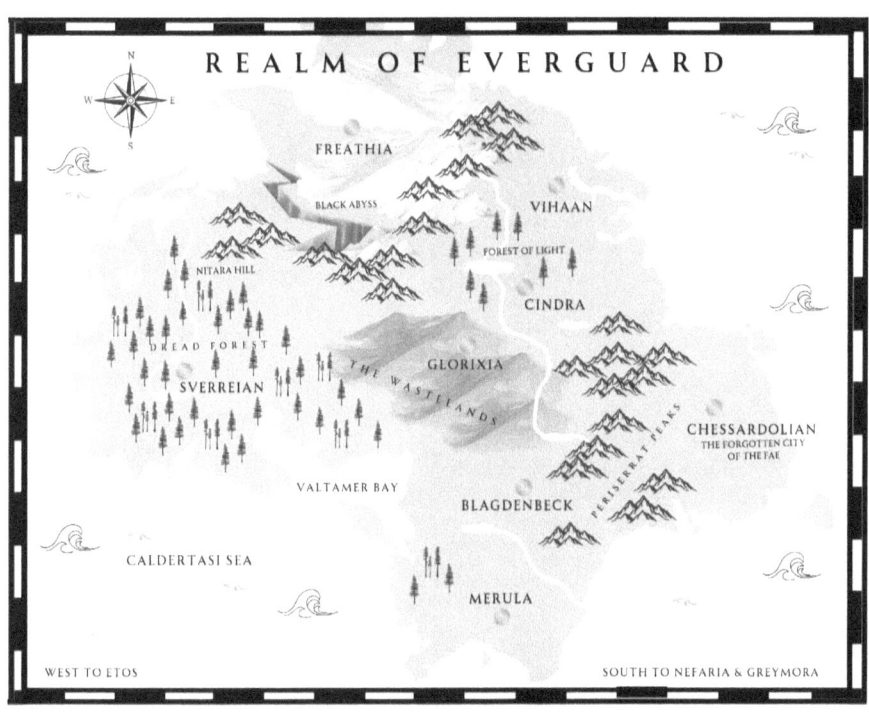

Note from the Author

Hey there, reader!

Just a heads-up: this book has some spicy scenes, some intense fight scenes, and a few characters might not make it out alive. So, if you're looking for something light and fluffy, this might not be the book for you.

But if you're up for an epic fantasy adventure with some sizzling scenes and maybe a few tears along the way, then buckle up!

Fair warning: There's gonna be some steamy stuff, so you know... reader discretion is advised.

I hope you enjoy the ride!

Chapter One

"*You're my muse... I can't live without you.*"

Thaddeus' voice, a chilling echo, twists into a grotesque parody as his blood, hot and slick, drips from my hands. I stare at my trembling fingers, unsure if the tremor is from the biting cold or the sheer, numbing shock of what I just did. The flashback of his body lying sprawled upon the damp forest floor, his skin already taking on an ashen hue, and my dagger, an angry, defiant shard of steel, sprouting crudely from his eye.

Thaddeus was here, and he was with me for one reason only. Though it had nothing to do with feeling anything for me.

And now he's gone.

The uneven earth seems to fight each footstep. In the absolute darkness, I can't tell if I'm placing my foot on a soft patch of moss or a treacherous tree root. Between my halting, stumbling steps and the hot tears blurring my vision, my progress is agonizingly slow.

I want to scream. For Baylor. For Gryphon or Licia. But Thaddeus' vicious threat still claws at my ears, and my neck still throbs, raw and bruised, from where his cold fingers held me, making sure I understood the deadly consequences.

Finally, through the shifting shadows of tree branches, the fire's orange glow pulses into view. A silhouette stands before it, unmistakably Baylor's strong outline. My arms shoot up, waving frantically, desperate. But Baylor's back is to me. He can't see me. Where are Licia and Gryphon? I can't see past the small, flickering circle of light.

A branch snaps sharply underfoot. Baylor's head whips around. I can't make out his face in the dim light, but I watch as his relaxed shoulders snap rigid, instantly alert.

I launch myself forward, my movements heavy, sluggish. Every muscle screams in protest, but I have to close the distance. I have to get away from the dark, whispering treeline and into our open clearing.

"What the fuck, Roe?" Baylor's voice, rough with concern, is a sudden, unexpected anchor. His warm, familiar arms wrap around me as I barrel into him. He doesn't falter, holding me steady, his thick arms enclosing me in his embrace.

A wracking, guttural sob tears from my chest, muffled by his shirt. His arms clench tighter around me. I can feel the tension in his body, the unknown threat he's instinctively scanning the darkness for, his chin grazing the top of my head.

I allow myself only one moment to fall apart. Now is not the time. Baylor needs information. And we need to get out of here. Our night of rest is definitely over.

I take a shaky step back, warmth still radiating from Baylor's hands as they grip my shoulders. He searches my face, the furrow in his brow deepening with my stunned silence. "Thaddeus?" he prompts, his gaze flicking past my shoulder, searching the dark wood behind me.

"Thaddeus."

That single word is all I can voice. An icy chill swims up and down my spine at the memory of his cold fingers around my neck. His arrogant swagger as he confided his *true* reason for being here. For getting close.

"Ombretta isn't who we thought she was, or hoped she was. She's queen. Queen of the North." My words stumble out as I try to even out my breathing. "She wants me to be the one—my blood, instead of hers. She's strong, not weak."

I can't stand still any longer. The image of him lying so peacefully on the ground, as if merely asleep, except for the dagger protruding from his eye socket, is too vivid. I shove my bedroll into my pack, attempting to drive down the frenzied panic taking over by recounting what just happened in the woods to Baylor over my shoulder.

"He tried to take me. To go to the North without you and Licia and Gryphon." My whole body goes rigid, a shuddering echo of the squelching sound my dagger made as it slid straight through his eye replaying in my head. "And then I stabbed him."

"Thaddeus is dead?" Baylor's steady eyes snap from my face to the forest, confirming Thaddeus is not walking out behind me.

"He didn't move. I stabbed him. And he just lay there. He didn't move." My words come out halted, distraught, a raw string of disbelief as another shudder rolls through my body, his prone form flashing through my mind again.

As my sorry tale ends, Baylor douses the fire. "I'll ready the horses. You grab Gryphon and Licia's things. Where did they get off to?" He takes a step toward where he left the horses to rest, but I grab his wrist.

"Please. Don't leave me." I look around us in the dark, my voice raw and crazed with fear. The embers left of the fire are not enough to even light our faces, but I think he hears the panic in my voice.

"I thought our camp was just over here." Gryphon's whisper sounds from the other side of camp. "Look what you do to me. You've got me all turned around."

A muffled laugh rises from the darkness, along with the sound of soft kisses. "I'll gladly take the credit, but you wouldn't be able to find your way out of a glass jar."

"We're over here. Hurry up, you two. We're leaving." Baylor's tone is all business.

"What?" Gryphon and Licia question in unison, both now stiff and alert, trying to make sense of Baylor's words. "What about sleep?" Gryphon asks. "I thought you said we're far enough from the castle that they won't find us here."

"Now." The word leaves no room for questions. And they move accordingly. Licia grabs both their bedrolls, and Gryphon grabs what's in my hands to take over to the horses. "You'll sleep on the road. Gryphon, you stay with Roe while I ready the horses."

I can feel the question in Gryphon's gaze, but I'm thankful for the shroud of darkness. I can't say it all again. Not right now.

He reaches for me, though, and when his firm grip finds my shaking hands, he knows enough. He doesn't need more of an explanation than this. "Lys, hurry. And bring one of those blankets over here. She's ice-cold." He rubs his hands up and down my arms, the friction creating a warmth I don't feel.

We ride through the night at a fast clip, and I think Baylor would've had us continue if he weren't such a softy for his horses. But as the sun rises fully, he slows us near a stream and jumps off his horse. The water curves around the land, creating a safe pocket. One where we'll be able to see anyone approach well before they're upon us.

"The horses need a break," Baylor says unnecessarily. I stay mounted, though, not wanting to get down. This place is different enough from where we were hours ago, but I can still feel his phantom hands around my neck, lifting me off the ground and restricting my air, leaving me unable to scream, unable to breathe.

"Let's let Navi rest," Licia says, patting the horse's white nose, as Gryphon's hands close around my waist, deftly lifting me down. "You need to rest, too."

Licia guides me to my bedroll, which she's already laid out between the small fire Gryphon's building and the curve of the stream. She's placed my blankets between hers and Gryphon's. So close there's no grass peeking through. That's a small comfort as I settle down between them.

As I watch Licia move toward the stream, my eyes catch on Baylor, who's brushing down the horses by the water. His eyes keep flicking over to me as if at any moment I could burst into flames. Or tears. And that's not too far from the truth.

Licia sits in front of me, a bowl and cloth in hand. She dips the cloth in the bowl and brings it to my face, gently dabbing at my cheekbone and up to my hairline. A shiver courses through me as I realize what she is cleaning off.

She begins slowly, "Do you want to tell me—"

I cut her off with a sharp shake of my head. It's too soon. I can't recount it. I can't think of all that Thaddeus represents right now. But she persists.

"Do you want to tell me why we're on this adventure in the first place?"

I forgot she didn't know. She's here in blind support of me. And the fact that she gets to spend all her time with Gryphon sweetens the deal.

I'm so tired. The last time I slept was on the floor, propped up against the door, miserably waiting for Killian to return and take me to a wedding that was never to be. But it's the same for everyone here. And they're still going because of me. Because I said I was strong enough to do this for our people. My people. Because of their belief that I'm something more.

Licia deserves to know. So I brush off the tiredness for just a little longer and smile to myself, knowing this will bring us closer together. It just drove Killian and me further apart.

"We left the castle so we could rescue my sister."

I look up to gauge her response. Her brows knit together and her lips purse, but her head tilts in a way that invites me to continue. So I do, knowing she's here for me, for the bond between us.

Licia doesn't interrupt once as I tell her what I've learned since I returned to the castle. She doesn't even flinch when I mention Ombretta. That Thaddeus led me to believe she needed me to save her, which is what put everything in motion so quickly.

I smile up at her when I finish, ready for the snarky comment I know is coming. But the shock and disgust staring back at me is anything but the response I thought Licia would have when I finally told her.

"You're Fae?" Her nose scrunches, just slightly, as if she's trying to hide a snarl.

Suddenly, I don't know how to respond. I thought she'd be surprised, but would take it in stride. Back in Merula, she jumped in front of us so she could come with us. She's been so supportive since I've been back at the castle. She's my best friend.

But her hand comes away from my face with a wariness. Like if she makes a sudden movement, I'll strike out at her. To her, I'm a feral beast.

"I am, yes. But I'm still your sister." I say each word slowly, with care, but I don't grab for her hand, even though mine is itching to pull her back toward me. "Don't worry. I'm your sister first."

"Oh, I'm not worried." Her eyebrows knit together again, and she wrinkles her nose. "I'm not worried, because if you are who you say you are, you're no sister of mine."

The bowl in her hands spills across my bedroll as she abruptly stands, as if she can't even bear to breathe the same air as me for a moment longer. Gryphon and I share a look, and I'm sure the shock on his face is mirrored on mine.

"Licia, wait!" I call after her, but she's already trekking across the clearing.

Exasperated, I fling myself onto the bedroll. Space. She just needs a little space, and it will all be fine. She can't possibly harbor the same hatred Hadeon and Killian do for the Fae. She's always been able to think for herself. And all her sources—her little birds—wouldn't they tell her what's true about our realm and what's manufactured?

Except that the part that's manufactured was done so by King Hadeon himself. Our father. And it's been a lifetime of lies.

Suddenly, the tug of exhaustion is too strong. Even as I worry over Licia's inability to accept me, the sleep that's been chasing me finally catches up.

"I can't believe you knew all this time!" The sound of Licia's strained whispers penetrates my dreamless slumber. "You knew and never said anything! I know you and Roe go way back, but I thought we were something too. That should count for something." Her voice rises and falls as if she's fighting for control, trying not to yell.

It's fully dark now. I thought I just closed my eyes for a few moments, but it's been longer. I wonder how long Licia and Gryphon have been fighting.

"If I've said it once, I've said it a thousand times. You are my heart. But, Lys, this is bigger than us. I wanted to tell you. Frankly, I'm surprised all your flitting birds didn't figure it out."

I don't want to interrupt, but I also don't want to eavesdrop. I lie frozen in place as Licia and Gryphon move closer. Luckily, I don't have to decide between my curiosity about their budding relationship and my honor, because Baylor's heavy footfalls tread from the shoreline. I have a feeling he's making himself known by exaggerating his steps, because Licia and Gryphon fall silent.

"If you guys are going to bring every guard and vagrant for miles upon us, then we'd better haul out. The horses are rested, and that's good enough for me." He stops beside the embers remaining of the fire, and I can read the exasperation on his face.

"I can't go with *her!*" Licia grates out, and I sit up.

"What do you mean?" I ask, my voice still heavy with sleep. "I'm still me. You're still my sister. Nothing has changed between us."

"Everything has changed between us." She looks between me and Gryphon. "You tricked me!"

Everything in me wants to look at Gryphon for reassurance, but I fight the instinct. I know if I do, it will only get worse.

"Lys." Gryphon says, his tone placating. "What do you want us to do? Take you back to the castle?"

"Yes! That's exactly what I want!" She starts stuffing her bedroll into her pack as if it's decided.

"We can't do that." Baylor's voice is steady and calm, as if Licia is a colt in his stable ready to bolt for its freedom. "And you know it."

"Then I'll get myself back. I don't need you." She starts moving toward the horse she and Gryphon shared. "You said it yourself: the land is crawling with guards. No doubt they'll find me sooner or later and return me to the castle. I can't stay here. I can't remain a moment longer in the presence of a *Fae*."

My shoulders reach my ears as I wince, glancing at Baylor to see how he takes her tone.

He seems unfazed. "I hate to point out the obvious." He struts toward Licia, taking her sneer in stride. "But you didn't have a problem with us hours ago when you begged to come along."

"Everything is different now." She repeats her new mantra, and Baylor rolls his eyes at her, unimpressed with the princess and her tantrum.

"Let's get on the road. We can split hairs along the way. But we're leaving."

Baylor strides back down toward the stream where the horses have been resting, and I look to Licia to see how she feels about being bossed around. She raises an eyebrow, but continues packing her bag.

By the time Baylor returns with the horses ready, we've scattered the remains of the fire and removed any trace of us being here, and then we're riding into the night in silence.

Chapter Two

Only when the first rays of sunlight peek over the horizon do Licia and I speak again. Our horses slow, cautiously maneuvering around the suddenly rocky terrain. Rock formations stand as tall as trees on either side of us, enclosing the path. The sun hasn't yet made its presence fully known, and the cold nips at my fingertips and nose until I can't feel either.

The path opens up again in front of us, and I wish Navi would pick up the pace and get us out of here already. It doesn't feel safe.

I look at Licia. "I'll always be on your side. You know that, right?"

"I get it. I get what you want to do." The horse she and Gryphon are sharing rides up next to mine and hope blossoms in my chest like a flower. A soft, conciliatory smile brightens her face. "But you can't do this, you know." The venom is gone from her tone and has been replaced by a soothing, placating quality. "I know you think you can, because you're full of hope—which I've always loved about you—but this is too far. You can't just ray-of-sunshine your way out of this. It's too much for you."

Her comment hits right where it's intended, and I rub my chest, trying to make room for the pain. Have I been blinded by my hope? Tricked by the very optimism that's kept me afloat all this time?

"I can do this," I insist, but even as I say the words, they shake and bend out of my mouth. "I have you and Gryphon; together we've always gotten ourselves out of any mess."

She shakes her head. Her eyes don't meet mine. "This is bigger than you and me. And as soon as Father finds out, let alone Killian, that'll be the end of all this." She turns in the saddle, holding tight to Gryphon for balance, and waves a hand in the air to indicate our surroundings. Gryphon's spine stiffens.

There may have been a few details I left out in my recount of recent events. Such as Killian locking me in my room or Hadeon taking a sword to my collarbone. And the tiny detail of me driving Hadeon through with a sword.

Now is not the time to fill in the blanks and tell her our father is dead by my hand, so I just nod along with her. At least she's speaking to me. I can work with this. But as I open my mouth to reply, the horses come to an abrupt stop. The hair rises along my arms as the sound of Baylor nocking an arrow fills the air. His taut bowstring matches the tension humming around us.

Lost in my thoughts, I hadn't noticed the change in our surroundings, but as soon as I turn to Baylor and see the way his back straightens while he continuously scans the road, it makes me think he's picking up on something that eludes me. I frantically turn my head from side to side, trying to see what he and Gryphon have sensed.

And then I see what they knew these long, torturous minutes.

Seven of the king's guards step into place, encircling us, leaving nowhere to go. They deftly draw their broadswords as they move closer to our group. Their helmets gleam, and the curling snake sigils of the king on their breastplates glint in the morning sunlight.

"Morning, men. The Wastelands are a little far for your morning excursions, aren't they?" Baylor speaks lightly, but his teasing question is laced with warning. He's pulled his hood up, masking his face for now.

The guards ignore him, marking him as harmless, and turn to us. "Princess Rowandine and Princess Licia, we have orders to return you both to the castle immediately," says a tall guard with dark features and a dark beard. "The king awaits you, along with your betrothed." He eyes Baylor, bow nocked and menacing, and Gryphon with Licia clinging to his back, and then he scoffs, as if he thinks this is just a silly child's attempt to run away, a lovers' tryst. "Your sorry excuse for a quest is no match for us," he tells the men. "It'd be wise of you to return to the castle as well, before the king realizes the princesses didn't act of their own accord."

Surprisingly, Gryphon moves his horse forward and stares down the guards with all the haughtiness of a royal brat. None of his usual playfulness dances in his eyes. "Neither Rowandine nor Licia will be returning with you. It'd be wise..." He pauses to let his tone sink in. "To forget you saw us traveling at all, and return to the castle at once."

For a moment, I think this will work. That Gryphon's demanding tone and noble stature will force these guards to turn and go, empty-handed. But then I remember that these are the king's men. And they do not answer to Gryphon. They'll certainly not leave without us. Not when the two princesses sit before them, and we are easily outnumbered.

The tall guard sizes up Gryphon and Baylor once more, eyes resting on Baylor's hooded figure, as if he's the unknown of the group. He widens his stance and then smiles at his men. In a low growl, he says, "Come with us, ladies." He sneers. Licking his lips like he's about to bite into a juicy leg of lamb. "Or do you think your gentlemen friends are ready to die for you?"

The guards are upon us quickly. They move in so fast that one has grabbed my reins before I even think to reach for my sword. I kick at him with my left foot and try to prod Navi into movement with my right.

Out of the corner of my eye, I see Baylor riding straight at the tall guard and the two men at his sides. He leaps off his horse in one graceful movement and swings his sword in an effortless arcing motion while drawing a short sword with his other hand. His movements are smooth and practiced; there's no hint of the easygoing stable master. The guard closest to him falls to the ground in a heap. The tall guard and his other men spread out, realizing quickly that they have sorely misjudged this fight.

Without a glance toward the fallen, Baylor moves against two more guards, his cherished bow forgotten on his back. Watching him, I distantly wonder when he's had time to learn such skillful swordplay. I'll have to ask him if we make it through this without being dragged back to the castle.

In all the commotion, Gryphon and Licia still sit astride their horse. Gryphon has lost his haughty look and is frantically fighting off a short yet sizable guard without losing the reins.

I finally realize what I need to do. I hastily draw my sword. The guard with Navi's reins pauses for a quick moment, but decides that even with a sword, I'm a minor threat. I channel the small amount of defense Patton was able to teach me before we left, cursing myself for not listening harder or learning faster. But really, there's little I can do besides strike. And so, without further hesitation, I bring my sword down on the guard's head.

A dull vibration reverberates up my arm as the flat of the blade makes contact. The guard looks at me, stunned, as he shakes his head back and forth. As he realizes his head is still attached, he laughs, resting both hands on his belly to drive home that I'm no danger to him.

I can't believe I used my one chance of surprise to strike him with the flat side of my sword. He begins his advance again, even more confident than before, while Navi bucks against his tightening grip.

I quickly adjust my sword and aim once again. With as much power as I can muster, I slice it down his cheek and across his upper arm. He looks at me with burning disdain in his eyes before the momentum of the blow causes him to fall, grabbing at his shoulder with one hand and his eye with the other.

I immediately learn that to swing a sword while remaining in the saddle is no easy task, instantly falling to the ground from the force of my swing and the weight of the blade.

As I land on my back with such force the breath leaves my lungs, I distantly hear my name being called. It's Gryphon.

I twist my body around just in time to see a sword catch him straight through the stomach.

His eyes lock on mine as they go wide in disbelief. I'm frozen in place, watching him grasp at Licia before he falls off his horse and lands with a sickening thud.

Licia half jumps, half collapses to the ground beside Gryphon. Her hands instantly find his wound and cover it with layers of her skirt. The blade that injured him now lies harmlessly beside them.

Still breathless, I pull myself closer to them. But I'm unable to move fast enough.

In one quick movement, a guard grabs Licia around the waist and hoists her up into his saddle, so she's perched in front of him. She kicks and screams and scratches, tears streaming down her face, her eyes locked on Gryphon's prone form, but the guard's grip remains strong. He gallops away at full speed with his prize, putting distance between himself and the rest of his men.

I look around, stunned. Trying to find someone to help Gryphon or go after Licia. Baylor makes quick work of taking down the tall guard. His movements are so fast I can't track them.

He's slain one guard, but the others keep him occupied.

Scanning the scene in the brightening sunlight, I count who's left, and realize there is one more guard somewhere.

A sharp tug on my scalp tells me he has found me. I twist in his grip, ignoring the pain and trying to angle myself toward Gryphon and the fallen sword. My scalp burns and tears blur my vision, but I can clearly make out the slash oozing blood across his cheek. He's back for round two, and looking to even the score. My hands grope in the hard dirt, desperate for a weapon. I finally clutch the cold metal in my fingertips, and not a moment too soon.

His fist wrenches me closer, the smell of stale sweat causing me to gag. I spin toward him while my hands go up, the sword still in my grasp.

The weight of his heavy body meets the tip of the blade.

I strain to stay conscious as the pain in my head radiates through my bones and pulls me closer to oblivion. With all my strength, I hold tight to the sword as his body continues to crash toward me. I focus on the bulkiness of the hilt between his body and mine until it's the only thing left.

Suddenly, there's a feeling of warmth pouring against my hands. Relief mixed with disgust washes over me. The strong stench of his sweaty body is overpowered by the rich scent of blood. I push and pull at his body to loosen my grip on the sword so I can wiggle free from under the impossible weight of him. He refuses to budge with my feeble attempts.

Fuzziness clouds my vision, and my arms drop to my sides.

Everything darkens.

Until a warm hand grasps my own.

The grip is weak and desperate. The hand squeezes, barely, but I feel it. And that's all I need to renew my strength.

Gryphon needs me.

I can heal him.

I must get up.

I grunt and strain against the weight of the guard until I finally get enough of my body out from under him. I swallow down huge breaths, only now keenly aware that his weight was suffocating me.

I roll toward where Gryphon lies. Every inch of my body aches, barely following my desperate plea to move faster. When I pull myself onto my elbows, I find him with one hand weakly pressed against his wound and the other still reaching out toward me.

For a moment, time stops. It's just Gryphon and me here together. Tears mixed with dirt are streaming down his face. Thick layers of blood surround him and coat my chest and elbows.

There's shouting behind me and the clashing of what sounds like more swords, but I can't spare time to see if this is a good or bad thing.

I gather my strength and kneel beside Gryphon. His skin already looks pale, even in the warm light. I find where the dark stain is growing and pull his shirt up.

Blood is everywhere. I feel around desperately for the wound.

In the time that Licia was carried off and I was busy fighting my battle, Gryphon lost a lot of blood. Too much blood.

His eyes dance wildly around, then settle when they find me. The fear falls away from his face and he instantly relaxes.

"Hold on now, Gryphon. I can heal you. Just give me a moment. You'll be just fine in a minute." I gently swat away his hands and find his wound, pressing just enough to stanch the bleeding so I can focus.

I close my eyes and fall deep into myself. But what I find terrifies me.

There's only a small glow left within me. I pull desperately at it. Drawing it up, out of my center and into my hands.

The warmth sluggishly obeys. The small glint rises and moves out toward Gryphon. It hesitates at my fingertips, as if it cannot find its path, as if I am making a mistake.

How could I be making a mistake? I must save Gryphon. This is the only way. I push through the hesitation. I can feel the glow turning green as it moves out of my fingertips toward Gryphon's chest.

There is no place for it to go.

My power hesitates once again, not knowing where to begin. There is too much damage. I begin to panic and lose my focus. The pull of my power drains me further, and I can feel darkness creeping into my vision.

I must hold on just a little longer. I am sure there's something I can do. I just need to figure out what. But it's hard to concentrate with the darkness pressing in, even as my power searches Gryphon's body, trying to find a beginning or an end to grasp on to.

He grabs my hand and pulls me close to him. His skin is so cold, and each short breath comes with a straining effort. "Roe," he gasps, blood bubbling across his lips.

I hush him, but his desperate plea is all I need.

The ring on my hand begins to glow with a faint green light. I take its cue and keep searching for more. I reach beyond myself and pull from the now thrumming earth below me.

The small vibrations begin in my knees and toes—the parts of my body connected to the hard ground. As they grow up my legs, the warmth of the earth strengthens my confidence, and I pull harder, greedily. This power, although many times more potent than what I am used to working with in myself, is easier to direct. As the vibrations travel from the earth, my bones rattle and shudder, all the way from my toes to my teeth. I try to rein in the vibrations, and suddenly, instead of a turbulent shaking wracking my body, the feeling settles. The power from the earth becomes a thick, velvety river, coursing through me. Light swirls up through my limbs, and I direct it straight toward Gryphon, whose chest barely rises with breath now.

The waves of warmth pulse through me into him, blanketing his wounds—for there are too many to count. I can see them all clearly now, and I use this new sight to wrap them in the gleaming power from the earth. There is nothing else now, just him, and me, and the power swirling through us.

And I can tell something has changed inside of him. It's working. The bleeding has slowed, and the wounds are stitching themselves back together under my now confident instruction.

Then Gryphon gasps for air. His eyes fly open, searching blindly before they land on me. The whoosh of air around us is the retreating guard, his horse picking up speed. He rides too close to us—and fast. Something has him spooked.

I quickly look up, scanning for Baylor. I can't trust what I see, though. Three silhouettes are outlined by the glowing sun, each with a sword in hand. At first it appears reinforcements have shown up to finish the job, but I can make out the tip of Baylor's bow, and with the way the sun hits them all, it almost appears as if he stands with these new figures, not against them. But who could they be? Someone fierce enough to make a king's guard flee? But my attention is quickly pulled back to my friend as he groans underneath me.

"Gryphon! Oh, Gryphon." I gently trace my fingers across his forehead, brushing his hair out of his eyes, but managing only to trail sticky blood across his skin, making him look worse than he did moments ago.

He squeezes my hand and his eyes shut tightly again.

"Where does it hurt?" I search his body, unable to feel any abnormalities with my newly humming strength, but amid all this blood, I can't tell what's old and what's fresh.

His brows pinch together, and he pulls my hands into his own, stilling my search across his body. "Licia?" It comes out as a squeak of a question.

I shake my head, not trusting myself to speak. Tears slide from his blinking eyes as I manage a few words.

"They took her."

Chapter Three

I don't remember getting back on my horse, but the trotting motion beneath me gently pulls me from a sleepy daze. The hooves hitting the packed dirt bring me out of my dark dreams. Strong, corded arms wrap around me, forearms weighing heavily against my thighs, holding me in place while guiding the reins.

I can tell we're not riding Navi. This horse has longer strides and runs like the wind, as if it costs nothing to move as quickly as it does while carrying two riders.

I can't bear to open my eyes. They feel swollen and raw.

And then I remember.

Licia. Gone.

Gryphon. Almost dead.

The weight makes it difficult to breathe. My whole body shudders as I gasp for air.

"Whoa there." A deep, rolling voice comes from behind me, reverberating from his chest into my back, causing me to involuntarily take a deep breath in. "Take it easy. Small sips. Take small sips of air until you find your balance."

In my not-fully-aware state, I realize this voice belongs to the man holding these reins—but it's neither Baylor nor Gryphon. Man or male?

My head spins, but not because of the pain. The last several weeks flash through my mind: my arrival home after Avicii's mysterious death. The confusion I felt at my father's announcement that I'd be married off to the King of Etos, used once again as a bargaining chip, this time to the surrounding lands of the humans.

And I'm not human. Thaliya's mantra sing-songs in my head: *Know yourself, know your path.* Her gentle, careful words as she recounted my true past. My father and mother were king and queen of a peaceful Everguard. At least, until Hadeon's malicious strategy played out. Instantly, I miss the comforting warmth of her office while she told me I was not an Aeronwick, and not human.

Like her, I'm of the Fae. But unlike her, I was raised to believe Fae were evil, along with the other races—Shifters, Ancients, Conjours, and Elementals. And if all of this wasn't enough to turn my blood to ice, Thaliya said the fate of Everguard was in my hands.

The weight of it all is stifling. And now, we're headed back to the castle. Which means it's already over. The king's guards have taken us. We're on our way to our imminent death.

Hesitantly, I open my eyes to take in how bad my situation has become. In my hazy state, there's only so much I can make out. But I can see this guard does not wear the armor of the king's men. I can feel the warmth of his broad chest pressed close against my back. He wears worn brown leather pants instead of the usual silver mail the guards wear to protect their thighs.

Sharp pain bolts up my neck and back as I turn my head to the right, but beside us, Baylor rides his horse, with Gryphon's following close. The sight of them both fills me with relief. Gryphon's bruised body and bloody clothes only hint at the fate he almost met. He sits tall in his saddle, a little pale, but with the determined look of a warrior set across his brow.

Baylor's features are lined with exhaustion, but he seems whole and well. There's another rider on his right, dressed in the same riding leathers as the one sharing the saddle with me. And Navi is beside her.

I breathe in, as the man suggested, and inhale the rich scent of woodsmoke and leather. The smell settles something deep within me.

With a fresh breath of air, I realize once again that our group is no longer whole. We made it less than a day's ride from the castle before everything went to the hells. Licia has been taken from us. A stabbing pain tightens in my gut. How could I have been so careless? There was no reason for her to be traveling with us, other than my selfish need to not be alone on this journey. And now, who can guess at the fate that awaits her? Surely Killian will punish her, break her, for going against him in this way.

Oh, no. I never had the chance to tell her about Hadeon. That his death was at my hands. And now Killian wears the crown.

I fall forward in the saddle as a sharp pain grips me low across my ribs. In answer, the rider's strong arms wrap snugly around me, attempting to soothe the ache within.

"It's been a rough start. We're almost to the forest, where we can make camp safely." That same warm voice again. It sounds the way dark chocolate tastes, rich and velvety, and I can't get enough. It barrels through my pain and scatters it with its timbre.

I have no response. Instead, a storm rages within me, and I have no strength to quell it. The torment keeps rolling through me like thunder while all the mistakes I've made pound against me, pelting me with each infliction. My body feels too heavy, and I don't want to be left with my thoughts, so I let my eyes close once again and drift away.

I'm not sure if I wake minutes or hours later, but when I do, I've been placed on my bedroll, close enough to the fire to feel its warmth. The sun isn't yet at its highest point, or perhaps it's already on its way down. I can't tell.

I hear voices on the other side of the flames. One sounds like the same warm, deep voice from before. His words are quick and harsh, but I can't discern exactly what he says. It sounds like he and Baylor are arguing.

"She's an Aeronwick; she should be dead."

I sit up straight as this blood-chilling statement comes from the person I was just riding on the same horse with. He wants me dead?

Momentarily distracted by a rustling sound, I can sense even before I turn my head that Gryphon has plopped himself beside me. The ease with which he sits causes me to turn to look at him, and a jarring pain shoots from the bottom of my spine up to the base of my skull. I groan and fling my arm across my eyes.

After a moment, I slowly open my eyes to chance another look at Gryphon, this time careful not to move too quickly. It hardly matters; every small movement causes my muscles to cry in pain.

"Did he just say he wanted me dead?"

Gryphon was smiling broadly down at me, but at my question, his smile turns to a frown. He brushes my hair away from my face and looks behind us, then leans in close. "Apparently, he's *the* Ultor Regni."

My eyes go wide, and after a moment, Gryphon uses one finger on my chin to close my gaping jaw.

"Are we safe? Am *I* safe?" I say under my breath, stealing a glance at the person I thought for sure was just a myth until now. Whispers about the Ultor Regni were always quickly silenced around the castle, but from what I've pieced together, he's a force to be reckoned with. Not only is he one of the elite Wardens who protect the lands that were once Glorixia, but the mention of *Ultor Regni* particularly makes my blood run cold, as the title was created specifically when Hadeon took the throne. The man standing before us has vowed to the kingdom to rid Everguard of all Aeronwicks. A plague, he calls our family, one he has made his life's work to wipe from this realm. Hadeon hid behind the walls of Merula, an impenetrable village, making it impossible for a strike to be made against our family so far, but I've just made this all too easy for him.

Suddenly, those king's guards aren't looking so bad.

Just as I'm about to see if I can catch up to them somehow, Gryphon says, "For now, I think we are. He and the other one just saved our tails back there, after all. And I think Baylor's convinced him you're worth keeping around—at least for a bit longer." He winks, but I can see the way his smile doesn't completely reach his eyes, leaving a small pit of doubt to bloom in my stomach.

"You almost died." The words leave my mouth with tremendous effort.

"*You* almost died," Gryphon answers as he comes around so I don't have to move to get a better look at him.

I peer up at him, confused, wanting him to explain, but realizing I don't have the strength to ask.

"They said you pulled too much power from the earth, too quickly. You glowed so bright you almost exploded. All I remember is feeling warm all over, but they said it was a sight to behold."

I try to search our surroundings for the "they" he speaks of, vaguely remembering the scent of woodsmoke and leather wrapping its comforting arms around me. Figures move into my vision, and when my eyes adjust, I see Baylor, his blond curls spilling over his wide-set eyes, which scan me from head to toe, worry marking his features. He appears satisfied I'm not hurt physically, just exhausted.

He looks back at the two who saved us. The Wardens. They're both dressed in lined brown leathers, and as they get closer, I note the one who was riding beside us, clearer now the morning haze has lifted. Her dark, textured hair, a halo around her head, frames her striking, cat-like features. She's smiling, her turned-up eyes twinkling. A stark contrast to her partner, the Ultor Regni, who I can tell is already frowning at us, even through his thick, unkempt beard.

He approaches with his arms crossed across his broad chest. "Your power runs deep." His voice is full of awe. I instantly recognize its deep hum; he's the rider from behind me. "But you're reckless."

I shudder as his words bite deep into my marrow, as the vision of Licia's fear-stricken face and the desperation in her pleas as she was dragged away from us looms in my mind.

"Give her a break, Niko. She's just been to the hells and back. She doesn't need you to admonish her for saving a life at the moment."

The other rider puts herself between me and the Ultor Regni, the man who must be Niko. Black ink swirls across the backs of her hands and up her neck, the only skin exposed beneath her thick riding leathers. In one swift and graceful movement, she kneels beside me, pulling one of my hands into both of her own, gently warming my fingers.

"Excuse the brute over there," she says as she brushes her fingers gently across my brow. "He doesn't have a sympathetic bone in his body." Her smile reaches her bright, oddly violet eyes, which dance with laughter as she continues gently taking stock of my injuries. Seemingly satisfied that I'm no longer in peril, she sits back on her heels. "I'm Gayle, and this is Niko. We are Wardens of the realm."

She presses a canteen into my hands and encourages me to drink. I look from Gayle to Niko and then to Baylor and Gryphon, trying to make sense of her words.

"These are Wardens of the realm, Roe." Gryphon looks at me, his eyes growing wide with meaning from our conversation. The clanging of swords dances faintly across my memory. They must've stepped in against the king's men.

I take in their worn leathers once again, the belts around their hips and across their chests lined with knives of different lengths. Their skin is dark from traveling for days at a time across the lands. They look just like the stories say they should. Hardened by countless battles and lonely nights on the road. These two riders are members of the elite group who have given their lives to ensure the safety of the realm and the secrets of Glorixia. But if Glorixia is nothing more than an abandoned desert now, why would they still exist?

Confusion must cross my features, as Gryphon moves protectively closer to my other side. "She needs more rest, that's all. And some space."

"You'll both feel better after a bath," Gayle replies.

Gryphon and I exchange a look. No matter how miserable I feel and how much my body throbs, I can't help but agree with her. A bath always makes everything better, but Gryphon's confusion mirrors my own.

Gayle turns. "What are you waiting for? I know a place." She throws the words over her shoulder as she strides beyond the treeline. My body screams with pain as Gryphon hefts me up so we don't lose sight of her quickly retreating form.

Chapter Four

I feel weightless as I dissolve into the tranquil water. There's an extraordinary buoyancy here, adding to the featherlight feeling that makes me just want to float away. The gentle trickling of the deep pool doesn't just wash away the blood and the painful memories of the day; it seems to cradle me, resonating with a soft hum beneath my skin.

At least for now.

My body throbs with pain, but beneath it, something else stirs. Energy? Power? Unable to properly separate the new feeling from the lingering ache, I push them both aside, until memories of our recent attack swarm over me. Each scream from Licia, each agonizing memory of Gryphon almost bleeding to death, is a new pinprick of pain to add to my already bruised being.

The sunlight peeking through the trees plays across my closed eyelids, creating shapes and patterns that distract me while I weightlessly float across the surface, washing away so much blood.

The lively conversation of the others bends around me. I have no room for their mundane words. Not after what just happened. I can't help the sinking realization that this is all my fault. But between Licia being taken from us and Gryphon being brought within an inch of his life, no one seems one bit fazed. Even Gryphon is recklessly throwing himself off the ledge into the water, following Baylor and Gayle.

And here I am, completely useless. Not like Baylor or the two newcomers who saved us at the last moment. They've all had a lifetime of training, and I've had what? Mere days?

I should've listened. We should have waited. Trained more. Prepared better. This has been nothing but an epic failure. And it has cost me and my realm.

What was I thinking? I can't do this. I should just mount Navi and ride back to the castle right now. Tell them I just wanted one more adventure before I happily settle down with the King of Etos. That wouldn't be so bad, would it?

It wouldn't be worse than my decade lost with Avicii.

But I can't go back. Nothing is the same. Everything changed with the knowledge that I have Fae blood coursing through my veins. In time, I hope I will see this as a gift, something that is for the better. The betterment of myself. The betterment of my kingdom.

But right now, blood stains my hands.

I'm drawn out of my miserable reflections by movement up on the rocks. Lifting my head and shifting my body upright, I note Baylor climbing high onto the rocks, his wet skin glistening in the sunlight. Droplets dance along his dark, chiseled frame, clinging to him as if the firm muscles of his chest are too good to let go of.

His face glows with remnants of energy from the hard day's work. His suntanned skin is a beautiful contrast against the setting sun shining low behind him. He shakes his head, and the reluctant droplets spray from his long golden curls, creating a halo fit for a god. He even still has a bit of the glow from when Thaddeus saved his life.

I wonder what the repercussions of that horrific night are. I can't help but think Baylor seems to have made peace with it. Bright laughter bursts freely from him as he and Gryphon run full speed toward the edge. Beside him, Gryphon's lean frame stands out as unfinished, his skin pale compared to that of the Fae male beside him. Even at thirty-five, Gryphon has yet to fully grow into his lanky, tall legs. But the smile on his face is unmatched. For a man who's spent his whole life behind castle walls, this is an adventure of a lifetime. Despite my black mood, his laughter is catching, and I fight the small smile that plays across my lips.

Moments later, the calm water rocks and churns with the turbulence Baylor and Gryphon have created. The small ripples send me closer to the bank, where Gayle lies stretched out along one of the sun-warmed rocks. I don't see Niko, who must've gone ahead to set up camp. But we're better for it. If I thought I was bringing the group down, he seems to do the same wherever he goes.

I watch the men and their strange energy, in stark opposition to how I feel at the moment. They're completely carefree. Gayle, with a small, knowing smile playing across her face, also seems to not have a care in the world, her voluminous hair now spread around her like a proud lion's mane. Her delicate features bely the strength and power just under the surface of her bronzed skin.

"Out with it." Gayle breaks the bubble of peaceful calm that the water has created. She sits up on her elbows and looks down at me from her perch on the rocks.

"Everyone's acting so normal."

That's what I say aloud, but inside I'm screaming at them for swimming and laughing and basking in the sun like it's just another day. Maybe for them, that's exactly what it is. While my heart is breaking into pieces, it's just another fight for them. Just one more notch on their belts.

"Is this so normal to you all?" I gesture to Baylor, splashing and diving into the deep, warm pool, to Gayle, and even Gryphon, who's taking part in the light mood. "What just happened was life-altering. How is everyone so unaffected?" My voice rises slightly with frustration and sadness, but I try to tamp it down, reminding myself that we don't know each other that well.

She looks at me like I'm a lost kitten, like she's unsure how many of life's hard truths I can take. "Fighting—and killing—is not pleasant, but it's familiar. You know, kind of like when you get tossed around by the waves in the Caldertasi Sea, and the salty water shoots up your nose. You don't love the feeling, but strangely, it's a comfort."

"I know the feeling well." Unfortunately, this does nothing to quell my unease. It just causes me to get lost among fond childhood memories for a brief, glorious moment. And then the look on Licia's face and the guttural scream she gave when she realized we couldn't get to her flash through my mind, and I cringe at how I've suddenly become so scared.

Gayle watches me. "I'm not saying you'll get used to it, because you won't. But you'll harden a little more to it each time. Like building calluses on your hands."

I look down at my hands, newly blistered from my recent plunge into training with a sword. I wonder if I have it in me to harden this way. Thirty-five years of being doted on at the castle have left me soft. Softer than I care to admit.

I'll have to learn quickly if I am to fulfill all that has been asked of me. At this moment, I decide that if I'm going to do this, I have to go all in. It will be arduous and bone-breaking, but a lot is riding on this.

The fate of my entire kingdom, to be exact.

"Then I have to learn. Quickly." I look up to Gayle, and she answers my resolve with a slow-spreading, cat-like grin. "Will you teach me?"

"I would be honored, Princess." She dips her head in a playful bow.

After we dry off, Baylor and Gayle decide now is as good a time as any to begin a training session. Baylor raises his closed fists and dives right in, charging at me headfirst. His swaggering speed and years of training quickly leave me dizzy in his wake. I'm still having a difficult time reconciling the stable hand I knew as a child with the Fae warrior in front of me.

Gayle keeps up with me, though. Each time she lands a blow, she walks me back through the sequence, showing me where I faltered and how to improve.

"You could pull your jabs in tighter and they'd be more effective." She shows me how pulling my arms in closer to my body allows more power to flow as I rotate my torso. "But your awareness of space and the way you use it is exceptional."

She doesn't sugarcoat anything, doesn't treat me like a child. Maybe more like someone she hopes will fight at her side one day. And I quickly grow to feel the same about her.

"I'll sit this one out," I manage to force out an hour later, as I collapse to the ground in a jelly-like heap.

"Can't hang with the big dogs?" Baylor grins at me, but his eyes trail to Gayle.

"You two go ahead. Show me how it's done." I wave them off and don't even move from my perch on the sun-warmed rock beside Gryphon.

"Gladly." Gayle's eyes flash as they square off to face each other.

She circles Baylor as a predator stalks its prey, her powerful movements graceful and silent. Baylor drinks in her fierce stance, as if there's nowhere else he'd rather be. But quickly, both their bodies become tense as bowstrings, neither one eager to land the first blow.

I sit up a little straighter, ready for whatever comes next. Without weapons, they look like two animals facing off, rather than the seasoned warriors they are.

Baylor laughs, like this is the most fun he's had all day. And before I can even blink, he moves in to land a powerful punch, square on Gayle's jaw. He uses his strength boldly, unafraid to jump right into the fight.

Completely undaunted, a primal growl sounding from deep within, Gayle launches herself at him with explosive speed. Baylor is ready for her attack, though. He pivots, easily dodging her as he becomes a quick blur, sending her stumbling to catch herself while he stands tall above her.

She quickly repositions her stance and delivers a swift set of jabs and crosses to his midsection. He doubles over, but instead of truly being hurt, he uses the opportunity to get low and kick her feet out from under her. Before she has a chance to find her footing, he lifts her above his head and throws her across the rocks, as if she's nothing but a sack of grain, giving himself a moment to reset.

Somehow, Gayle lands lightly, in a crouched position on top of a soft moss bed beside the pool. She takes a moment to shake her wits back into place. Determination is written plainly in her blazing eyes and feral grin. She charges full speed across the rocks, leaping gracefully from boulder to boulder.

Baylor's Faeness is apparent in his every movement. His motions have a controlled fluidity about them, each precise and calculated strike hinting at decades, if not centuries, of honing his warrior abilities. But Gayle matches each blow with one of her own. Is she Fae, too? She's a Warden of Glorixia, which means she must have some special abilities. Absentmindedly, I wonder if there's a polite way I can ask this.

Growing up, King Hadeon only entertained humans at court. He always said the Fae, Shifters, Ancients, Conjours, and all the other magical races had their own ways. That they thought it below them to join us in Merula.

But now I wonder.

Are people sometimes more than they seem? Do Fae and Shifters live together in other parts of the realm? What about the mysterious Ancients of the North? Do they really hole up there in those jagged mountains drinking blood from goblets, or do they venture all over the land?

"Give it up, kitten." Baylor laughs as Gayle races at him, taunting her by motioning her closer with both hands.

He sidesteps her advances at the last moment. As she continues forward, he grabs her by the throat with one hand, pulling her close against his body. Close enough to whisper something I completely miss into her ear.

He pauses, a victorious smile breaking out across his face, but Gayle is fast.

Rather than succumbing to him, she uses her seemingly vulnerable state to her advantage. She swiftly twists out of his grip and side-kicks him away from her. He staggers back from the forceful blow and tries to compose himself, realizing the fight is not yet won.

"Wow, you're good," I say, staring between them, trying to lighten the mood as they continue to dance around each other across the rocks. "Where'd you learn to fight like that?"

My words seem to break the spell they are under. Gayle gives Baylor one last look before striding over to where I sit in the warm sun.

"What? You're done already? I was just getting warmed up." Baylor flings his arms wide, welcoming Gayle back into the fray.

She doesn't take the bait. She plops herself beside me and says, loud enough for him to hear, "I like them a little more feisty than that." She gives me a wide, knowing smile. "I have eight older brothers. My mother was ecstatic when I was born. But animal instincts and big brothers won out. A girl's gotta be able to protect herself. I never so much as looked at a dress." Gayle meets my eyes, then looks out over the pool of water. "My mother embraced every second of it, though. Until she was gone."

I glance up at her, the sadness in her voice stopping me from asking more, leaving me curious about her past.

"It all worked out, though, as things tend to do. I became a Warden, and now I get to spend my time traveling the realm, helping where I can. The only drawback is that I have a bear of a partner." She rolls her eyes, letting me know she's only half kidding.

Chapter Five

We find Niko and our camp for the night easily enough. And after hours of flip-flopping between Gayle's firm training instructions and catching quick naps in the warm sun, we welcome the cozy campfire.

The delicious scent of roasted fish fills the air as we arrive in the clearing. Baylor proved impressive with his makeshift fishing rod at the pool, once again reminding me that despite having known him all my life, I don't know anything about him at all. Ever the mother hen, he sits by the fire, fussing over the fish, astutely turning them on the spit as they cook. As I pass, he gives us a wide smile, and I am grateful for his familiar face, especially after everything that has happened in the past twenty-four hours.

Though, we seem to have walked right into an argument. "You want us to take *her* to Sverreian?" The other Warden, Niko, sits outside the glow of the fire, head bent and braids trailing down his back. His focus on sharpening the many blades lined up in front of him gives him a stormy air. He gives a distracted nod as we pass, grumbling something as Gayle kicks the heel of his big boot.

She obviously understands the husky remark, because she responds, "Get it yourself, you overgrown lizard. And forgive me for butting in, but if we take them home, it'll get Killian off her trail. He won't look for her in the middle of the Dread Forest."

Confused by the insult, I look back at Niko, confirming that he is the least lizard-like person I've ever seen. He's big and scruffy. His huge frame compares more to a bear than a lizard scurrying between cracks.

He catches me staring, and the look he gives me does nothing to clear the angry bear image from my mind. His large brown eyes pierce right through me. And even though his unkempt beard disguises the bottom half of his face, I don't think he's smiling.

"You want us to go to Sverreian?" I break eye contact with Niko and direct my question to Baylor, who must've started this conversation. "Isn't that out of the way?" I know the Shifter village is on the northwestern coast of Everguard, and it would probably take us days out of our way north.

"I think it would be good for us, for exactly the reason Gayle pointed out. If we lie low in Sverreian for a week or two, Killian will lose our trail."

Gryphon nods along with his reasoning, and I know it's not really because he agrees so much as because he's always wanted to meet the Shifters, and heading to their village would be a dream come true.

"Yes, that makes sense." But in my heart, the thought of wasting any more time before getting to Ombretta tears me in two. Despite what Thaddeus said, she's been alone and at the mercy of the Ancients for too long. Every day counts now.

Our next move decided, I trail Gayle past Niko and Baylor, across camp. She sits down in front of the fire, upwind of the roasting fish. I can't help noticing the seat she's chosen keeps Baylor right within her sight. I wonder if there's something off between them, or maybe the spar was a little too intense for her liking.

He flashes his flawless grin at her, and she bares her teeth in response.

I know I'm sitting beside Gayle and sharing in her united front against him at the moment, but I can't help but notice how that smile accentuates Baylor's high cheekbones in a very flattering way. All this fresh air also seems to highlight his flirty, arrogant persona.

Before I get too lost in my heated thoughts, Gayle elbows me in the ribs. "That one is dangerous." As she says this, she follows my gaze toward Baylor, who's suddenly paying very close attention to the fish.

I elbow her back while rolling my eyes, knowing that the warning was all for show, as if she's reminding herself, not me, not to get involved. In an attempt to drive the conversation in another direction, I comment on their sparring session. "Earlier, you and Baylor seemed to have different styles in the way you fight."

I look between the two. There's a difference in the way they're built, Baylor being so tall and sinewy, every ounce of him lean muscle. Gayle is maybe a hand shorter than me, but with her voluminous hair, she seems bigger than life. While she's built thick, she is all strength and power.

But it's more than just their size. Even my untrained eye caught the way Baylor dove right in, full strength behind each strike he made, while Gayle seemed to attack with quiet determination, using her surroundings to her full advantage. She was constantly aware of how her vulnerabilities could be used against her and instead, she leveraged them to her benefit.

"I should hope so." She laughs, a big, warm belly laugh that permeates the darkening space around us. "If I stomped around the way he does all the time, I wouldn't have made it all these years. Not to mention made it to Warden status before forty." Her pride radiates from her amiable smile. "But in all seriousness, you're right. And that's a fine observation, Roe. They fight differently in the North and have different strengths than those from the Dread Forest. You must be aware of your strengths for where we're headed. Your weaknesses, too. Because you better believe your opponent will take note of both. So, tell me, who are you these days?"

I stare at her a moment, wondering if anyone has ever asked me such a loaded question, but the tilt of her head assures me she's honestly wondering. I open my mouth to respond, but where do I start? Up until very recently, I did as I was told and worked hard to keep those around me satisfied—namely, Avicii and Hadeon. But look where that got me. I've just recovered enough memories to know I was responsible for Avicii's death—self-defense, of course, but he died at my hands. As did Hadeon.

Ever since I learned of my Fae powers, my world's been tipped over. I'm just like that tortoise who'd regularly visit my garden, that one time I found him stuck on his shell, unable to flip upright. I know who I am not, and I know where I need to get to, but who am I right now?

Taking in what must be my completely horrified expression, Gayle takes pity on me. "Let's start with something easier—what are your strengths, Roe?"

What are my strengths? I involuntarily exhale like I've just been punched in the gut. How is that question easier? Stars, if only I had strengths. Or one strength. I'd take just one.

"I don't think I have any. Growing up in the castle was so different from the little I've seen out here on the road." I flick my hand to encompass our small encampment while envisioning the dining hall, where I would usually be at this hour, plate piled high with steaming food dripping with thick sauces and glazed with sugar. The constant chatter and bawdy laughter ringing in my ears. The stiffness of my corset digging into my ribs until I couldn't take another bite.

The differences are glaring. I return to the quiet, where the only sounds are the sizzling oils falling from the fish into the flames, the constant drag of Niko's blade against his whetstone, and all the night creatures surrounding us.

"I know it was different, but that doesn't mean you weren't good at anything. What did you enjoy? What did you do in your spare time?"

Gayle looks sincerely interested, so I give it a shot. "When I was little, I spent many evenings in the library, where I'd beg Killian to tell me stories. Unfortunately, the only stories he'd ever agree to tell me were of battles that he'd read about in books, or the few he witnessed as a young boy."

As I recall the many nights I spent curled up in his lap while the fire burned low, I wonder what he's doing at this moment. And then I quickly attempt to block out the image that fills my mind: one of him staring at a map, planning the best route to follow to return me to the castle as quickly as possible. Or worse, kill me on the spot for leaving right before my betrothal.

I look to Gryphon, who grounds me in this moment. "Growing up, I spent all my free time with Gryphon, exploring the castle—finding or causing trouble. Or I'd be in the healer's wing with Thaliya. I helped her by making poultices and healing those who came in sick or injured. But I don't know how any of this will help me while I'm out here."

I look up, surprised to see Gayle smiling at my answer. Now I'm even more confused. She must be mad. Stars, and I was just starting to like her.

She must see as much on my face, because she says, "You're close, Roe. You're right there. You just don't know it yet."

She pushes off her knees, moving with slinking grace toward Baylor, who's dishing up fish stew, and the way she fingers his broad shoulders confirms her warning was for her, not me. My stomach growls loudly as the scent reaches me. It smells like the heavens. Especially since jerky, cheese, and bread are already getting old.

I stare into the bowl Baylor hands me, seeing not the stew, but my thoughts swirling around in the broth. Is Gayle right? Am I so close I just don't see it yet? Does she see a hint of the warrior within me, too?

I frown, realizing I was so lost in thought that I've just eaten the entire bowl without even tasting it, even though I had so looked forward to the special meal. Defeated, I roll out my bedroll and sit on it, staring up at the stars, which blink and shine through the shifting branches above. Questions dance through my head.

What if these obstacles aren't just obstacles, but the journey itself? Maybe this is the right path for me.

How could I have been so selfish? How could I have so foolishly thought we could make it north without consequences—fatal consequences?

"Your thoughts are rather loud this evening." Gryphon breaks through my spiral as he takes Gayle's vacant seat beside me and pulls me in close.

"You almost died." I lean into the arm he's draped around me, breathing in his warm cinnamon-and-fresh-linen scent. It reminds me of the castle. "We weren't prepared. Reckless. That's what Niko said. Should we just go back? Make sure Licia's okay and—"

Gryph's flinch causes me to stop, but before I can apologize, he fills the silence. "You're anything but reckless. That big brute? He looks like he's taken too many souls to know what feelings are anymore." I stifle a laugh, and he continues, "Everything's harder out here. I don't have to tell you that."

His shoulder brushes mine in solidarity as he gives me a knowing look.

I shudder at the thought of my marriage to Avicii. Everything about it was hard, not just living outside the castle walls. But he's right. It was a difficult ten years.

"You made it, though. We can make it through this, but you're right. We're not prepared. But we can work at it."

"It's all too much." What I don't say is *I don't think I can do it*. But he sees it written across my face.

"The hard things are always worth the effort." Though his words are gentle, their impact is immense. "You don't need to decide tonight. Sleep. Think on it. We'll decide in the morning. And anyway, Licia will be just fine." His words are almost too low to hear, but losing her clearly weighs heavily on his heart.

"Were you going to do anything about *that*?"

I cringe as I recognize Niko's deep voice behind me. I turn, shielding my eyes against the glare of the morning sun to see what he's referencing. I follow his gaze to the campsite. There's a clear outline where Gryphon and I slept last night, but otherwise, it looks like no one's been here, including the way the fire's ashes have been scattered.

"I-I..." I stammer as I look from Niko to the site to Navi, who's saddled and ready to go. "How'd you all do that?" I thought we were better at covering our tracks. No wonder those guards found us so fast. Now, there's no trace of the others at all.

"I suppose respect for your surroundings isn't something they teach at the castle." He huffs as he returns to the site in question, scattering sticks and evening out the ground as he goes. As he does, I have to scold myself for watching the way he bends over, the way his leather pants hug his hips and outline the tree trunks that are his thighs. There's no reason to find him the least bit attractive—he has a beard and reeks of nature. He wants me dead. And I haven't had the best luck with men lately. Is he always this grumpy, or is it me in particular who brings out this mood?

But as I look back across the campsite, I have to admit he knows what he's doing. Nothing at all stands out anymore.

"Thanks," I say as he passes me on the way to his horse. He doesn't respond.

As the sun climbs higher in the sky, the cold becomes bearable. When we stop for a quick meal and to rest the horses, Gryphon and I take up our swords to practice a little, but mostly to stay warm. My sword, Ivy's Embrace, is starting to feel like an extension of my arm.

"You're being too hard on yourself." Gryphon says when we're back on the road, nudging his mount forward until our horses are in step with one another. "I can tell by the fall of your shoulders and the way you keep looking south, as if Licia is just going to ride over the horizon at any moment."

I'm not surprised at Gryphon's read on me, but now that he's put it into words, tears fill my eyes.

"I miss her too. But you know Licia. She runs that place. Killian has the title, but Licia has everyone eating out of her hand." He's smiling, but it doesn't reach his eyes. I know he's suffering too.

"You're right. We'll return to the castle, and she'll have a celebratory feast waiting for us to introduce Ombretta to all of Merula. Her birds are already a step ahead of us, even before we arrive." I play along with cheerful words, but the unspoken sadness flows between us. This is what we both need: to be able to talk about her. The rest will fall into place, eventually.

We ride in companionable silence as the afternoon passes into evening. Baylor and Gayle lead the way, and I don't think they've stopped their back-and-forth the entire day. Niko brings up the rear, and I swear I can feel his eyes on me. At any moment, he could throw a dagger and end my life. One Aeronwick down. I wonder what Baylor said to him to make him step down, go against his vow to the realm.

To take my mind off Licia and the male staring daggers at my back, I focus on our surroundings, attempting to make a mental map of how far we've come. I know we're headed to Sverreian, the village of the Shifters, but on all our maps in the library, it looked so much closer. I thought we'd be there by now. I need to reevaluate my navigational skills. But it seems like we have the edges of the remnants of Glorixia to the east, and we're hugging the Dread Forest to the west. We have to be getting close.

There's something about the forest, the way it almost leans in toward us, like a friend looking over our shoulders, that reminds me of the way the vines in Merula responded to me, helped me, saved me. And I've hardly reached out since then. I wonder if the earth misses me the way I miss my connection to it. As soon as I think it, I laugh. What an odd thought. Nevertheless, I reach out to the trees beside us, curious.

Even though Navi is between the earth and me, I can still feel my connection to it the way I can feel Gryphon's comforting presence riding beside me. I close my eyes, focusing on that connection, picturing it as a warm green light reaching toward me. It engulfs me with a peacefulness I haven't felt since the last time I was with Thaliya, in the healer's ward. And

I realize this warmth, this healing earth energy, is as much a part of me as my hands are.

Even though we're going to the Shifter village, I wonder if I'll be able to find more answers about my heritage. I know Thaliya would've given me all the answers I needed, but there just wasn't time. The small diary I carry comes to mind, and I wonder if Baylor would be able to read the ancient Fae inside. I'll have to ask him next time we stop.

When I open my eyes, little white flowers that weren't there before wink at me in the growing night. Moonflowers. All along the ground, weaving their way into the coniferous trees lining the edges of the path. This is such a gift, to be connected to nature in this way. And to think, the connection has been there all along, just waiting for me to recognize it for what it is. I've lived a lifetime before this, yet there's so much more of me to discover.

As I stretch out on my bedroll, enjoying the small curve in my spine to counteract a whole day in the saddle, I open the small book I've carried with me from the library in Merula. I trace the markings as I flip through the pages. The looping curves are a beautiful mystery, for now.

"You brought a book along with you on the road, Datura? Maybe you're not so impractical after all."

I turn to look over my shoulder, where Niko is standing above me. "By impractical, do you mean living on borrowed time? I am yours to dispatch." I roll my eyes and turn back to my book, but not before I see his reaction to my challenge. At first, an eyebrow raises, as if he's taking my measure, but then one corner of his mouth twitches upward in a ghost of a smile.

Out of the corner of my eye, I see Gryphon and Gayle exchange a look, but I ignore it, thinking about what he called me. *Datura*. He must've noticed the moonflowers earlier. I don't know if it's more amusing that he knows what a moonflower is, or that he picked the more poisonous of them as an endearment.

So he knows flowers and likes to read. If he didn't want me dead just because I'm an Aeronwick—*was* an Aeronwick—I might be intrigued. But even if I could look past his life's work to end my family line, that overgrown beard is something else entirely.

Even so, because he despises me and because he's completely awful, I don't need to think about the fact that he enjoys my favorite things. And I definitely don't need to watch him walk away. I bring my attention back to the swooping, unintelligible words on the page, but can't help but watch Niko's warrior braids move in time with his steps as he sits on the other side of the fire, just out of sight.

As I'm flipping through the diary and waiting for Baylor to get off watch, my eyelids grow heavy. Eventually, exhaustion wins out and I drift off.

I sleep in fits and starts through the night. My dreams begin in my garden. The rows are neat and straight, the crops grown tall and sturdy, still moist from the morning dew. Safe. I was safe here once. The thought worms its way through the rays of sunlight warming my skin. *Once* meaning *no longer*.

Then it all changes. The solid bounty of the earth surrounding me twists suddenly into blurry lines of blues and greens. Neat rows of cabbages and kale surrender their space to thick, waving seaweed. The air in my lungs leaves through bubbles drifting skyward, except there is no sky. Just darkness, all around. I can't see any farther than the hands I bring up to my face, hesitantly checking to see if only the world around me has blurred beyond recognition, or if I have as well.

Before I can discern anything either way, a silky-sweet voice drifts around me in the current, beckoning me closer, deeper. The warmth of the waves surrounding me lulls me into a soft reverie.

A moment of understanding and recognition sweeps through me as a lithe figure appears in front of me. Her dark hair cascades in sleek sheets past her shoulders down to her waist. Her large eyes are sunken and dark, any life in them long since lost.

Despite the shivers running down my spine, a sense of security and self washes through me, although what I recognize within this hollow wraith is lost to me. It's unmistakable, though. I know her, and she knows me. The need to reach out and touch her overcomes me, and as I reach out my hand, hesitant at first but then never more sure of anything in my life, her smile grows, and the scene changes...

The same inky darkness tinged with red surrounds me, but this time, there's a familiar comfort to the swirling shadows. Rather than choking me, they twist and spin around me, their soft caress tingling across my skin.

You're on the right path, they seem to whisper.

A chill breaks through the shadows, somehow pushing them just far enough to clear space around me. My eyes flutter open, and I instinctively pull my blankets tighter around myself. The wind has picked up. Wind was wrapping around me, not shadows. Wasn't that what I thought it was?

Confused, I sit up, the campsite coming into focus. Gryphon, asleep next to me, reaches out his arm. Even in his sleep, he's trying to get closer to Licia.

The morning sun still sits low on the horizon. It must be early. The fire is low as well, but the grumpy Warden looks like he's attentively tending to something.

Reckless. That's what he called me. Powerful and reckless and... on the right path? My mind reels, trying to make room for everything swirling around inside it.

"Looks like you need a mug of this."

Gayle hands me a ceramic cup, and the heat radiates up my arms and warms my whole body, chasing away the morning cold as well as the last chill from my dreams. I pull the mug closer into the nest I've created, blocking it entirely from the wind. The steam rises, and the calming scent of chamomile and lavender adds to the comfort that arrives with Gayle. She seems to be hyperaware of her surroundings, including me.

A weight lifts, and I exhale—*that* I can answer. "It's exactly what I need."

Chapter Six

"Slow! There's something up ahead." Gayle pulls on her reins, causing us to stop short behind her. Baylor, beside her, puts a hand on his bow, waiting to see if he needs to draw it. Niko stops beside me and Gryphon. "I'll go ahead to check it out," Gayle says.

"We stay together." Niko's response is blunt, but I agree, and Baylor nods too.

We approach slowly, but as we get closer, a child runs toward us, hands waving and beckoning us forward. Gayle rests a hand on her belt of daggers, but lets the child approach. I try to get a glimpse, but she and Baylor block the sight of what's ahead.

"Help us!" The child's voice is small and desperate. His slight frame is swallowed up by the too-large shirt he wears, only staying on due to the rope he's tied around his waist. His arms are still waving and pointing to the formless shape ahead. "My mama is hurt. She's stuck."

"Well, which is it, boy? Hurt or stuck?"

Stunned by Niko's blunt question, I throw my legs over the saddle, dismounting immediately to help.

"Wait, Roe. It could be a trap." Gayle's tone is gentler, but still hesitant. Before she finishes her sentence, though, I've got my hand in the child's small, dirty one as he guides me back to his mother.

"What happened to your mama?" I ask in the most soothing voice I can summon as we run across the sandy road, closing the distance between us and the motionless form.

"We're going to Cindra. Mama says we have family there. But the king's guards came so we hid."

Cindra is across the continent. I wonder why they'd be going on foot.

The boy's words start to run together with emotion, but it sounds like something landed on his mother and she can't get out. He leads me around the figure I thought was the mother and toward the treeline, constantly looking back to make sure I'm behind him, even though he still grips my hand tightly. Right before we dive into the trees, I look back at the pile of cloth beside the road. If I squint back the way we came, I can make out several packs piled together—not a prone body. I wonder how many of them there are?

"Roe, don't follow him into the woods!" Baylor shouts as their horses ride closer. Niko has already dismounted and is poking the pile of packs with his sword, and Gayle and Gryphon are rushing to secure the horses.

The cool, crisp air welcomes us as we enter the break in the trees. Branches caress my arms as we make our way deeper. There's a group of children sitting in a circle several paces in, and as we get closer, they all scurry away to hide behind trees.

Niko and Baylor break into the brush with their swords drawn—an impressive picture of masculinity, but unnecessary, I think. I swat at them as I walk toward where the children were seated. "You're scaring them. Put your swords away!"

The boy pulls me toward what appears to be a large hole in the forest floor. Peeking from behind the trees are at least eight children in shirts too big for them, their dirty faces giving them the look of little woodland creatures.

"Mama, I brought help," the tiny boy beside me calls into the hole. As I move to kneel beside the hole to get a better look, Baylor steps in front of me while Niko eyes the trees surrounding us. The little faces have all disappeared, and the silence left in their wake is palpable.

A weak voice makes its way from the innards of the hole. "Cato, is that you?"

The boy peeks over the edge and waves, his shoulders relaxing when he hears his mother's voice.

I frown at Baylor and gently shove him out of my way. Kneeling as close as I can to the hole, I'm dismayed at what I find. The woman below, pinned beneath a rotted log, looks like she's been down there for days. She's dirtier than all the children combined, and her tear-streaked face speaks volumes of the pain she's in.

It's no wonder they couldn't get her out. The walls of the hole are all mud; there are no rocks to grab onto or roots sticking out. I look back down; the woman's eyes are wide, and she's shivering.

"We'll get you out. Don't worry."

She nods at me, fresh tears making trails along her dirt-stained cheeks, but with a new light in her eyes—hope.

I lean back on my haunches, looking for a way out. The men are still eyeing the trees, as if waiting for the children to spring a trap on us. They're completely useless.

There are plenty of sticks lining the forest floor, but none big enough to reach down to her. Trying to stay calm for the boy's sake, I take a few deep breaths, weighing my options. I can go deeper into the forest to find a long vine or root strong enough to hold her, or maybe if I edge my way down, I can lift her. But then I'd be stuck.

I rub my hands together, trying to stay warm, and my ring catches my eye. I wonder if I can create some roots to hold on to. The boy looks expectantly at me with big, round eyes. I nod to him and hold up one finger—*just a moment*. Closing my eyes, I reach into myself, and deeper, into the earth beneath my knees. I place my palms onto the earth, too, to sharpen my focus.

The roots surrounding the hole answer my call immediately, and there's a gasp from the boy beside me. I ignore it, pressing on and guiding more roots to the surface. In my mind's eye, I see them work, the paths of the roots below the forest floor and the ones that make their way into the hole to aid us.

Opening my eyes, I see there are now many holds for the climb out, and many eyes upon me. Baylor and Niko have moved closer to watch what I'm doing, and the children have resumed their spots surrounding the hole.

I scurry down into the hole, hoping I'll be able to move the log on my own. But then, dirt begins falling on my head from movement above. Niko is right behind me, now making his way into the small space. I'm surprised at first, but as a Warden, this is what he does. He protects and helps the people of his realm. If only he could see that's what I intend to do too.

"Datura," he nods, and we work in silence, as one. Niko lifts the log high enough so I can pull the woman out from under it. High-pitched cheers sound from above. As he moves the log out of the way, I can't help but think maybe a part of him does see me.

"Are you in any pain?" I ask the woman.

"My leg is broken, I think." Her voice is still weak, but her smile is radiant, a glowing light down here underground.

Sure enough, she's right. As I gently work her loose pant legs up, the right one looks fine, but where the log sat, there's a clear break. The unnatural angle has Niko turning away, and if I'm not mistaken, a little pale.

"We'll have you fixed up in no time, won't we, Niko?" I wink at the woman, who's also noticed the way he's turned his back to us, as well as the gagging sounds he's trying to hide with a cough.

"Mama?" Cato yells from above, the other children leaning in as I look up.

"I'm going to be okay, little ones," she says, giving them a wave with both hands. "You are all so brave." But when she looks back down, the sob she swallows is unmistakable.

"It must be a daunting endeavor to travel with so many little ones across the continent on your own," I say as I check the break and assess the damage. Before, I would've added a poultice and used a splint. It would've taken her weeks to heal, and she would've been unable to travel. But now, I can do more.

"We do what we have to do for those we love," she says, before she winces and swallows a shout of pain.

I nod and rest my hands lightly on her shin. I focus on the light within me, drawing on the power of the earth surrounding us. The same way the roots answered, my light answers and grows, lifting from deep within me with each breath, moving from my core to my fingertips. I can feel the moment it flows from me into her, directing it straight into the broken bone.

I wait as the feeling of something broken becoming whole again fills me, causing the light within to grow brighter.

There's a collective sigh of excitement from above, and the woman before me gasps, just as her son did when he saw what I did with the roots. Niko turns to see what's happening. His lips quirk to one side, and the beads in his braids clank together as he shakes his head. The astonishment on his face is in childlike opposition to the dark ink covering almost every inch of his arms and what I can see of his neck.

"A little help here?" I say as I try to help the woman to a standing position. Niko shakes off his surprise and joins me. As we work, his arm brushes mine, and the warmth—and something else—I feel sends a shimmer of something I can't quite place brushing through me: recognition, maybe, though it's too strong a word.

If he feels it too, he's better at hiding it than I am. As the woman stands, her legs shaky from days of disuse, he asks her, "Where were you and your pack headed?"

I look at him and then back at her. Pack? Of wolves? Is she a Shifter? A wolf Shifter? How does he know?

She looks more closely at him and then, if I'm not mistaken, gives a slight bow. "We're headed to Cindra. I have family there."

"What family does a wolf Shifter have in Cindra?" he asks, returning to his wary state.

"Mama! Can you climb up now?" a little girl yells, her dark hair standing on end, framing her face.

"Their father," the woman tells Niko, nodding to her children.

He narrows his eyes. According to my studies of the realm, Cindra is where those who study magic live—the Conjours.

The woman pointedly ignores him and tests the roots stretching out just above her. "Thank you for saving us," she says as she gives me a hand out of the hole. Niko climbs up right behind me. "Thank you all." She turns to the others in recognition, then kneels beside Cato and gives him a tight hug. "And thank you for being so brave."

They head out of the forest to retrieve their packs, and we follow them. When I turn, Niko is watching me with what may be a hint of respect, but he doesn't voice it. "Just like I said. Completely reckless."

He moves forward, but I step into his way. "What you call reckless, I call strength."

I gulp as he folds his arms across his chest. This close, I can see his muscles twitch in frustration.

"Too reckless to even know the difference between trust and naivete." He moves around me, striding to his horse.

I raise my voice to be heard across the distance. "I've trusted you not to slit my throat in my sleep these past few nights, Ultor Regni."

He's immovable, like an old oak with the most gnarly roots dug way down deep. My hands ball into fists at my sides, and I huff a big sigh. Turning around, I'm met with smiles from Gayle, Baylor, and Gryphon. Their faces range from entertained to impressed.

"You're in a good mood this evening," I say to Gayle as Navi brushes up against her mare. The two horses seem to have taken a liking to each other.

"We've saved a life, and we're close to home. And there's a village that Niko and I like to stop at along the way. It's the most picturesque spot. I can't wait for you to see it. The entire village backs up against a small bay, and there's a waterfall you can see as you approach from this end;

it's absolutely gorgeous. And the village tavern!" She gasps. "They always serve the most delicious stew." She almost sings the words with delight as our horses travel along the sandy road I've gotten so used to. The forest continues on our left, just as it has since we started, but now it seems to beckon us toward it, and despite its name and the impenetrable darkness, I look forward to seeing what's beyond the treeline we've been tracing this whole time.

The night moves slowly, and the only progress I note is the moon's path across the sky. The leaves rustle gently, and I begin to fight against sleep. Gayle's promise of a warm bed and a hot dinner is the mantra I keep repeating to myself.

I know we must be close as the moon begins its descent. I'm so hungry at this point that I can almost smell the tavern cooking our meal. I'm starting to imagine what we'll have when a sharp curse wakes me from my reverie.

Smoke surrounds us; I wasn't imagining it at all. Baylor points toward the sky. At first, the leaves are too thick for me to see anything, but I keep moving forward, and when the leaves break for just a moment, a wide cloud of smoke fills the sky.

Niko and Gayle look at each other. Disregarding the rest of us, they drive their horses in a full sprint into the heart of the fire. Without hesitation, we follow. My grip on Navi's reins tightens, and I cannot tell if it's because of the speed or what we'll find when we reach the village.

Smoke grows thick quickly, and soon I can't see past Navi's head. I slow her pace and dismount when I realize her sight is the same. The woods around us begin to thin as I lead her forward, and just when I think the smoke can't get any worse, I see the village.

But instead of the picturesque scene Gayle promised, the sight before me breaks my heart.

The reason for the smoke becomes apparent quickly. Homes and buildings are aflame everywhere, clearly in the aftermath of an attack, fire traveling easily from straw roof to straw roof. Bodies are strewn across the ground, warriors and villagers alike, struck down by arrows or brutally maimed by swords. No one has been spared.

I pull my shirt up to cover my nose as the smoke and scent of burning flesh become too much. My vision blurs, but I refuse to give up. I'm determined to help.

"This way."

I hear Gryphon's voice and direct Navi toward the sound. I follow Gryphon toward the clash of metal on metal, all the while cringing at the wreckage left in the wake of such a heartless action. It sounds as if swords are meeting all around us. I keep telling myself it must be a trick of the smoke, but I'm unsure if this is true as I see the fear I feel reflected in Gryphon's face.

I walk straight into a solid figure, not realizing it's Baylor until he shushes me and grabs my arm to keep me from tumbling straight into two skilled swordsmen locked in a struggle. Until now, I've never witnessed such speed in sword fighting. Despite their large and imposing stature, they're also remarkably stealthy and powerful. The involuntary grunts each man expels when they're met with a block or parry illustrate their raw power.

The pair spin and shuffle across the village meeting space, and I realize one of the males is Niko.

"Shouldn't we help him?" My question comes out almost inaudibly as I try to make myself very small next to the brawl happening before us.

"I think that's unwise." Baylor's whisper is as low as my own. "We would only get in his way."

Across the open space, Gayle stalks the outskirts like an animal pursuing prey, never taking her eyes off Niko's progress, ready to pounce at the first sign of struggle. But Niko doesn't need her to interfere on his behalf. The rage emanating from him would be enough to send me running. Mixed with the precision of each strike and the honed skills of a Warden, it's a deadly combination.

Soon, it becomes clear the straggler is no match for this force of destruction. Upon delivering his final blow, Niko drives his broadsword straight through the soldier's middle—and then keeps pushing until its pommel meets the man's rib cage. He snarls something, but his words are too low and laced with anger to hear.

He kicks the body off of his blade and returns the sword to his back without taking even a second glance at the soldier left staring sightlessly toward the heavens. The sound of his stomping steps is the only thing he leaves behind.

My eyes meet Gayle's for a moment. Tears are shining there as her gaze follows Niko until the thickening smoke swallows him up. She looks back toward us, and the expression on her face devastates me. The sense of loss there is clearly not for the man left on the ground before us. I wonder if this scene is all too familiar to two Wardens of the realm.

Wordlessly, we follow Gayle's retreating form back the way we came.

"Let's head out." Her voice cracks as she leads us through the burning ruins of the village back to the horses. Baylor and Gryphon are beside me as we walk through smoke-filled streets, and I get the distinct feeling they're trying to block the scene from my sight. But even with them flanking me on either side, these images are burned into my mind forever.

This is what Hadeon's—now Killian's—men do to the people of Everguard.

The charred bodies we pass each tell a story. Three bodies, men, by what's left of their taller frames, lie before the remnants of a house, as if they fell defending what's inside. Their swords lie beside them, and I can't tell if they were finally taken out by the heartless guards or the fire.

It's too much. Part of me wants to close my eyes to everything as we pass, but another knows the importance of bearing witness to such tragedy—each twisted face silently screaming for someone to save them, each small hand peeking out from what they thought was a safe place.

The soldiers left no survivors.

Besides the crackling flames that have run out of places to spread, the only sounds left are the buildings falling around us and the distant sound of Niko ahead of us, taking down any soldiers who fall behind. So far, he's made quick work of them.

But then, something changes.

"You're right! This is Rowandine Aeronwick!" a triumphant voice yells.

I'm yanked off balance and pulled backward. I thought Niko's blind rage had taken out all the remaining guards, but the woman who's wrapped her arm around my waist in a vise grip and holds a small knife to my throat is quickly surrounded by several others, judging by the shuffling boots at her back.

Gryphon and Baylor turn around first, both assuming a defensive stance at the disruption. Gryphon's face is a mask of anguish, but quickly his resolve becomes unmistakable. He sinks into his stance and tightens his grip on his sword. Baylor, choosing a sword over his bow for such close combat, has pulled a dagger as well, and doesn't miss a beat.

Gayle, though—when I search the flickering shadows behind Gryphon and Baylor, I can't see her short, fierce frame. Dread seeps through me. I knew it wouldn't be long until the Wardens left us to our own devices. Especially after whatever that disagreement between Baylor and Niko was. There's no reason for them to stay.

"Let her go now, and you can all leave in one piece," Baylor shouts across the flames.

"King Killian expects his sister to return to the castle. Don't worry, we'll get her there in one piece." The woman's grip tightens as she delivers my fate, pinning my arms to my sides. "I can't promise she'll stay in one piece, though."

"She's not returning to the castle. It's just a question of whether you all are." There's a slight waver to his threat, but Gryphon holds his ground. He even takes a step forward. His eyes widen slightly, and I turn my head to see what he's looking at.

As the flames lick the buildings surrounding us, the rest of the guards are no longer hidden in the shadows.

This is worse than I thought. There's no chance the three of us make it out of here. There have to be at least twenty of them. Some are on horseback, not even pretending to be worried about a fight. Instead, they look at us with a mixture of boredom and disdain.

"I'm not returning to the castle with you." Even as I say it, I know my fate is sealed. But just as I'm trying to find the courage to go with them, a voice that sounds like sand shifting in the wind comes from the shadows beside us, from the burning building itself.

"If you know what's good for you, you'll step away from the princess, turn, and go."

Niko and Gayle step out of the building, blades drawn—Niko with a menacing broadsword and Gayle with throwing knives. The fevered look hasn't left Niko's eyes yet, and even though we're sorely outnumbered, it's that look alone that gives me hope we'll make it out of this.

But the hope is quickly doused as the female's grip only tightens at his words, and she laughs. A deep, throaty laugh that suggests a lifetime of smoking. "Forgive me, but—"

Her thought is never finished. While the guard's attention is on Niko, the whoosh of a throwing knife sails past my right ear and directly into the guard's shoulder, throwing her off balance just long enough that I'm able to fall forward onto my knees, scooting close enough to Gryphon for him to scoop me up and pull me behind him and Baylor.

As I turn around and gather my wits, I'm just in time to watch as Niko viciously spins his broadsword and it easily takes off the head of the closest guard. Gayle throws another knife with enough force that it sinks into the temple of the guard who held me, finishing the job she started.

Baylor and Gryphon don't need any further encouragement. They drive forward together, brandishing their swords and cutting through the guards one by one.

I think of Licia, and the last words she spoke to me. *You can't do this. It's too much for you.* And then the look on her face as the guard carried her off—a mixture of surprise, fear, and something else. Something that looked a lot like regret.

Did she regret her last words to me? Regret coming with us? Either way, I will not find myself in the same place. I will continue this path I know is right, and everything else will come.

My sword is heavy but familiar in my grip. The flames lick at my ankles, urging me into the fray, and I launch myself at the chaos before me.

Our small group stays close, but it quickly becomes apparent we can't take them all down—so what *can* we do? Exhaustion pounds on me from all angles with each clang of my sword. Out of the corner of my eye, I see Baylor yell out and grab at his torso. Gryphon is at my other side, and we fight as one, working together to ward off the advances. We have a slight advantage—they want us alive. But they don't make it easy. With each parry, I can tell I'm in over my head. Fear creeps in. The best I can hope for is that I can hold them off a little longer.

Over the continuous chorus of metal meeting metal, I hear Baylor and Niko arguing beside me. Is now the time for this?

"I won't!" Niko barks as he fights off three guards at the same time. "She's—"

"That's exactly why you have to! You're the only one who can get her out of this fast enough," Baylor bites out between strikes. The fight is even wearing on him.

The distraction costs me. I didn't think they'd attack me. But as I try to move closer to hear the rest of their conversation, the uneven ground takes its toll. The guard before me takes advantage of my loss of balance, swiping upward along my torso. The pain is instantaneous and blinding.

"Now! Go!" Baylor shouts as I stumble off balance, trying not to fall.

"Fuck!" Niko growls, but a second later, right before I hit the ground, forearms the size of tree trunks settle beneath my knees and back. Gayle and Baylor cover us, and Niko jogs away from the fight, further into the burning village.

I crane my neck to catch a glimpse of Gryphon, who's staring after us—torn between helping Gayle and Baylor or running after me.

I twist and turn to break Niko's grip, and manage to free myself. "I have to go back. I can't leave Gryphon."

"We're not leaving them. We'll go around and attack from the back. Close in on them. Let's go." Niko turns to lead the way.

This makes sense. We were losing ground quickly. If we close in from behind, maybe Niko and I can catch enough of them by surprise to make a difference.

Just as I turn to follow, flames shoot out from a falling building, blocking my path and my view of Niko completely. Panic rises, but I take a deep breath—it's only fire. I just need to find a way around, but there's no sign of Niko.

The heat sears my skin as I turn in circles. The fire engulfing the walls that came down in my path seems to be growing, though. I can't follow Niko through. To my right, where the building once stood, it looks like maybe I can squeeze around the stone foundation and make my way around the fight that way, hopefully finding Niko along the way.

The smoke thickens, but I make quick progress, weaving around what's left of homes and shops. The grating noise of rusted metal sounds above the flames, where a sign is hanging off its hinges. *The Drowned Dragon*, it reads, and the memory of Gayle's excitement about this town makes my stomach sink.

Pushing on, I don't get too close to anything; the heat radiating off the charred walls and frames warns enough.

I can't believe Killian could do this. I won't. Although, there's a niggling feeling pulling at my mind. The conversation with him about the mining town and how Hadeon—and Killian—planned to raze it to make space for their purposes. Could they be going after the entire realm? Killian's words: *Fear is easy to root. Love and respect take more time.* He can't carry on in this way, ruling by fear. There is so much more to him than this. At least, there was before Hadeon dug his claws into him. I can only hope something remains within him that knows what's right.

The rolling sound of rocks is the only warning I get. At first, I think I've caught up to Niko, but there's no sign of him as I spin in circles, trying to decide where the sound came from. I look for a wall, anything, to back up against. But all the buildings are gone; besides the haze of the smoke, there's little to hide behind.

"Niko?" My voice comes out weak and is swallowed by the darkness.

"Have I been replaced so soon, Princess?"

A melodic voice I thought I'd never hear again comes from right behind. So close that I jump and back right into him.

"Thaddeus—what are you doing here?"

The true question in my mind is *You're alive?* I left him for dead. I thought I killed him—driving that dagger straight through his eye, into his brain.

I shove away from his proximity, and when I turn to look at him, I can't help but gasp at what I find. He's still strikingly beautiful, his high cheekbones taking me back to our trysts beside a blazing fire, but I shove the memory away as soon as it surfaces when he smiles at my surprise. Where his pale eyes were once balanced atop those cheekbones, now only one stares back at me. Where the other once was is a still-raw wound, healing quicker than normal due to his Ancient powers, but gruesome nonetheless.

"I'm fine. Thanks for asking." He nods in my direction, that small smile still playing across his lips. He's clearly enjoying my shock. "I thought I'd offer you another chance to come north with me. Ombretta is eager to meet her sister. You don't want to keep her waiting. It will break her heart." He reaches out to touch a strand of my hair, pulling out a curl beside my cheek and letting it spring back into place.

Despite his calm tone, I can't help but gauge my circumstances, noting there's no one around. The sound of the flames feeding on the surrounding homes is too loud to yell over. Memories of the last time Thaddeus cornered me spring to the surface: the surprising force of his icy fingers closing around my neck. The way the bark of the tree bit into my back as I fought to get away. I touch my collarbone, knowing the bruising is faint, but still there. He follows my movement and grimaces.

"It won't be like last time." He reaches toward me again, and I shrink away, remembering the last time he touched me. "I lost my temper, and it won't happen again. It's never happened before, has it?" He's trying to bargain with me, but I know where that path leads. I've taken it one too many times.

"You helped me." The words come out unbidden, but now that I've started, I can't stop. "I'll always remember the short time we shared. Because you helped me find myself and learn about my past. But—but…" I stammer, the words thick in my mouth.

"Don't do this, Roe," he pleads, reaching toward me. "We can achieve so much more together. Don't draw this line."

I back away, the heat from the flaming buildings uncomfortable on my back. "But you gave me nothing, and now that's not enough. I'm…"

Stars, where were we headed? I tilt my head, knowing Thaddeus would be the fastest way to Ombretta. And she's where I need to be. But not like this. I shake my head, more firmly this time.

"I'm not going with you." I start backing away, not wanting to put Thaddeus at my back, knowing how much it cost me last time.

"Come with me, Princess." His voice is soft velvet in my ears. I can't help but pause, remembering the way his nimble hands roamed my body. I melt, just for a moment, thinking how much easier it would be to go with him.

But then he reaches out, offering me his hand. The flames, getting closer, flit across his hand the same way the moonlight highlighted his fingers just before they wrapped around my neck.

My feelings are at war with each other, but I've made my decision. I will not go with him.

My dagger glows in the firelight as I pull it from my belt. Now it's his turn to flinch. "Turn and go, Thaddeus. I'll find Ombretta on my own. I'm not going with you."

The fire licks at his heels, but he's completely unaffected. Me, on the other hand—sweat drips down my face and blurs my vision. The heat is unbearable. I start looking for my exit, because I can't stay here. Not with Thaddeus, and not while this village burns to the ground around me.

He takes another step. I don't know if I have the strength to defend myself against him again. The feel of my blade sinking into his eye socket still haunts my dreams. But I stand, feet apart, my weight balanced and ready in case he strikes. The ground beneath me pulses as if in answer to my fear, my defense. And then I remember: I'm not defenseless. I have more than a dagger at the ready.

My toes wiggle within my boots, grounding me. I want to close my eyes, knowing it would make this easier, but I don't dare take my gaze off him. The earth beneath my feet rumbles in response to my grounding. First, a light tremor, but the answer to my call emboldens me. I can feel the power beneath me, ready and willing.

Thaddeus pauses his advance, tilting his head as if listening. His eye narrow, as if he's trying to decide if he felt the ground beneath him move. He shakes his head in dismissal and continues his approach, now only a stride between us.

He still looks like the same Thaddeus who saved me from slipping over the balcony at our first meeting. The same Thaddeus who came to my room, making me feel things I had never felt before. But was he ever that Thaddeus? Didn't he always have a reason for pulling me back from the balcony ledge? For getting so close?

In hindsight, it's obvious. He never had feelings for me. He got close to me so I would trust him, go back with him. But now, I know better. I can't let anyone in. It's never for love. There's always something else. Avicii, as the king's right hand, was hungry for my name only. Wanting to be linked to the crown alone. And Thaddeus only wanted my blood. Only wanted me to return to Freathia with him to relieve Ombretta, who has shared so much of her Fae blood with the Ancients that she is now something else entirely—not Fae, not Ancient.

I can't let anyone in. Not again.

This time, the tremor in the earth is unmistakable. What's left of the weakened buildings around us crash to the ground, enveloping us in clouds of smoke and ash. The heat burns the inside of my nose, but I stand my ground.

"Suit yourself." Thaddeus shrugs, and I think I've won, but instead of turning to go, he grabs for my wrist. My knees buckle instantly, and as they hit the ground, I can only think: *He's got me again.*

Chapter Seven

"She said she's not going with you."

A deep, rumbling voice breaks through my pain, and the sparks flying from the downed buildings get closer—too close to our small circle.

"A Warden." Thaddeus' annoyance is clear. "Savior of all and protector of Glorixia." His grip tightens around my wrist, and a whimper leaves my lips. I press them together, not wanting to appear any weaker than I already do. "I didn't think there were any more of your kind. Don't you know? Glorixia is gone, buried by greed and sand."

Niko gives a curt nod in response, watching, waiting. He slowly steps forward, angling himself between Thaddeus and me, but says nothing.

Thaddeus' lips curl up on one side in annoyance. "A Shifter, Roe? Interesting company you're keeping now that you know you're Fae." His gaze pulls from Niko to me, goading me into playing his game, whatever that may be. But I'm distracted by what he said. Niko is a Shifter? I never considered this. There were no tells. But I suppose it was the same with Thaddeus—I didn't realize until I was too far in.

Well, it doesn't matter either way. As Niko growls beside me, I take in his untamed beard and tattered clothing that hint that he hasn't bathed in a very long time. That would be enough to repulse me alone, but in addition, he hasn't said more than a few words at a time, and when he does talk, it's never kind. But Thaddeus doesn't need to know that. He can think whatever he wants; he doesn't have a part of me anymore. He lost that privilege when his ulterior motives finally surfaced. Just like with Avicii.

There's no point in loving someone. I silently thank Thaddeus for the harsh reminder as I reply, "It shouldn't matter to you what company I keep."

For a moment, his good eye drops to the ground, and he almost looks chastised. But before I can think what that means, he lunges again, trying to take both Niko and me off guard. He's quick, and his Ancient speed makes him quicker. But it's as if Niko saw him coming. One of his daggers is in his hand, and if Thaddeus takes one more step, he'll end up impaled.

I close my eyes, unable to watch. Their movements are too fast to follow, anyway.

When I open my eyes, they're both standing as if frozen. Thaddeus is stiff with anger and incredulity while Niko growls, the sound barely above a raspy whisper, "She said she's not going with you. Touch her, and you die."

My gaze flits between them. Aggressive masculine pride emanates off both of them like the heat off the flames surrounding us. Thaddeus' eye slides to me, and he opens his mouth, about to reply, but I'll never know what he was going to say. The building closest to us comes crashing down in a cloud of fire and fury.

The flames consume Thaddeus, even before the wood and stone crash to the ground. The whoosh of fire heats my face, but before it touches me, I'm yanked off my feet and we're moving away from the billowing explosion, the fire growing with new life as it sucks in the fresh night air.

I try to pull my hair away from my face long enough to see where we're going, but everything is a green blur because of how fast Niko runs. It seems like we're moving further into the woods, not skirting the village to help the others like we planned.

"We have to go back. They don't stand a chance without us." I press against his chest, a vain attempt to slow his speed or loosen his grip.

"You stay, we all die. You underestimate Gayle. She could take them all single-handed. She has Baylor and Gryphon. And with an angry Thaddeus in the vicinity, the humans will retreat." His words are sharp but steady, despite his rapid pace and him bearing my weight. "Stop squirming. You need to hold on."

Momentarily confused by his words, because I *am* holding on, I stop squirming. The dense trees don't even slow his quick pace.

"We can't just leave them!" Again, I attempt to loosen his hold. "We have to go back." If we don't return now, it will shatter Gryphon. The look on his face said as much. He just lost Licia to the same guards. I can't imagine what's going through his mind right now.

Niko doesn't answer.

My anger rises at his lack of emotion. "Put me down! I can run on my own!" I push against his chest, but it does no good, and he continues to ignore me.

Minutes pass. The only sound is the snap of twigs beneath his feet. The air this far out is fresh; there isn't even a hint of the fire.

I'm thinking I might be sick because of the constant jostling when he finally speaks. "Ready? Hold on."

"Ready for what?"

I turn to where we're headed, but all that's in front of us is a—

"Have you lost your mind?" I screech as he runs the last several steps over a cliff's edge.

My entire body tenses as I feel his other foot leave the last bit of solid ground behind. I thought he was running to save us, but why then are we suspended in the air, falling?

The air whooshes around me, but then my stomach drops as we stop. My mind rushes to catch up with my body. His grip loosens, and he lets go—just for a moment, but it feels like I'm falling for an eternity. I choke. The air in my lungs isn't sure which way it should go. My whole body isn't sure which way it's going.

Niko's form changes underneath me, becoming solid and long. I find my breath, and at the same time, my body and mind stop falling and level out. But we didn't meet the ground. Far from it. We're still so far above it that the trees look like tiny ants. He's still supporting me, but instead of his hands coming around me, there's something solid—something scaly—beneath me.

My support shifts once again, and my mind finally registers what my body has sensed since we leveled out. I'm seated. And we're still moving closer to the clouds above.

As the realization dawns on me, my hands fling out in search of any purchase. Rough, cool scales meet my fingertips, and when I look down, I can't believe my eyes. Pearl-white scales as big as my favorite sweet rolls overlap all around me, reflecting iridescence in the light of the moon.

We're flying. In the air.

My body shifts for balance as we climb higher. My breath catches in my throat again, but is it from the motion this time, or the massive dragon now between my legs?

A steady beating sound distracts me, and I look to my left and then my right for the source. Wings spread out around me, gracefully riding the breeze.

A remarkable wingspan.

They must reach as wide as the east end of the castle walls are long. They go on forever.

Wings. Scales. Niko is a dragon Shifter. I didn't think that was possible. I thought the dragons were wiped out.

"Niko?" My voice is unsure and gets swallowed by the wind. I try again. "Niko, is that you?"

In answer, the dragon's long, pearlescent neck snakes around, the wings not missing a beat. The eyes are the same soft, rich brown as Niko's—just bigger, and set into a reptilian face. He huffs at me and then surges higher.

I buckle forward, grabbing for purchase on something, anything. But all I find are scales. The smooth ones at the base of his neck have just enough space for me to hold on. As I wrap my fingers around them, I'm finally able to relax.

The air smells different up here. It's the sharp, clean scent of conifers and damp earth, and it fills my lungs with an invigorating cold. It tastes of the wilderness itself. I take several deep breaths and release what's left of the smoke from the world below. The crescent moon hangs low, a single luminous petal left behind by the sun. Below, the forest is a sea of dark, shaggy peaks, starting as a thin sprinkle of jewels on the horizon that quickly blossoms into a lush velvet curtain of evergreens as we near our destination.

I try in vain to crane my neck to see if everyone else is okay, but we've put too much distance between us. I hope they all got away. Gryphon must be in a state. I hope he knows I'm okay.

The sound of Niko's wings changes from a powerful beat to a whisper-soft glide. The distant cliff, once a faraway silhouette, now looms directly beneath us. He banks in a gentle arc, our descent a slow, deliberate drop until he settles onto a ledge just wide enough to cradle his immense form.

The scratch of his talons meets the rock first, the impact jolting me forward. My thighs tighten around his body, and I grab on just before I tumble to the unforgiving ground below. The view from up here, the way the dense forest runs right into the bay, is breathtaking.

Two dragon eyes, each as big as a horse, block my view. Niko huffs again, and this time it sounds just like his impatient grumbles. I look around, trying to figure out how to gracefully descend from this height. There's no way to jump from up here; the impact would shatter my teeth.

I look back at Niko's looming dragon face. "How do you expect me to get down from here?"

He rolls his eyes and crouches down, getting as close to the ground as possible, while his iridescent wings, glittering in the moonlight, fold in close to his sides. His hesitancy makes me think he rarely has someone on his back. From this angle, though, I'm able to swing my leg around and slide down his scales.

"Oof." The granite is unforgiving, and as soon as I land on my ass, I wonder if I need to heal my tailbone before moving. But the view surrounding us keeps me rooted to the ground. The view from my chambers in the castle tower doesn't even come close to this. An endless expanse of conifers spans as far as the eye can see. We're at the apex of the bay, and the water looks black in the predawn shadows.

The sound of scales transforming to flesh has me turning around. Niko stands there, magnificent and unashamed, his human form as powerful as his dragon form.

"Is there a problem, Princess?" he drawls, clearly enjoying the flustered expression I must be wearing. My cheeks heat with misplaced embarrassment. "Here." He holds out a hand.

Even though his words are full of disdain, the deep, gravelly voice has me pausing before I put my hand in his, because the reverberations, mixed with the proud show before me, do something powerful to the area just below my core. I bite my lip, thinking *don't look down, don't look down.*

After I regain my composure, I reach for the outstretched hand. He pulls me from the ground effortlessly. His arm comes around me, brushing against my elbow, and I lean into the heat radiating off him. But he gently shifts, reaching into an alcove right beside me, hidden among the rocks.

As he retrieves a bundle of fabric, he doesn't look away. A challenge. And I'm not strong enough to look away, either. The loose pants he pulls on sit low on his hips, highlighting his stomach muscles and that V I've learned only a certain type of man has. His shirtless body creates a palpable warmth that beckons me closer, that I'm hungry for after the time spent in the constant wind. The fresh air mixes with his scent, a heady combination. I almost reach out to touch him, as if I'm under a spell, but then I remember who the man before me is. His soft features transform straight into uncloaked hatred for me, emanating from him as clearly as the warmth. The questions and anger that have been simmering since he shifted resurface.

"Why'd you bring me here? And what about everyone else?" I push against his chest, my palms meeting rock-hard muscle. Being separated from Gryphon and Baylor after Licia was just taken is too upsetting, even though I'm safe with this man. *Male*, I automatically correct myself. He's a Shifter—not human.

He stands firm and unmoving. "I thought I was clear. With you there, everyone was in danger. Once the guards saw you, they weren't leaving without you. If we removed you, everyone else was safe and could make a run for it." He watches me warily for my reaction, waiting, gauging.

What he says goes straight to my core. The very thing I fear most. It's me. I'm the problem. If it weren't for me, everyone would still be at the castle, safe.

"Don't make this about yourself. It's not."

I falter, as if his words were a physical blow. I try to ignore the way his muscles flex and twitch at my response. "You think I'm making this about myself?" My voice is a low growl. Years of Avicii telling me I'm overreacting, telling me to back down, flash through my mind. It floods with memories I tried so hard to forget: cowering at his yelling, the blues and purples of the bruises the next day.

Niko's eyes smolder as he takes a step closer to me, but I stand my ground. We're locked in a staring contest, and this time, I won't back down.

This is about me. It's my life. My family—Hadeon—has torn apart our kingdom. And now, Killian sits on a splintering throne. One he doesn't intend to fit back together, and one that is rightfully mine.

That last part still doesn't sit right on my shoulders.

The air between us practically thrums with a dangerous energy, a tangible blend of our mutual fury and something more, something unspoken.

"You have no idea." Niko turns and stalks off to the rock face.

Too riled up to be dismissed, I run after him.

Chapter Eight

The darkness around us shifts in the growing morning light, and the mouth of a cave appears before me. Niko is about to disappear into its black maw when my fingers close around his wrist. The contact is a shock, a sudden anchor that forces him to turn back to me. His stare, heavy and intense, is a physical weight that presses against the tangled knot of feelings I have for him. From the look in his eyes, he's just as caught as I am.

The last of the moonlight paints us in a soft glow, causing his bright brown eyes to sparkle. His hands grasp my hips, firmly drawing me closer, his eyes watching mine, waiting for consent. I stretch up onto my toes and press my palms into his hard chest, bringing my lips closer to his, showing him I want this. A delicious mixture of anger and fire warms me, beckons me closer. Fury burns within me, and the same heat reflects behind his eyes.

Our lips collide with urgency.

His tongue explores my mouth, and there's a delicious all-consuming heat I can't get enough of. Any distance remaining between us immediately dissolves as he lifts me, his palms supporting my thighs, and we move as one into the black mouth of the cave.

As the shadows engulf us, the rest of my senses heighten. Vines of moss brush against my upper arms, which are wrapped around Niko's shoulders. His scent of woodsmoke and leather engulfs me as he moves deftly through the darkness, our kiss never breaking. The warmth of his body devours me as surely as each kiss.

His steps slow, and my back roughly meets a stone wall. The bite of pain intermingles with pleasure and sends a shiver through me, from my neck down to my toes. "Ah," he growls, seemingly in appreciation of the sounds escaping my lips.

This is madness. He's just called me self-centered and reckless, and yet here I am, pressing against him as if my body has a mind of its own. A small, rational part of me screams to pull back—to preserve the biting jabs and clever remarks that have been our only language. But this feeling... this charged, dangerous connection fueled by our mutual fury and fierce passion... it feels like a truth I can no longer ignore. So I stop fighting. I lean into the fire of this moment. My fingers snake into his braids and give a firm tug, a silent demand for more as he opens his mouth against mine in a desperate, ardent clash. Until there's nothing left but him.

With my back pinned to the wall, his hands are free to claim me. His fingers trace a possessive, slow line up my waist, and I lean into every deliberate touch. He thumbs the bottom of my breast, suddenly heavy with need, then palms it, rolling my peaked nipple between his fingertips.

My body arches into him, demanding more. My legs loosen around his hips and slide down until my feet touch the ground. One of his hands continues up, gripping the back of my head, his thumb along the soft part of my neck, tilting my head back. My breath hitches as our kiss intensifies.

A shiver of pure surrender races through me, and my body thrums with every inch of contact. I moan, a low, guttural sound, as his hard length presses against my stomach—a stark, carnal promise. My hands desperately trace the potent outline of him through his pants, but it's a futile gesture. I need more, now.

My hands fumble with his pants, and a deep-throated chuckle leaves his mouth, but no words, and I think he appreciates my eagerness. I wish he'd appreciate me faster. As he takes off his pants, I try to help us along by pulling down mine, but he stops me. His hands rest atop mine until he traces along the waistline, taking his time—an unwelcome change from our frantic, eager energy. But I let him, reveling in the way he plants light kisses along my hips while his fingers tug my pants first off one leg, and then the other.

He moves to kneel before me, but I am too needy for him to waste time worshipping me. That chuckle sounds against my thighs at my impatience, but he rises, enveloping me once more, the back of my shirt giving little protection against the protruding rocks as he lifts me once again. I wrap my legs around his back and lock my ankles at the base of his spine as he brings the head of his cock to my entrance.

"This is what you want, Rowandine?"

My name in his deep, rumbling voice is intoxicating. I pause, relishing the way it rolls over me, landing deep below my belly button. But he takes my hesitation as something else. I can feel it in the way he draws away.

I pull him closer to me with my heels, my nails digging into his broad shoulders. The morning light peeks through the mouth of the cave, making it look like Niko is glowing from within.

"Yes. This—you are what I want."

He leans in and kisses me, our lips colliding, and at the same time, he enters me in one harsh movement.

The way the pain draws out the pleasure of him filling me shatters me completely. His scent mingles with the smell of our heightening arousal and sweat, a heady, animalistic combination. I rest my head against the cool cave wall, and he covers my neck with rough kisses, his beard scratching every spot he caresses. The contrast between his soft lips and the prickly scrape is a sweet torture that makes my body hum in response.

The satisfaction builds inside of me, as sure as my anger was rising in the moments before we kissed. I let go of everything, allowing myself to completely surrender to the way he feels entering me over and over again. The sound echoes off the walls of the cave each time our bodies meet, the rhythm picking up as my euphoria mounts.

The feelings are almost too much—almost. But I drink in the way pleasure and pain mingle together to create something beautiful, the way my anger has turned into pure, heated passion.

His movements quicken, and I drive down onto him, meeting each thrust, the sensations heightening within me until my whole body tingles with an ecstasy I've never known before.

"Come for me, Datura."

His words drive me over the edge, giving voice to the satisfaction building throughout my body, and then it bursts. A moan of contentment escapes my lips, and the way it echoes around the cave makes me self-conscious for just a moment, but Niko's last pumps inside me have him doing the same. A low rumble accompanies his final drive into me, intensifying the waves rolling through me until I'm dizzy and disoriented.

He releases me, but our shared gaze remains unbroken. My feet find the ground, and I watch as his eyes soften, their flecks of gold receding as his pupils shrink to their normal size. A hundred questions hang in the air between us, unspoken, but they are all there in the silent conversation of our eyes.

"That was…" He trails off, his fingers brushing a strand of my hair back into place.

"Yeah," I reply. The correct answer wars with all other words in my mind, too. The tension between us is completely dissipated, for now, at least, replaced with something else entirely. An understanding? A spark of some sort? I'm not sure, but what I do know is that this man can get under my skin in more ways than one.

He moves away into the open space surrounding us, but returns, handing me a cloth. When I look at him questioningly, he replies, "I'll go see what I can find for us to eat." He looks at the cloth. "I thought you'd like to clean up."

I feel my cheeks heat instantly, but even as embarrassment flushes my skin, the thoughtfulness warms me in a different way. The fury from moments ago has drained from me completely, and by the looks of it, from him as well.

One moment, there's only a soft morning glow surrounding me, and the next, a hearty fire adds its orange gleam around the space. I pull my pants back on, then wince a little as my arms stretch over my head, looking down to check the spot where one guard got a little too close for comfort. But then I turn, and I'm momentarily distracted. The fire grows, lighting up the cave walls. This place is well cared for and homey. Shelves upon shelves of small figurines and trinkets, all lovingly placed, line the room. The small space warms, and the chill of the night recedes.

"Every dragon needs a lair." His words are light, but tinged with loneliness.

"You come up here often, then, with damsels in distress?" My question dances around our fight from earlier.

"You're the first person I've brought up here." He looks up from adding more wood to the fire, his eyes reflecting the glimmer of the flames. "And you're anything but a damsel in distress."

I let his words settle over me, a truth I didn't know I was waiting for. All my life, I've heard the same refrains: *Just wait, I'll do it for you. Let me get that for you. It looks too heavy. You will marry; that is your purpose.* They all saw me as something fragile, weak, and easily broken. And until now, I saw myself that way, too. But hearing Niko put it into words feels like a shift in the earth—a reason to stand taller, to feel stronger.

His sudden kindness is too perplexing for me to dissect in my current state. Rather than warming myself by the fire—by Niko—I distract myself by studying the shelves. The care with which each of these items was placed speaks of a patient, sentimental person. But as I look for the owner of the cave, all I see points to Niko. There's one small chest against the far wall, with only one pair of boots beside it. I steal a look toward where Niko continues to immerse himself by the fire. Beside the small wood pile, there's an end table, and stacked atop it is only one set of a plate, bowl, and cup.

The room soon fills with the comforting scent of cinnamon. My stomach growls in answer.

"Here."

I turn back to the fire, and Niko hands me the bowl, making me smile.

"What?" he asks.

"You're back to your gruff, one-word sentences, I see," I remark, but my stomach's growl cuts the bite from my tone. Niko pulls the bowl back toward him, and I pause, a fleeting moment of pride battling a very real hunger.

The heat of the bowl seeps into my hand as I join him beside the fire. He holds up the silverware options: a fork and a spoon. Looking at the dense liquid in the bowl, I take the spoon. Without a word, he plunges the fork into his own food, the liquidy substance spreading across his plate.

My spoon hangs in the steam rising from the unfamiliar meal as he shovels the contents into his mouth. It looks like a liquid cloud, all the same, bland color. As steam clouds my spoon, Niko sets his plate down with a scrape, his gaze fixed on my hesitation.

"You've never had porridge?" His tone is a razor's edge of judgment, and his eyes narrow—a surprising amount of venom for a simple meal.

"It's so..." I'm not sure how to complete the thought, but the moan escaping my lips expresses my feelings perfectly.

"Creamy? Filling? Warm?" He reaches toward my bowl, ready to finish it off for me. I pull it close to my chest, and he backs off, waiting expectantly. I scoop up a spoonful and bring it to my lips. It smells a little earthy and a little like bread fresh out of the oven. The taste is the same, but with a hint of sweetness. It also tastes like childhood, like a warm fire on a dark morning.

"You made this?" I ask, now enthusiastically spooning each bite to my lips before I finish the last.

"That's all I had up here on such short notice." He shrugs, looking away and into the fire.

"It's delicious. A little like the sweet rolls I love so much on special occasions, but milkier and without the glaze."

"Glad it meets your standards," he replies, but he looks pleased with himself.

His words, though, remind me of the way he sneered at me and his argument with Baylor during the attack. The words were blurry because I was still out of sorts, but they fought, and it felt like it was about me. "What is it you have against all Aeronwicks?"

"What makes you think I have an issue with you?" He stands, a giant in this small cave, to take the dishes. I wait, a skill learned from Licia, knowing that if I stay quiet long enough, he'll continue. And it works. "But if you must know: Hadeon Aeronwick destroyed this realm. I'm a Warden. It's my duty to keep people—the realm—safe." His voice shakes almost imperceptibly as he ends his thought.

"And that's turned into attacking the king's guard and carrying off the royal family?" I stand too, not wanting to feel small in this man's presence.

"You're quick." He walks closer to the mouth of the cave, throwing some gritty pebbles into the remnants of food and pushing it around with his fork—it looks like he's cleaning it, but with dirt.

"But why?" I ask, remembering how his breath felt on the back of my neck, the way he held me in place, making sure I wouldn't fall off the horse while I was still groggy from healing Gryphon. Or the way he looked at me after we saved that wolf Shifter and her pack.

"But why, what?" He adds more gravel to the plate, rubbing it all around until he appears happy with it.

The brief truce of breakfast is over, and my anger flares hot. "Pick one, Ultor. Why were you and Gayle there? Why did you save us? Why did you lose control with that guard, and why in all the hells did you bring me all the way up here, alone?" I close the distance between us, undeterred by the narrowing of his eyes—a permanent fixture on his face, it seems.

A raw, unguarded emotion—is it hurt? Pain?—flares in his eyes for a split second, then vanishes behind a hard mask. "You needed help," he says, his tone clipped. "We were there." He shakes the last of the gravel from the plate, his movements precise and a little too deliberate as he rubs it clean with a worn cloth. "What's an Aeronwick doing with earth magic anyway?"

But before I can even formulate an answer, he rushes forward. My gaze follows his hands as he sets the now-immaculate dishes on the side table, and he meets my stare, his full attention once again fixed on me.

"Are you bleeding?" Niko shoots to my side, his eyes locked on my cream-colored tunic. I look down, confused by his quick movement. But as soon as my gaze lands on the red bloom, I know why he's so concerned.

"It's nothing. Just a scratch," I insist, trying to downplay it. "One of them clipped me on their way down, but there wasn't any force behind—"

Before I can finish, he's already taken a blade to my shirt, slicing the fabric from the hem almost to the neck. "You're bleeding," he murmurs, the words an incredulous whisper.

He starts pulling things from the shelves, filling the freshly cleaned bowl with water from our waterskin. His hands are unsteady as he dampens a cloth and presses it gently against the cut just under my breast. His touch is a stark warmth, like the heated stones the maids used to place at the foot of my bed. I could melt into it.

I shake off the thought. One, I'm bleeding. Two, I just felt a flicker of attraction to this man who thinks I'm completely helpless. If only he knew.

"I can—it's not that bad," I try to reassure him, reaching for the wrap he's started winding around my ribs. My eyes meet his, and I notice his hand just skimmed against the swell of my breast, but he seems oblivious, focusing only on covering the wound. In fact, he looks a little pale... a little gray around the edges. As my healer instincts snap into place, I pitch my voice low and calm. "Do you... have a thing about blood?"

"No, I—" He lifts his chin to meet my gaze, and the small, quick movement is his undoing. His dislike of blood, combined with the sudden motion, sends him crashing to the ground. I lunge forward to catch him, but can only manage to soften his fall, his body a dead weight against mine.

I'm on my knees beside him the moment he lands, my hands flying to the back of his head to check for blood. There's none, but I lean across his chest anyway to check the other side, just to be sure. The slight twitch of his jaw and the shallow flutter of his eyelids tell me his head didn't hit the stone, and he's coming out of it.

I'm about to sit back on my heels, satisfied he'll be fine and I can tend to my own wound, when his eyes open. I freeze, caught like a thief over a stolen treasure. But I'm not a thief; I'm just a healer doing my job.

Our eyes meet as I hover over him, our faces inches apart. I don't move, unsure if any sudden motion will confuse him, or if I even want to break the moment. This close, his eyes are a beautiful chaos of browns, the shades dancing and softening his usually stony exterior.

He's just as frozen. Neither of us moves, held captive in the space between our breaths. I can feel his steady exhale against my lips, and his eyes, dark and searching, burn into mine. They're asking me something, a question I don't understand, but one I suddenly, desperately want to answer.

And then I understand. He's not waiting for me to move; he's waiting for me to kiss him. The quick, nervous lick of his lips, a sudden vulnerability, is a powerful invitation. The raw, masculine heat of his chest, still bare, is a siren's call. I begin to lean forward to answer it.

Don't make this about yourself; it's not.

The words echo in my mind, sharp and cold, a slap of reality. The thought is a painful bite that makes me push against his chest and sit back on my heels.

"So you're the great Ultor, a ruthless Warden who can't handle a little blood?" My hands rest along the makeshift bandage he started wrapping around me. Already on the ground, finding power to draw from is simple, and I close the wound in no time. It doesn't even seem as if Niko takes notice.

His jaw tightens, a subtle flinch at my words. "It never used to be an issue," he admits, his voice low. "It's gotten worse as I've gotten older."

At his honesty, so disarming, a surprised laugh escapes me. He's just like everyone else. At my reaction, his lips quirk on one side, a fleeting smirk that's more self-conscious than confident. It's the first truly unguarded expression he's ever shown me.

One moment, I'm filled with the familiar fire of anger toward him. Next, I'm lost in a confusing tide of curiosity and attraction. The air between us is a living thing, heavy with our past antagonism, but he's just pierced it with a moment of genuine vulnerability. I let our temporary truce linger, content to simply watch the layers of this complicated man unfurl.

Chapter Nine

Niko finally responds to my previous question as we make our way down the cliff face.

"I've been trying to put this land back together for decades. Hadeon's poison was strong and thorough," he says. "What makes you think you have the remedy when so many before you have failed?"

He throws my question back at me, and I can't tell if my struggle to find my footing is because of that or the trail he's leading us down.

The rock face seems to mock me, alternately shrinking and expanding, a cruel optical illusion. Niko promised only a morning's hike, but we've been on this relentless downward march for what feels like the better part of the day, each step jarring.

What makes me think I'm different? I don't know. But now that I know there's a problem, I can't just turn a blind eye. It will just take some time. With each new problem that sprouts through the ground, I realize this land is no different from my gardens on the mountainside of Merula, and if we just take time to propagate the right cuttings and cultivate the right conditions to grow, we can fix this.

"I have to try," I bite out between steps. If I thought riding horseback all day was rough, I was sorely mistaken. Descending this mountain is more of a climb than anything else. When I'm not pressed up against the cliff face, holding on for dear life, I'm attempting to keep up with Niko's brisk pace while trying to avoid breaking an ankle on any of the uneven rocks sticking out along the path. "There's got to be a better way."

"There is," he huffs over his shoulder while he traverses a felled log as if he's walking on clouds. "There are many better ways. But Hadeon chose to take any other path. He preferred destruction and fear over peace." He turns around when he gets to the other side, his dark eyebrows raised in expectation.

I look at the log. It's thick enough, except it's fallen over a deep ravine. A deep, rocky ravine. The fall alone would kill me. I look back to Niko, shaking my head. "I'll find another way around. There's no way I'm crossing this."

"What happened to your sunny 'I can' attitude? It's not that bad." He points down at the gaping hole in the ground as if we're looking at two different things.

"You made it look so easy," I say, incredulous that he expects this of me.

"Thank you." I can see his grin through his thick beard.

"But how?" I can't fathom the amount of confidence it would take to even move one step further. This is impossible.

"Remember? I have wings." He points to his shoulders.

I roll my eyes, but at the same time, I can't help but think how nice it would be to have my own set of wings. Even if only for moments like this. Just knowing that if I'm about to fall, I could shift and fly up, would add a layer of protection.

"Don't worry. If you fall, I'll save you."

I purse my lips at his implication that I can't do this. Even though it would seem I completely agree. But that's the irony of the situation. I must try. I must cross this log. This is only one of the many travails I will face.

The sun continues to rise as we trudge silently on. Despite the chill in the air, sweat trails down my back, and the front of my tunic sticks uncomfortably to my body. I glance up, hoping to see flat ground up ahead, but instead I trip on a rock as soon as my eyes move upward. I catch myself grunting with the effort it takes.

Niko turns to make sure I'm upright. "We won't ever get there if you keep tripping over every rock on the path. Are your eyes even open? With all the racket you're making, we would've been stealthier if we'd arrived as a dragon."

"And why didn't we?"

"Why didn't we do what? Fly down? I thought arriving on foot would be more inconspicuous. I prefer to make a slightly less audacious entrance if I can."

"I feel like I'm doing alright for someone who has just traded balls and gowns for boots and sleeping rough."

He responds with a low growl and turns to continue. I glare at his back, although my expression quickly softens as I remember the way his kisses trailed across my collarbone as he had me pressed against the wall.

"So we've returned to the big, bad, silent Niko, I see," I spit out between gasps for air.

I stumble—again. It's impossible to keep up with his long strides on such uneven ground, and to make it worse, I keep getting distracted by our surroundings. I don't think I've ever seen so many evergreens in one place, all different types and all as tall as giants. I feel like an ant in a field of sunflowers; my gaze is anywhere but the ground. At least the land has flattened out at this point. And I can't tell if it's just my wishful thinking, but it seems like his purposeful strides have slowed just a bit in this last hour. I think we're close.

"How long has it been since you've been back to Sverreian?" I ask, realizing that with the state of his beard and roughly worn clothes, he could've been gone for weeks or even months.

"It's been a year or two." His voice is deep and unreadable.

"Then I'm sure you're happy to be back. Should we hurry? Do you think Gayle and the rest have made it already?" I'm excited at the thought of seeing Baylor and even Gayle again, but especially Gryphon. I hope they've had no issues along the way, and that Gryphon hasn't been too worried about me.

"They won't arrive until after noon. They've got a long way to travel on foot. I know it didn't seem so far last night." He pauses, turning to inspect me as he says this, checking to make sure I'm still whole.

"They'll be alright, though?" I ask tentatively, now realizing we left them there to fend for themselves with an angry Ancient close by.

"I don't think Thaddeus would have given them any trouble. He seemed to have more important things to tend to first. That eye wound looked pretty fresh. Even for an Ancient." He looks pointedly at me with raised eyebrows—I'd think he's impressed, if I didn't know better. "And he wanted you; he wouldn't have bothered with them knowing you'd already disappeared. I'm sure by now he's pieced together that I shifted and carried you far away. He'll regroup and be back, though." He looks up at the sun, gauging the time of day. I realize this is the first time I've noticed him looking for signs or markers. He must know these lands well. "And we'll be in Sverreian before too long."

Although his words are sure, his eyes look sad as we get closer to his village. I wonder what happened the last time he was home to bring him so much pain.

He feels my gaze on him and turns his head. "What is it?" His eyes search my features for an answer.

"You know, you've said more words this morning than you've said in all the days we've been traveling."

He hums, and his mouth quirks to one side in thought. "You're right. We're wasting too much time. Let's go."

As the path under our feet levels out and takes on more of a manicured state, I could fall to my knees and kiss the ground. I'm more relieved to see signs of comfort than I could've ever imagined. Even while I take in the strange village, the foremost thought on my mind is a bath.

People turn toward us as we walk into the center of Niko's village. Kids trail after us, pointing, whispering excitedly. Older people hide their surprise by bowing their heads while they look on. We draw a large crowd, but all eyes are glued to the return of their Warden. No one is paying a drop of attention to me. It's just like moving around the castle with Licia.

The pathway opens up wider and wider as we move closer to the center. Instead of the rows and rows of buildings that usually make up a village, here, the villagers have taken advantage of the larger-than-life trees. It appears they've hollowed out the centers of most of the largest ones to create their homes within.

Niko nods toward the people and animals gathering around us. I follow his gaze upward, surprised to see another level of homes and buildings lining the treetops. Above us, all the structures are made of wood and use the thick tree branches as a foundation to build around. People wave down from bridges high in the trees, attempting to get a better look at the commotion down below. Just as on the ground level, there are plenty of animals gathered as well—everything from squirrels and mice to exotic creatures I've only read about in books.

We're met in the village center by a group of warriors encircling a figure dressed all in white. Her snowy robes flow around her, giving her considerable size an even wider presence. The darkest of hair rolls down to her hips in stark opposition to her light skin. Her eyes are warm and crinkly in the corners. I feel her gaze fall on me before she studies Niko for a long moment.

He stands tall and remains quiet, so I do the same. He says nothing as this woman takes his measure.

Flanking her are six warriors on each side. They seem both more relaxed and more aware of their surroundings than any of the castle guards. The one standing closest to the woman's left exudes power, his legs spread wide to take up as much space as possible. His arms are casually at his sides, but the weapons at his belt suggest he'd be able to arm himself in seconds if threatened. His eyes are hard, but as he looks Niko over, a small smile spreads across his rigid facade.

The woman's serious demeanor cracks suddenly as well, and she smiles widely. "It's been too long, Cinderkins. Too long indeed."

Niko stiffens, and his whole face turns from a deep blush to a bright tomato red, then to a plum color in rapid succession. I hide my laugh with a cough, thinking only a mother would call him such. I stand straighter at this realization. If this woman, a leader in this village, is his mother, then Niko must be of some importance here as well. A prince, perhaps? If so, why wouldn't he have mentioned it before?

Her robe-swathed arms go wide, and she wraps them around him. Niko's arms come automatically around her, and he bends down to meet her embrace. She pulls away and grabs both his cheeks. Tears glisten in her eyes as she inspects him up close, patting his long, pulled-back hair and thick beard. For his part, he endures it well. I have never seen him with this much patience during our days of travel.

The tall sentinel closest to the woman steps forward. "Ultor Regni." His voice, thick with reverence, echoes through the square as he bows to Niko. The other guards immediately follow suit, each dropping to one knee, and the gathered crowd lowers their heads as if before a god.

My gaze snaps to Niko. He remains stoic, absorbing the deference, but a cold knot forms in my stomach. He truly is *the* Ultor Regni. He's the reason the king's guards whisper prayers in the shadows, begging the stars for safe passage beyond the city gates. He's the reason countless spouses of the royal guard curse the name that leaves them widowed.

I take him in again with fresh eyes: the shadowy tattoos crawling across his skin, the unyielding set of his jaw. These people venerate him, and he is the reason Hadeon and now Killian second-guess every move beyond Merula's walls, letting their guards do the dirty work. Both kings knew one step outside would mean their lives were forfeit to this man.

The memory of the day Niko and Gayle found us claws at my mind, sharp and cold. I was too numb with grief for Licia, but Baylor and Niko argued. Baylor must have been arguing for my life. The thought chills me to the bone. Even though Gryphon named what Niko was at the very beginning, seeing him now, in this new light, revered like a god—a god of destruction and vengeance against everything I am—my jaw must be hanging slack.

He glances over to me, his umber eyes utterly unreadable as they meet mine. The same eyes that devoured me only this morning. Heat, sharp and unwelcome, rises in my cheeks—not from embarrassment, but from a sickening surge of betrayal. Of course he, too, had an ulterior motive. The pleasure he drew from me, the vulnerability I showed… I never should've lowered my guard. Not even for a single stolen moment.

Niko's jaw works as everyone rises again, and he takes in my reaction.

"You're too thin. And in dire need of a bath." The woman's nose crinkles as she inspects him further. She looks between us, reading more than I want her to. "Good that you've come home just in time for the midwinter celebration." At this, she steps back and smiles at me. "Thank you for bringing him home safely," she says as she cups my face with both hands.

"Mother," Niko interjects, taking a swift step forward as if to intercept her words. "This is Rowandine."

"Rowandine?" Her eyebrows shoot up, her gaze sweeping over my face, from my forehead to where her hands still rest on my jaw. Her voice drops to a stunned whisper. "Rowandine Agroterra, of the Glen? As in, the last of the Fae royals?"

The words hang in the air, a bell tolling. My breath hitches, not at her question, but at the sharp, ragged intake of breath from beside me.

"No, Mother, Rowandine Aeronwick. Of Merula." Niko's head whips toward me as he says the words. Is it my imagination, or does he spit them? His usual mask of stoicism has cracked just a little, making room for his mother's truth about my lineage.

But she only shakes her head, a slow, certain movement. Her steady, knowing gaze remains fixed on me. "No, Nikodemus. She's of the

Agroterra line. She's Fae."

Chapter Ten

The name Agroterra confuses me, yet she finds whatever truth she seeks written on my face. With those words, she drops into a deep, sweeping bow. The warriors follow, and there's a ripple through the crowd that seems to be the entire village as all heads lower in unison.

My entire life, people have stumbled over their words in my presence. Crowds have bowed; grown men have knelt at my feet. It comes with the territory of being a princess, the weight of a crown that never quite fit.

But this moment is different.

This is not the compelled respect given to a princess; this is profound, heartfelt veneration. Today, they recognize my heritage and know my purpose. Today, these people look at me with hope igniting in their eyes.

Exhilaration washes over me, quickly followed by a crashing wave of doubt. The acknowledgment from this entire village causes a flood of uncertainty. The realization that these people, and many, many more, expect great things from me weighs heavily on my shoulders.

I turn to Niko to see what we do next. He looks as puzzled as I feel. But even as his eyes narrow with confusion as he weighs his mother's words, he tilts his head in silent acknowledgment that this moment is completely mine.

Mine? What does that even mean? My decisions have always been made by someone else, part of a greater scheme. Now, after more than three decades of doing as I'm told and being told what I want, I can make my own decisions. A heavy blanket is lifted from over my eyes.

I pause a moment, while all these people kneel to me, and close my eyes. I look deep within myself. Most of my wants and desires, choices and actions have been sullied by the needs of those around me. I search and search, looking for a small, forgotten piece. That piece—that piece is me. In this moment, I vow to myself that I will nurture and grow this piece of myself until my whole self is genuine.

I open my eyes with this new seed growing deep within me. I will strength into my words, but fail miserably as I begin, "Rise, please, Lady…"

"Lady Alasie of Sverreian in the Dread Forest." She straightens, and everyone else follows. "Today is truly a day to celebrate. You both need time to clean up and rest, of course, but this evening we look forward to celebrating with you. Please." She gestures for us to follow, looping one arm through mine and one through Niko's, leading us away from the now fervently whispering crowd and toward one of the biggest trees I've ever seen.

Inside, the tree appears to be used as a meeting house. There are wide entrances to large rooms on either side. As we pass the rooms, I note groupings of chairs or cushions arranged in circles. Some take up the whole of the room, while other spaces are more intimate, with only three or four seats. Another room has a large wooden table and chairs spanning its length.

Lady Alasie notices my curiosity and gestures around her. "This is the Council House. Many decisions are made here for our people. Large groups come together here for meetings, but also for celebrations. On this floor are the meeting rooms and kitchens, but above we have rooms for visiting members of the council to reside in during their stay."

"The Village Council?" I notice that some of these rooms could hold more than double the number of people I saw out in the village just now.

"Well, yes, we regularly use it as such. But also the Realm Council." She throws a meaningful look my way as she says this, measuring my response. "Which we have been able to maintain all these years."

"You mean the other races continue to meet? I thought connections were destroyed when the Fae disappeared." My knowledge of the kingdom's history is shaky at best, so I am eager to understand the truth.

"Good. Yes. This is what the other races allow the humans to believe. It is better for them to believe they are in control and have destroyed everything except what's left of Merula. In fact, the complete opposite is true. We are in close contact with the Conjours and Elementals past Cindra, and have limited contact with what's left of your people." I quickly realize she means there are more Fae somewhere in these lands. "The Ancients mostly keep to themselves in the North. We also have contact with those across the sea. The only ones we've cut out are the humans, and that's only since Hadeon sat on the throne. Humans used to be a part of our council alongside us all. We were hopeful King Killian would be more amenable, but since you're here, I'm afraid my doubts about him are true."

Trying to find a shred of truth in all the lies I've grown up with, I ask, "But didn't all the races previously live together?"

"Yes. This is true." Alasie motions toward a staircase in the back of the meeting tree. It's mostly roots, but a few boards are placed strategically between some that grow too far apart. Never having been inside a tree, I have no idea what to expect as we climb the stairs.

At the landing, the stairs open to a wide, cozy room on one side, and a row of open doors on the other. On the common room side, the ceiling is low and slanted. Built into one of the tree's large knots is a stone fireplace with a glowing fire, bringing warmth into the room. The scent of old books wafts from the wall-length bookshelves on either side of the fireplace. Woven throw blankets are haphazardly strewn across the wooden furniture, adding to the welcoming charm. The way the room looks and smells reminds me of our library in the castle, except this place has a worn-in, well-loved feel about it that the royal library lacked entirely.

Lady Alasie guides me toward the first open door, which leads to a small room decorated in the same inviting way as the outer one. "Here you are, Princess Rowandine, your home for the time being. There's a bathing chamber through there. I'll have someone bring a few items of clothing that should fit."

"Thank you, Lady Alasie, for your hospitality. Your village is beautiful. I cannot wait to see more of it," I say as she backs out, leaving me in my *own* room with my *own* real bed. It's almost too much to ask for.

I glance at the large wooden tub in the corner, but instead, I promptly sprawl out on the thick, plush blankets across the bed. Sighing heavily, I thank the stars that we've made it this far, and hope that I'll get at least a few nights of sleep here, in this room with a ceiling and a big, fluffy comforter.

I stare at the ceiling, swirling with roots and knots, worried about Gryphon, Baylor, and Gayle. Shouldn't they be here by now?

My mind shifts again to the Ultor Regni. The swirls of roots mimic my emotions. This morning was so raw and beautiful. At the time, it was clearly just two people giving in to the moment. But on the way down the mountain, when he started to open up, I thought maybe there was something there.

At least now I have nothing to worry about. If it wasn't clear before that he dislikes me, it's clear as root rot disintegrating a vine now—there can be nothing between the Ultor Regni and an Aeronwick.

He wanted me dead. But now that he knows I'm not an Aeronwick, has that changed?

After a thorough scrubbing in the bath, I sit in the outdoor common area under a wide-spanning white cedar, basking in the feeling of being clean and refreshed. The afternoon shifts to evening, and the gentle glow of the fire before me has my thighs thankful I'm not sitting astride Navi.

I let my eyes unfocus as I enjoy the flickering of the huge flames. Here in Sverreian, I feel like I can relax fully, which hasn't been the case of late. It doesn't seem like these people are worried about being attacked at all. And rightly so. There's no way someone could navigate the depths of the Dread Forest without prior knowledge of it.

Thank the stars. I'm exhausted from looking over my shoulder. And now, I can fully appreciate the way this giant fire is thawing places I didn't even know had frozen during our trek west.

There's movement on the other side of the fire, so I bring everything quickly back into focus. A female interrupts my peaceful reflection as she sits beside me on the log bench. She hands me a small wooden bowl filled with freshly cut fruit and motions for me to eat it.

"Oh, yes, please, I'm starving."

She giggles as I shovel the food into my mouth, as if I haven't eaten in months, rather than the few weeks I've spent on rations of jerky and stale bread. The sound is so unexpected that I look up at her. I notice she is probably about the same age as me. Younger than I first thought, from the way she carried herself with so much confidence. Her dirty blonde hair is pulled in tiny braids away from her face, falling down her back. Freckles pepper along her nose and stand out against her pale skin. Her brown eyes are bright, and I can't help but think she looks familiar somehow.

I grab another handful of the sweet fruit she's brought and continue to scarf it down. Around chewing, I manage a muffled, "Thank you. This is amazing."

She giggles again. "Niko said you were a bit strange."

I'm taken aback by her frankness. Usually, the only person to speak to me in such a way is Licia, with her endearingly rude comments. I get ready to ward off her attack, but realize she's looking at me with more curiosity than malice.

Oh. So she's with Niko. I'm unsure why, but this realization stings a little more than I thought it would.

"You're... with Niko?" I'm unsure how to ask such a bold question straight off, but for some reason, this answer feels important to me.

She actually snorts in response. And now she's lost in a fit of laughter. I take the moment to ungracefully tip the remnants of the fruit into my mouth. Is that such a funny question because it's a ridiculous thought? Or because it should be obvious that she's linked to him? I guess I should've kept the question to myself, because I'm even more confused now.

"You've come a long way in such a short time. You must be run ragged." She looks me over matter-of-factly, as if the proof is written across my face.

Unsure how to respond to her laughter and her judgment, I sit quietly, staring at her, wishing she would get up and leave now that I have filled my empty stomach.

"I'm sorry, you must think me completely without manners!" She shakes her head and begins again. "I'm Priyanka." Her hand comes up and touches my shoulder, and she waits. She smirks as if thinking I must be a complete loon and waves her hand. "Never you mind. Call me Pris. Come join us—we're setting up for supper just over there, but you looked like you needed something before you fell over." She points across the clearing to where both people and animals are setting the long, low tables for a large meal and bringing out piles of pillows.

"I appreciate it." I nod in thanks as she takes my empty bowl and turns back to the bustle of people.

A male catches my eye as he takes a cask from two others and carries it over, placing it at the end of one of the closer tables. He continues around the table, helping two females with their arrangement of wildflowers. Set in the middle of the table, the tall flowers tip the vase. In one smooth motion, he's able to keep the vase from spilling and evens out the tall forsythia so it has balance once again.

As soon as he's satisfied with the arrangement, he dismisses himself and begins heading my way. I scan the scene for Pris or Alasie, or anything to busy myself with, but there's nothing for me to do but wait for his approach.

The stars themselves must favor the man striding toward me. He's as tall as an oak tree, and might as well be as broad as one, too. His dark hair is freshly braided away from his face and gathered loosely into a tie at the bottom of his neck. His white shirt moves against his skin, giving glimpses of the muscles below. His features come into focus, and his bright brown eyes sparkle with knowing.

As he approaches, the smell of woodsmoke and leather washes over me. I do a double take. I must be mistaken. "Niko?"

He's cleaned up. The layers of dirt and grime have been washed away to reveal deeply tanned skin underneath. His beard is trimmed close, revealing his strong jawline. His fresh clothing fits snug in all the right places, reminding me of the morning we spent together in his dragon cave.

Right before I swore myself away from love—There's no need to try that mess again.

He gives me an easy smile, and those dimples almost bring me to my knees. The smug look on his face says he knows the effect he has on me, but I have to say, I feel pretty smug right about now too—I've slept with this god of a man.

"You clean up nicely, too, Rowandine." His gravelly voice brings me back as he waves to someone behind me. I lose my footing at once as I try to spin to see who it is. In one swoop, he places me back on my feet, pats my shoulders, and moves past me.

Shaken, I turn to see who he's striding toward. A tall, raven-haired beauty wraps her arms around him, and I turn away, not wanting to see where that goes.

Before I have time to wonder about what she means to him, my eyes alight on a pleasantly familiar sight.

"Gryphon!"

Chapter Eleven

At once, I take off at a run and jump into his arms. I'm so glad to see someone I know in this strange, if not welcoming, place.

Gryphon spins me around, looking just as glad to see me. "We saw the dragon. I mean—Niko. We knew you were in good hands, but we still came as fast as we could." Words tumble out of his mouth as he checks me over and decides I made it here in one piece. He pulls back and looks at my neatly braided hair wrapped in a crown around my head. He gives a playful sniff and sighs. "You've bathed! That sounds amazing!"

I look at him again, noticing he's covered in dirt and his clothes are a bit more torn than usual. "You look as you always do. What are you complaining about?" I laugh and hold my nose as he tries to get closer to share his grime.

Another person crashes into me and wraps me in a hug. "We were so worried!" Gayle's melodic voice chimes in. She takes in the bruises along my jawline and the scrapes along my face and hands. "You fought well, it seems." She gives a nod of approval as she moves on to Niko. They embrace, and I can tell they're exchanging quick words before they pull apart, just before Gayle is tackled by big, hulking males I can only assume are her brothers.

As she gets swallowed up, Baylor steps in. "You did well out there. I want to hear about what made Niko shift, but before all that—Patton would be proud." For the stable boy who always talks slow but thinks fast, he is all kinds of wound up. Endeared by his obvious distress, I give him a big hug.

As we step back from each other, I notice the village has once again gathered in all the happy commotion. Alasie approaches slowly, giving us time to compose ourselves. She gives Gayle a long hug and touches Baylor's left shoulder. She waits, hopeful. He takes a hint better than I do, because he raises his right hand to her left shoulder. Alasie nods approval and does the same with Gryphon, who takes the cue from Baylor. She welcomes them all.

"Tonight we celebrate the return of these two honored Wardens of Glorixia."

Cheers go up all around us, and both Niko and Gayle are swarmed with hugs and greetings. Cold horns splash with golden liquid as they're placed in my and Gryphon's hands, and we're pushed to the outskirts of the celebration. I can feel Gryphon's eyes on me as I watch Baylor lead all the horses to the stall. I bet he could find his way to a stable blindfolded. I don't know how he does it.

"Are you alright? Niko is a dragon Shifter? We've been traveling with the legendary Wardens of Glorixia? Are you alright?" Gryphon circles back to his first question as the firelight dances across the bruises and scrapes.

"Yes, I'm okay, I think. I'm alive and here, at least."

He pulls me into a brotherly hug, crushing my ribs and then backing off as I wince. "So what happened?" He pitches his voice lower, even though we're well outside the rowdy crowd.

"I'm not sure I'm ready to relive it all quite yet, but basically, Thaddeus isn't going to play nice. And apparently, Ombretta isn't either."

A hole begins to grow in my chest. I rub at my heart. In the past few weeks, I've learned I'm not the human I thought I was, that the people who raised me are the very ones who destroyed my family as well as the kingdom, that I have a twin who needs my help in the North, and now I've realized she's hunting me. So rather than saving a sister I didn't know I had and then, together, reuniting our kingdom once again under Fae rule, I have to figure out what's next.

"Huh," Gryphon grunts as he leans back against a tree. "So what's next?" His thoughts eerily mirror my train of thought.

"I can't even think about it right now." And with that, I empty the cup I'm nursing. The drink is refreshing, tasting a lot like the fruit Pris gave me earlier, except with more layers of flavor. The sweetness hits my tongue first, with a tartness to the finish. Whatever it is, I've never tasted anything like it. It warms my belly going down, and I sit in silence next to Gryphon, attempting to find peace while my insides twist and turn with the knowledge that whatever decisions I make, the consequences will weigh heavily.

Torchlight twinkles all around us. Trees reach toward the night sky as we sit on pillows on the forest floor. The table before us puts the royal table at the castle to shame. It is at least twice as long, and angled in a U shape. The entire village is seated along the pillows as dish upon dish is set on the table.

Pris sits next to me, her legs folded under her. She appears at ease with herself, even in the company of so many people. Or perhaps because of them. She spoons thick noodles soaked in a cream sauce onto her plate and then passes the dish to me. The rich, savory scent of the sauce wafts my way, and the mixture of fresh basil and garlic has me taking much more than I'll be able to finish. I pass the dish to Baylor, who sits on my other side. I quickly realize I'm in the middle of what could easily become a very fun night for those on either side of me. It's already clear Pris enjoys Baylor's easygoing nature, and I'm sure his good looks don't hurt, either.

A loud guffaw sounds from the head of the table. Niko sits beside his mother in easy conversation. The lines of discontent from the road have now smoothed, and by the looks of it, he's entertaining that end of the table with tales from his travels, all while making sure everyone's cup is full.

The twinkle in his eye and the relaxed set of his shoulders remind me of this morning in the cave. We haven't had a moment to discuss it since we've arrived back in his village, but this version of him is a stark contrast to the Niko who stared daggers at me while he introduced me to his mother and then eyed me appraisingly when Alasie called me Rowandine Agroterra. I wonder which is the true version of himself and if there's more to his gruff exterior than he's letting on.

I toy with the idea while focusing on all the delicious food in front of me, each bite more flavorful than the last. My ears perk up at the mention of tomorrow's training session, and I'm momentarily distracted. I look to where two females converse, both sitting tall on their cushions. From the easy way they move and the way their clothes sit, I can tell they've honed their muscles. Most of the techniques they mention go right over my head, but I can pick out that they must practice hand-to-hand combat as well as with swords. It sounds intense, and I wonder if I'd be able to keep up with any of it.

"Care to join, fledgling?" One of the females looks toward me. I'm more obvious than I thought.

"Really?" I answer hesitantly. "I'd love to. I don't think I'll be able to keep up, but I'd at least like to watch."

"We'll be out at dawn. See you then." They turn back to each other, deep in further conversation about training.

As people finish their meals, they move toward the large fire near the middle of the village. Some of them pull out drums and flutes and begin playing rapid rhythms that quickly get people moving.

The sight reminds me of the Moon Festival. When Gryphon and I would ride the rush of danger, sneaking into town and staying out late, the beat of the drums filling me up to the brim. That night seems so far away. The stakes seem higher now, with how far we've traveled and how much I've lost since setting out.

Pris sidles up next to me along the outskirts of the dancing. Sweat is already spotting her brow, making her look as if she's glistening in the torchlight. "You dance?" she asks, out of breath.

"Not right now, I think." Even though the pull of the music is strong, I would rather remain on the outside, not quite ready to take the plunge.

"Oh, you just wait." She shrugs and dances back into the crowd, her light braids swaying along with her hips.

"Tonight..." Lady Alasie booms, and everyone gathered under the canopy of the trees falls silent. "We have much to celebrate!" Cheers sound all around. "We celebrate the return of these two distinguished Wardens of Glorixia, and the return of the Fae royal line in Rowandine Agroterra.

Along with one of our most sacred evenings, the Darkest Night."

More cheers go up, and Niko and Gayle are swarmed with greetings and hugs. A cold horn full of a pale, sunny liquid is placed in my hand as the rest of our small group is gently pushed to the outskirts of this happy celebration.

"The Darkest Night? What have we gotten ourselves into?" I lean into Gryphon's warmth as we fade into the background of the merriment.

"It's how the Shifters celebrate midwinter. The Darkest Night of the year is just that: the new moon closest to the winter solstice."

I look to the sky, searching for the moon, and realize I haven't missed its light because of the torches lining every path, and the big fires in all the common areas.

"We didn't celebrate the Darkest Night at the castle," I say, looking around at all the preparation that has gone into this evening. There are streamers in all the colors of the rainbow tied along the torches and draped from the bridges high in the trees.

"There wasn't much we could celebrate there. I'm just glad we were able to sneak out long enough for the Moon Festival. This year, Merula went all out, knowing the castle was busy with their celebrations."

As we sit in silence, clouds of blues and reds fill the sky. In the crowd, people are throwing small sachets of powder at each other. "So we're celebrating the darkness?" I look around, confused that there's so much light and color surrounding us.

"Sort of. When the winter solstice and the new moon coincide, it's extra special. The Shifters celebrate renewal and rebirth as the sun returns and the days begin to grow longer."

All the ribbons and streamers waving in the breeze radiate hope and renewal with their bright hues swaying. The torchlight wards off the night and creates a glowing bubble, where these people revel in the promise of the growing days to come.

My mind travels to both Licia and Ombretta, and I can't help but think my darkest days are yet to come. I exhale a big breath at the thought of all we still have ahead of us.

The night explodes with all shades of the rainbow. If I thought the streamers were pretty, then the small packets of powder being thrown around, bursting everywhere into clouds of blues and reds, greens and yellows, are more than words can describe. The music is loud and spirits are high as the streets crowd with more people and animals than I thought could fit in this small village.

"Can you believe we've made it? An entire village of Shifters?" Gryphon remarks as he returns with his refilled drinking horn. He raises his glass toward all the animals in attendance, along with those in human form.

"I wonder if they prefer their animal form."

Gryphon looks back at the crowd. Everyone is now covered with splashes of dye from the powders filling the air, their light clothing now stained with clouds of pink and orange, even their skin painted in rainbows.

"You're completely unscathed." He looks down at my spotless clothes, frowning. The only tinge of powder on me is where his shoulder brushed mine in greeting. He, on the other hand, has enjoyed all aspects of the celebration. "Let's get you out there."

"I'm quite enjoying being so fresh and clean. I'm fine right where I am now, thank you very much." My tone is prim, leaving no room for argument.

We watch in comfortable silence for a few moments, me taking small sips of the amazing wine and Gryphon gulping it down as if he cannot get enough. He finishes and gives me a wolfish grin. He tosses his empty horn to the ground, grabs my hand, and pulls me into the pulsing crowd.

The mingling scents of smoke and sweat hit me like a wall as we snake through the crowd to the center. Gryphon doesn't loosen his grip until we've found Baylor, who's dancing with Pris and Gayle. Baylor nods to us, a knowing look on his face, acknowledging Gryphon's triumph at getting me out here.

Within moments, splotches of color stain my pristine tunic. But instead of turning and heading back the way we came, something causes me to pause and stay. Everyone around me is covered from head to toe in powdered patterns. And now, the streaks of pigment stand out on my clothes, too. The glow from the fires surrounding us is just enough light to make out the broad lines of those around me, and it reminds me of the last time I found myself in a writhing, churning crowd. Back in Merula, at the Moon Festival, the people of the village were a part of me, and I them. Can I become a part of this as well?

"I knew you'd find your way." Pris smiles, and I decide to stay.

Chapter Twelve

There's no moon passing across the sky, but by the ache in my thighs, it must be the early hours of the morning now. There's little talking, but I'm getting to know Pris and Gayle in a different way. Pris' high energy matches Baylor's, while Gayle's movements are rhythmic and smooth. Gryphon can't stay in one place and keeps bumping out of our group and back. Which is why when I'm jilted for the millionth time, I don't even flinch, just laugh and spin back to the group, as Pris squeals with delight. The high pitch hardly registers over the music engulfing us, but her face is alight, and I look for what has her so excited.

"I never thought I'd see the day—I mean, night!" Pris waves a hand toward who I thought was Gryphon returning, but it's not. The broad frame, in contrast to Gryphon's tall lankiness, is a solid presence beside me.

Niko sways a little with the music, mostly looking uncomfortable as he shrugs at Pris. "Don't get too excited. I just came—"

But Pris pulls him forward and into our small circle, so he never finishes his sentence. The way they interact—comfortable with each other, yet more friendly than romantic—makes me wonder what their history is. Could they be just friends? Maybe they had something long ago, like me and Baylor? Or it could be something else entirely. But I can't deny that they're at ease with each other.

As I wonder at what brings the two of them together, my eyes are drawn to the way Niko moves. Here, amid all these people, his body is tense and his motions are rigid, not at all like the way he was in the darkness, with only me to witness his smooth, sensual movements. But that's not what holds my eye. The tattoos that whirl around his arms and legs don't stop there. His bare chest is covered with patterns and swirls—all except the spot over his heart. The muscled, tan skin is a stark contrast to everywhere else.

I can feel his eyes on me and snap my attention upward. The blush of being caught stings my cheeks. I hold his gaze for a moment, but his stare is too searching, and I have to look away. I attempt to dampen the pull between us, still too raw from my connections with Avicii and Thaddeus. There's no reason to waste time. I know how this will end.

Scanning the crowd, I notice most everyone has a tattoo, or several, tracing their bodies. At first, I assumed it was a cultural thing, but now, I wonder if it means more than that to these people. Gryphon seems to notice the same, because he asks, "What is the significance of the body ink? Almost everyone here has markings."

Pris answers, "A marking is a great honor. Each one shows how many lives one has saved."

All eyes dart to Niko, who has barely a blank patch of skin left. I can't help it when my eyes go straight to the only place there's bare skin—over his heart.

Gayle notices and cuts off the question I'm about to ask. "Yes, he stays busy. Being a Warden does that to you." She shows off her legs, where most of her tattoos are placed. Niko looks uncomfortable, so I let my questions go unasked, allowing the music to drift over us instead.

My body begins to sway again. But instead of the frenzied, upbeat motions of Pris and Baylor, my movements are slow and measured, and despite my efforts not to, I fall into rhythm with Niko. I watch him watching me and it's not the first time I wonder if there's more to him than meets the eye. Because what meets the eye is incredibly alluring, and that's all I thought this was at first.

His fingertips brush along my cheek, and his fingers come away with blue and purple smudges. I realize I must be a sight, and wonder what I look like through his eyes. Am I the human princess who doesn't belong here? Or something else?

"You're out on the dance floor?" The tall, raven-haired woman is back, and she effortlessly slides between Niko and me. "You never come out dancing. It looks like you've changed since you've been gone."

"A lot has changed, Reinette." Niko casts a look at me over her shoulder, but Reinette quickly snags his gaze again.

I tell myself there's no reason I should care that she put herself between us, but my chest hurts as I turn to find Gryphon and the others again. For the rest of the night, I can't shake the heavy weight that's settled right over my collarbone.

After dancing until the first rays of sunlight start peeking through the swaying pines, I fully regret my conversation with the two warriors. I am no longer looking forward to the early-morning training session. But here I am, dressed in an incredibly short top that doesn't even cover my belly button and pants that act as a second skin, tight down to where they cut off at my ankles. I don't miss the bodices and full skirts of Merula, but I feel too exposed in such form-fitting clothing, so I pull on another layer.

The warmth of the loose wool sweater braces me against the cold to come.

On my way out, a tray of fruit and baked goods catches my attention. I grab a warm sweet roll, one of my favorite treats from my time at the castle. Doubting anything could ever match the talented bakers there, I take a bite. The dough melts in my mouth, and I have to fight back a groan. This baker and those at the castle have a thing or two in common. For just a moment, I'm glad to be reminded of home.

The training takes place along the bay, in a forest clearing right before dirt turns to sand. Many people are already there, stretching and warming up. I realize quickly that my cropped clothes seem to be standard for training. All the females are dressed similarly, and most of the males wear slightly looser pants, some with shirts, some without, despite how cold it is. I automatically scan for Gryphon and Baylor; neither of them is here.

Gayle notices me and waves me over to a group she's stretching with. She introduces me to Delsie, along with Saleen, Reinette, and Holden. Delsie has the most beautiful golden-bronze skin, and she's dusted with freckles from head to toe. Her sun-bleached hair is short and curly, neatly pulled back with a wide headband. Saleen is all legs, and her deep red ponytail sways as she folds easily to touch her toes. Reinette's dark curls are cropped to her chin in a style I have not yet seen on a female. Holden is currently the only male in this group, but he seems to get along well with the others here. His skin is the darkest shade of mahogany I've ever seen. His dark hair is braided in tiny rows from his forehead to the nape of his neck.

All of their arms and legs are corded with muscle. If training with them will help me look like that, count me in.

As I watch Gayle with her friends, I notice how easy the banter is between them all. None of them seems to work too hard to impress or be noticed. I wonder if they grew up together. I can feel the friendship between them, and I now see that such friendship is so much more than the frivolity my instructors always made it out to be.

My knowledge of physical training is limited, as Patton only worked with Gryphon and me for a few weeks before we left. Baylor continued the work on the road—I know he's been throwing everything he can at us, but it's also been rushed and incomplete, to say the very least. But watching this group move is magical. The ones who are most experienced, such as the two who invited me, are as fluid as a coursing river. They have complete control of their limbs at all times and can anticipate their opponents' upcoming moves as if they're written across their faces.

"Stop gawking and start moving," Gayle warns, as she kicks my feet out from under me again. "You'll get hurt if your attention is elsewhere. Again," she demands.

"You don't play like a girl, do you?" I ask, amazed at how fast she moves and how hard she strikes.

"What are you talking about? Damn straight I play like a girl. Try to keep up!" She flashes me a toothy smile as she continues her drills.

We spend the entire morning practicing balance and foot placement with a little running and strength training sprinkled in. Despite the cold day, my clothes are dripping in sweat, and I'm swaying on my feet. Baylor's training was not nearly as rigorous as this.

"Those who sweat more in training bleed less in battle." Gayle holds her hand out to pull me up once again.

I groan as I rise to my feet. "I'll keep that in mind."

"We're done for the day, Roe." She looks hard at me. "Keep moving, but get some rest."

She has another think coming if she plans for me to do anything other than promptly return to my wondrous bed and take a nice, long nap. And after that, I think I'll find the largest, warmest bath I can and sink deep into it for the rest of the day, even though we haven't even reached midday yet.

"You'll be better for it if you keep moving for a while. Trust me." She nods sagely at me and then saunters with light steps in the opposite direction. She's rubbing it in. My legs strain against each step I ask of them.

"Maybe tomorrow, you'll whine less and work harder," says a voice behind me. I spin to see Reinette.

My hackles rise. Taken aback by both her tone and my reaction, I attempt to continue on my way. But the animalistic anger taking root is hard to ignore as she moves in front of me, blocking any further progress.

"You have no idea what you're doing, do you? And you're the one planning to save Everguard? King Hadeon did a great job raising you to be nothing more than a shiny object."

The truth whips me across the face as surely as any slap would. I wonder if she knows how close she is to voicing my very thoughts. Does everyone think this of me? Will I just be a sacrificial lamb to move King Killian out of the way?

I shove past her, tamping down my desire to rip her insides out and stomp on them. The image comes unbidden to my mind, and I shake it off, wondering where it came from. My hands shake as I walk past, the only outward sign of the effort it's taking to hold myself back. From what? Attacking her? What would that achieve?

The thoughts whir through my mind as I focus on putting one foot in front of the other. I'd probably hurt myself more than her anyway; my muscles scream in pain as I brush against her rock-solid shoulder.

"That's enough, Reinette."

I spin to see Niko leaning against a tree, watching the entire confrontation.

He moves to stand between Reinette and me. His back muscles flex as he stares her down. "Can't you see she's nowhere near your level?"

I don't need to see Niko's face, because Reinette's smirk says enough. It's clear by the way he steps in that even he thinks I'm nowhere near capable enough to take her on.

Before I can react, flashes of Avicii, the husband who constantly pushed me around, go through my mind, followed by Hadeon's manipulative words and the way my brother brushed me off. And the most recent: Thaddeus. A shiver runs down my spine. That wound is still fresh. He didn't just see a weakness when he looked at me; he found a way into my bed—and maybe, if I'm honest with myself, into my heart—and *created* a weakness, just to expose it to the elements.

I was starting to think that with Niko, it's different. I thought he was starting to see the true me. But I'm only kidding myself. He only sees a princess playing at being a warrior.

"It must be all that royal blood making her think she could even take me on, don't you think, Niko?" Reinette smiles sweetly at him, looking right through me.

The anger rising within consumes me, and I snap. It's as if a blood-fury ignites within my veins, and all I see is red. It almost reminds me of the Warrior's Peace I found with Patton, but this time, instead of peace, all I feel is unbridled rage.

I move with a speed I didn't know I had, rushing toward Reinette. Her smirk is replaced with confusion, and then, if I'm not mistaken, a little bit of fear. I can feel myself growling as I crouch low, ready to tackle her.

As my feet leave the soft dirt, strong arms come around my waist, pulling me backward. My back hits Niko's chest hard, and his muscles strain to hold me against him.

"Whoa there. There's nothing for you there."

His voice, so close to my ear, snaps me back into myself. The feral rage subsides instantly, and my head falls back against his chest.

What just happened? All of my senses seem stronger than they usually do. My breaths come in fits and starts, as if I've just awoken from a bad dream. I'm too aware of the drops of sweat along my forehead as well as the ones trickling down my back. Niko's chest pressed against my back, his arms holding me in place, feel as hard as a dry garden bed, yet as welcome as the petals of a rose across my skin. I shiver, feeling too many things at once.

Reinette scoffs before she turns on her heels. As soon as she leaves the practice ground, his bear grip loosens around my midsection slowly, as he tests my reaction. The tension hasn't subsided completely, so I shrug him off, still disbelieving that he thinks I can't protect myself from a scuffle with Reinette. He doesn't move to stop me this time, so I guess the damage is already done.

Chapter Thirteen

My muscles hurt less now. I've been training with the Shifter warriors for four straight, unrelenting days. My clothes already fit differently, and I'm not sure if it's because of the training or the amazing meals each day. Either way, I feel much stronger and more energized than I did just days ago. I'm even feeling more myself. Maybe more than ever before.

This is a new feeling, and one I'm slowly leaning into. I can hear the difference in the way I think. I listen more to the whispering voices of my thoughts and feelings rather than shoving them further down and making my decisions based upon the thoughts and feelings of those around me. I pause often throughout the day, surprised that this little purr of a voice continues to bloom within me. The more it grows, the more often I reflect on this knowing inside me.

I walk into the planning room, as we have so lovingly dubbed it, chosen for its central location in the Meeting House and its proximity to the kitchens. We meet here each afternoon to discuss the latest intel coming in from the scouts and how this affects our plans to continue north.

"I still say we'd be better off going northwest, deeper into the forest. Then we can cross the river right outside the walls of the North." Baylor prefers the straight-arrow approach, even when talking strategy.

"As I've said before," Gayle retorts, "one: both the Ancients and the humans will expect that, and they will plan accordingly. And two: although that way is more of a straight shot, it won't be easy." Her fists come down on the table, and she looks to Niko for his final vote.

We have spent the past week gathering information from scouts and any of the villagers who know the northern terrain well. Many of the elders have been eager to share their knowledge and reminisce about their journeys of long ago. We have mapped out several paths toward the North. Now, all we need to do is pick one.

We've been arguing for two days straight.

"What if…" I begin, but step back when all eyes turn toward me. I have spent very little time talking in this room. Compared to everyone else, I don't have much of an eye for strategy and even less for travel. But perhaps spending my childhood listening to Killian drone on for hours about battles and troop movement will finally come in handy, just this once.

"Go on." Niko sweeps a hand over the table strewn with maps. "New eyes could be helpful."

My eyes rise from the ground, and fall on Niko. I expect to find laughter shining in his eyes, to find him ready to slam my idea before it comes out. Instead, his strong gaze holds mine for a brief moment in encouragement.

Baylor runs his hands through his hair—something he's done many times already, his curls sticking straight up like a child's after a good night's sleep. Gayle begins pacing as I move closer to the table.

My fingers trace over the castle that was once my home and move northwest, following the path we have traveled thus far. I circle our current location on the west coast of Everguard in the middle of the Dread

Forest. Then I continue along the trail that leads northeast, just as Baylor suggested. "What if instead of crossing the river near Cindra, as both Ombretta and Killian would expect, we remain on this side of the river, using Nitara Hill to shelter us as we continue north? As long as we can make it through the Pass, we'll end up right at the gates of Freathia. Before they even have a chance to react, we can already be inside."

Baylor moves closer to inspect the route I traced. "It could work."

"The Pass is not an option." Gayle forgets her pacing to stand beside us with her hands on her hips. "The name of Nitara Hill is completely misleading. I'll tell you now, there's nothing hill-like about it."

Niko begins nodding slowly, and cuts his eyes at me in surprised appreciation of my idea. "If we wait till spring, it might work. Especially if we feint toward Cindra, making it seem like we're looking for aid from the Elementals or Conjours."

"And once we get there, what?" Gayle's exasperation is clear in her tone. I don't blame her. We've been over all of this too many times to count. I know they just want to be sure we understand the plan. That I understand the plan.

"We find Ombretta," I reply. "If there's no talking her down, she has to die."

The last words feel like sludge in my mouth. I know they need me to say it and to believe it, but I keep getting stuck on it. Even if I've never met her, she's my twin. And it's more than just shared blood.

Even with Licia, whom I grew up thinking was my twin, I had a special bond. We understood each other better than anyone else. How will it feel when I meet my twin by birth? My blood thrums through her veins as well. Will I be able to save her? Am I strong enough to kill her to save our world, if that's what it comes down to?

Every time I think about it, my stomach twists into knots.

"You're getting that weird look again, Roe." Baylor's eyebrows have disappeared into his curls, and he tilts his head, trying to read me.

I can feel Gryphon step closer to me, right at my shoulder. The closeness is comforting, and I know he still has my back no matter what.

"I know what I have to do," I repeat for the millionth time. Still not completely able to believe it.

Gayle tilts her head as well, tapping her chin. "What if we take Roe to Iolanthe?" She looks to Niko as she says this.

"It could help. It certainly wouldn't hurt." Niko sizes me up once again. I've kept my distance since he stepped between Reinette and me, but it's as if he's offering an olive branch. Could he see me as the leader the realm hopes me to be?

"Who's Iolanthe?" Gryphon asks, so I don't have to.

Niko's thick finger traces a spot on the map where the forest edge meets the hills, right along the bay. "She's a healer. Some say she's as old as any Ancient. She can help people with wounds and disease, but also with their minds."

My lips purse as I try to swallow that. "You think something's wrong with my mind?" My arms cross as I give Gayle a look for suggesting such a thing.

"I'm not saying there's anything wrong with you. Well…" She trails off as she smirks at me. "This is a hard thing. It'd help to have as many strategies as possible. You've been training and accomplishing so much while you're here. I'm just saying it wouldn't hurt to train your mind to do hard things while you're at it."

Despite my desire to, I can't argue with that. I've learned so much already. The thought of how strong I could become with further training has me drunk on the possibilities.

Niko nods. "And this way, we can set off sooner, since Iolanthe is on this side of the Pass. Hopefully, we'll be sidestepping any eyes trying to find our trail later in the season." His eyes gleam as he says this—with excitement, I'd say, if I didn't know better.

Thanks to all my tossing and turning last night, I have a hard time keeping up with training this morning. Two hours in, and my arms keep buckling during pushups. Gayle pairs us off to practice our hand-to-hand sparring for the remainder of class. Hoping for someone who won't pose too much of a challenge, I cringe when I hear "Rowandine and Reinette!"

It takes all the remaining strength I have not to throw my arms up and moan. What is Gayle thinking? *Is* she thinking? Are we even going to be able to fight respectfully with each other? Or is this the moment I've been waiting for since Niko pulled me away the last time?

Instead of voicing my dislike, I stride confidently toward Reinette. At least, I try. Reinette gives me a feral grin, as if she knows I know she's about to eat me alive. My false swagger comes to a standstill in front of her, and it feels like everything I've learned so far drains out of me.

Gayle's yell to begin shakes me from whatever stupor I've slunk into. My mind begins to work again as Reinette's fist meets my jaw. I flounder, attempting to find my footing. I duck on instinct and her second blow goes right over where my head was moments ago.

She was not expecting me to recover this quickly, so I use it to my advantage. While her side is wide open, I give her two quick jabs. She doubles over for just a moment. When she rises, there's a gleam in her eye that terrifies me to my core. *Stars, what do I do now?*

I freeze again as she launches herself at me, snarling, and somewhere in my mind, I compare her to a wolf, or something else with sharp teeth. The sheer animalistic way she moves keeps me rooted in one place. Again, she swings, this time striking me high on my cheek and then on the opposite shoulder, which sends me spinning to the ground.

I hear her moving behind me. I tell myself to stay put and feign unconsciousness, but I don't think I could move if I wanted to. I reach down deep within myself while she slinks closer for her final blow.

She stands above me. With my barely open eyes, I notice her putting more weight on her right foot. I hear Niko's voice in my mind, reminding me to stay balanced, or someone will use it against me.

I strike before I even think my plan all the way through. I push my arms straight and swing my left leg around in front of me, connecting hard with her ankle. She lurches to the side. My swipe wasn't hard enough. How is she still standing?

A laugh swells from within her. As if it's funny I dared to try bringing her down. Although I'm starting to think she's right. I try to reach for that anger she sparked last time, but it doesn't come.

Get up, get up, get up. I beg my legs to listen. I stagger to my feet and sway a little before my vision focuses on Reinette, standing tall with one hand on her hip. She only looks slightly ruffled, while I feel destroyed.

She moves quickly, closing the distance between us on the balls of her feet. She crouches down low, and I can tell she wants to drive right through me.

Up, up, up, I yell at myself. Trying not to cower before the final blow lands. *Just take it like the warrior you one day hope to be. Up, up, up.*

And suddenly, my shoulder blades sting. A million bee stings, all concentrated in one area. I flex them upward, but something feels off.

At that same moment, my feet lift from the ground. I feel light, like a lone cloud in the sky on the sunniest of days. I watch from above as Reinette falls face-first to the ground rather than connecting with my body.

Shocked by my new vantage point, I spin around. Still, my feet find no purchase. I realize all has suddenly gone quiet around us. I have to adjust my gaze, aiming it further down. The ring of people who were cheering and jeering just moments ago are now stunned silent, eyes wide and mouths hanging open.

I turn around to see what they are looking at, to meet the same awestruck faces on the opposite side of the ring. Well? What is everyone gawking at? Am I dead? I pinch my arm and wince. It hurts almost as much as Reinette's blows.

The silence is broken when Reinette, now dusted with dirt, lifts from the ground to see why her body never pummeled into my own. Her eyes go wide as she finds me. Above her.

"Wings?" she shrieks. "You can't shift mid-fight!" She turns in circles, looking for confirmation from those around us, standing now with her arms out wide, pointing and gesturing in disbelief. I turn again to see what she's squawking about.

Over my shoulders, I find large, iridescent wings fluttering back and forth behind me.

As I realize what's happened, I feel the same pinch along my shoulder blades from before, and just as suddenly as I rose, I've landed hard on my ass in the dirt.

Once again on the ground while a livid Reinette stands over me, I wait for the strikes. A shower of dirt lands on me as she kicks the soil in front of me and storms off the training grounds, mumbling about Fae royalty and cheaters the whole way.

Gayle and Baylor run to my side, launching questions at me all at once. Still exhausted from the fight and confused about what just happened, I let them usher me to a quieter spot. The surprised exclamations from the crowd fade. When I look up, I find we've made it to the Meeting House. They set me down on the porch, and I look up at them, ready to show how grateful I am for their rescue.

Baylor winces at the sight of me. "Towels! Healer!" he says, then runs into the building at my back. I am left with Gayle looking at me with a self-satisfied grin on her face.

"I think that means I win," she says, staring at my many wounds.

"What?" I try to make sense of what she's saying.

"We were wondering what your first Fae sign would be and when it would emerge. I said wings. I win."

I tilt my head up and squint my good eye at her. Pretty sure my hearing is damaged, I wait for her to repeat herself.

I guess she's moving on, because she asks, "How'd it feel?"

"I feel like I was just run over by a stampede of horses."

"No, not the sparring-turned-fistfight. I'm sorry, by the way. I suppose this is all my fault." Despite her words, she doesn't look very sorry. "You look awful. You must feel twice as bad, at least. What I meant was, how did it feel to sprout wings?"

"Wings? Did that really happen?" I go to scratch my head, but am met with searing pain as I touch an already protruding bump on my scalp. I try to summon enough strength from the earth surrounding us to heal some of these wounds, but it turns out, Reinette did a number on me. I lean back, letting Gayle poke and prod me. "Stars, kill me now."

Baylor returns, saving me from having to decide what spontaneously growing wings felt like while fighting off the desire to close my eyes. He starts gently pressing a cloth against my wounds. When he pulls it away, it's stained deep red. I must be bleeding more than I thought. Gayle and Baylor begin to spin out of my vision.

"Stars!" Baylor curses, and I crumble against him into darkness.

Chapter Fourteen

I wake to a touch more gentle than Baylor's. There's a pleasant humming as hands tend to the cuts and bruises along my arms. The soft, familiar warmth of the blankets against my skin clues me in that I'm no longer on the porch. I must've somehow made it upstairs to my bed.

My eyes slowly open, revealing the soft light of dusk filtering through the windows. Lady Alasie presses thin circles of cotton to my arm and deftly wraps them with strips of cloth.

She must sense my movement, because without missing a beat, her humming stops and she begins, "There's a bit of bruising and a few scrapes and bumps, but nothing a strong tea won't mend." She hands me a mug and I inhale the warm scents of peppermint and chamomile, mixed with something else I faintly recognize but can't name through my haze.

I bring the mug to my lips and wince slightly at the pain shooting down my arms with the slight movement. The tea itself must be brewed with expert care. As soon as the first drops slide down my throat, I begin to feel slightly detached from my body.

"Lady Alasie?"

"Hmm?" She was walking toward the door as if to leave, but turns now and sits down in the comfortable chair she must've spent most of the day in, next to me.

"I have wings?" The first of many questions swarming around within me.

"It would appear you do, dear." Smiling, she pats my hand, and I rest the mug on my thigh. "Usually, Fae get their wings earlier, along with their other gifts. I suppose since you had never been exposed to someone with wings, you wouldn't know where to begin to look," she muses. "But as I understand, there were others around you, guiding you this whole time."

"Guiding me?"

A smile breaks across my face as Thaliya and Patton come to mind, the motion making me wince. Smiling hurts. I reach up, hesitantly. My fingers gently brush along my cheekbone, and a sharp pain runs through me. I guess Reinette's punches connected better than I thought.

Lady Alasie applies a warm compress to my cheek and continues, "As I understand it, chickadee, you have a gifted hand when it comes to mending. It sounds like someone's been by your side this whole time, slowly and furtively coaxing out your abilities."

I open my mouth to protest. But then I recall the many poultices I have learned to brew, always followed by Thaliya praising me for their complexity. I remember how she would always encourage me to "sit with it" until I could figure out what was wrong. Or how she would always tell me to "be still and know." I smile to myself, suddenly proud of all I achieved within the healer's ward.

"You've gotten a good start for being raised among humans. But consider the strength you'll gain with explicit instruction." Lady Alasie motions for me to continue drinking my tea. With just one more sip, my muscles relax even more, until the pain becomes only a slight, annoying buzz in the background.

"The wings—" I feel around my shoulder blades where they were, still not convinced it wasn't all a dream. My hands find nothing but smooth skin, and my arms are so heavy. The tea is working so quickly.

"There we are, now." Lady Alasie takes a satisfied breath as she sits beside me on the bed. "We'll talk about those wings and more when you're feeling better. I'll have someone bring some food up in a bit, but right now, get some rest. We can chat about all this later." She takes the mug from me just before it falls from my loosening grip and quietly leaves the room.

I wake to the door creaking open and find the sun has been replaced with rays of bright moonlight along the floorboards of my room. Niko sticks his head in, and in my fog, I find myself fascinated with his good looks. Has he always been this beautiful? I must smile at him, because he smiles back and takes it as permission to enter.

He crosses the room and balances a tray across my knees, then sinks into the chair Lady Alasie left beside my bed. He takes in the bandages wrapping my forehead and the smaller ones down my forearms from landing hard on the dirt. His hand reaches out to brush against my arm, hesitating a beat before he pulls it back before making contact.

"I hear you gave Reinette quite the runaround." He laughs, and then stops abruptly, perhaps unsure if it's time to laugh about it yet.

"I'm not sure I would say that." From under my eyelashes, I try to decipher if he's impressed or surprised. "I just let her kick me around."

"Well, everyone's talking about it. I was out on patrol when news of your sparring lesson made it to me out there. Quite impressive." He seems more surprised than impressed, but the way he stepped in the middle of our last confrontation still sits squarely between us.

"Glad I'm able to provide some entertainment. Makes me feel useful." Thinking about what he said, I realize just how far away he must've been. "Word travels fast here." I look at him questioningly.

"When it's that good? Sure does." He laughs again. This time, an unguarded gravelly boom fills the room. "I suppose it's one pro of shifting. Some creatures can travel as fast as the wind."

A few beats of silence pass, so I pick up the huge roll he's set before me. I haven't seen one like it before. It's as big as a horse's hoof and knotted together, so heaping puffs stick out every which way, allowing soft chunks of fruit to settle on top. The entire bun calls to me, its gooey glaze rolling off the sides. The smell alone causes my eyes to roll back into my head. An involuntary moan leaves my mouth as I inhale the cinnamony goodness.

Niko tries to hide his laughter by walking toward the window, but that low rumble does something to the deepest parts of me that I can't ignore. "What?" I ask through my first bite, instantly not caring what his answer is, because this is the most delicious treat I have ever tasted. The soft bun, the fruit, and the sweetness of the glaze all melt together into a buttery knot meant for my belly alone.

"I noticed you liked sweet buns. I asked Alasie to show me how to make these," he says, his eyes trying to settle on anything but my face. I must look ridiculous. Covered from head to toe in bruises and bandages, and now fawning over a pastry.

"*You* made this?" I try not to sound too surprised, but I don't think it works. He turns from the window and ducks his head sheepishly as he nods silently. I don't think I've ever seen him bashful before. This big, fierce dragon-man is blushing over baked goods. I can't help but smile, though I kick the part of me that thinks it's adorable. "This is by far the most amazing thing I've ever tasted. In my entire life. It's like you've baked the sweetest star in the sky." I know I sound absurd, gushing over a roll in between bites, but I can't find the words to describe how delicious this is.

"It was my favorite growing up. Alasie always made them on special occasions."

I stop with the bun halfway to my mouth. He's marking this as a special occasion? Stunned, now I'm the one who's not sure where to look. "That was thoughtful of you" is all I can manage. Because not only has he realized my affinity for baked goods, he's actually made me his favorite childhood treat.

What does this mean? Is it an apology for not letting me fight my own battles? Do I forgive him? Should I let him in?

"It sounds like you need some practice." His comment jars me out of my thoughts.

"Hmm?" I know I've been hit in the head one too many times recently, but is it that obvious that I'm currently swooning? Over both the sticky bun and the man who made it?

"With flying," he adds. Is that a smirk playing across his lips?

"Oh. Yeah. I suppose I would need help with flying."

"Just so happens, I know a thing or two about flying. I could help if you'd like." He says this hesitantly, as if suddenly not so confident in my response.

Should I take him up on it? Lately, he seems... different, somehow. Not quite as open as he was that first day in the cave, but it seems like he has a bit more to say, so maybe he's trying. He's certainly not as stoic and cold as he was at our first meeting. And it might just be my imagination, but it seems like he's gone out of his way to make me feel welcome here.

It's settled, then. "Yes, I'd like that. Thanks."

Satisfied, he raps his knuckles on the bedspread and dismisses himself from the room, leaving me with my thoughts. I realize I may have hit my head harder than I first thought.

Lady Alasie insists I spend at least one more day recovering before heading back to training. I don't put up too much of a fight. I'm not eager to face Reinette again. Or anyone else, for that matter. But I'd like to at least try to heal the remaining cuts and bruises.

I head out the back door of the Meeting House in search of a quiet place. I overheard some of the villagers talking about the community garden, and I'd like to find it. Right now, midafternoon, the morning gardeners will be finished for the day, and those coming for fresh vegetables for dinner won't arrive for another hour or so.

The perfect rows of greenery make my heart flutter. It's been too long since I've had my hands in the dirt, and they itch to be knuckle-deep in the cool, moist soil. I find a small spot between the hearty kale plants and the spinach, sitting on the cool earth in the afternoon sun.

I still can't believe I sprouted wings. Until now, I'd almost convinced myself that everyone had the wrong woman. That they confused me with someone else somehow. Surely I couldn't truly be Fae.

The time I almost died healing Gryphon flashes through my mind. My body tenses at the thought of not being in control of myself. Of being so reckless with both his life and my own. But I take two slow breaths and then reach out to the earth. She's there, and as soon as I open myself to her, bright green power floods through me. I don't even have to direct the flow.

The results are instantaneous. My remaining cuts and bruises heal and are replaced with plump, healthy skin.

A gasp escapes my lips as the power I haven't summoned since I saved the Shifter flows freely from the earth into me and back again. It's like a limb awakening after a night of sleeping wrong. And I didn't even know how empty I was in its absence was until it was back.

I figured if I didn't put too much thought into it, it'd all just fade away. But instead, I'm slammed with a reminder of who I am and what I must do.

It would be so nice, so easy to stay here. Train the mornings away and help heal minor things here in the village. It's certainly something I could get used to. Especially when the warmth of the bedsheets and thick quilt wrap snugly around me, in stark contrast to cold nights in the winter air, where I just had a small fire and the clothes on my back for warmth. Chills run up my back at the mere thought of all those nights out in the cold.

Unfortunately, this wonderful place isn't my life, in the same way the castle wasn't my life. My sisters need me. My people need me.

Licia. Poor Licia. If I ever see her again, I hope she's forgiven me and moved on. I hope she's found happiness, even without Gryphon by her side.

And Ombretta. Even though she wants me for a glorified snack, I still can't help but think if she met me, and we had time to talk it through, then maybe she would see.

See what? I'm not sure. That I'm her sister? That I can be more than just a fancy meal? That the Ancients have twisted her mind, and maybe, just maybe, I could be the one to help untie all the knots?

I know it's been too long. If she knows about me and still would rather have me meet the same fate she was forced into, there's little to hope for. But I can't help but hope, even if that makes me weak.

I know what we'll have to do when we finally reach her. I know what I'll have to do. But I keep imagining better scenarios working out in my head. Even if this imagining will be the death of me, I think I'd rather that than have to kill my flesh and blood.

With the appearance of these wings, the weight of everything settles heavily onto my shoulders. I wonder if this scholar at the base of the mountain will shed some light on my Fae abilities.

Thaliya's words echo in my mind. That the strength within me is stronger than she's seen in a long, long time.

"There she is."

My hands come protectively around my mug of tea as Baylor jostles me on the steps of the Community House. He pulls me in for a side hug, attempting to grab Gayle with his other arm. Gryphon is trailing them, looking a little worse for wear, coming from the direction of the training grounds. I wonder if they've ramped up his training to prepare him for our next haul. By the looks of it, it doesn't agree with him.

"No, you don't, Killer." Gayle ducks under Baylor's advances with impressive speed and moves to my other side. She drapes my arm around her shoulder, effectively turning us out of Baylor's reach. "You're looking fabulous. When are you returning to the training field?" She waves me off, uninterested in my answer. "Us girls are grabbing drinks tonight at the

Viper's Den. Care to join? It looks like you've made a full recovery. I'm sure you'd like to rub it in Reinette's face a little."

"I would never!" I respond with sarcasm, but honestly, I would leap at the opportunity.

"Don't mind if I do!" Baylor smoothly inserts himself into our conversation, despite our best efforts. Gayle swats him back into submission, and he falls back to talk with Gryphon. They both wave to Pris over near the school rooms, and head her way.

Surprised to be pulled into the group, I respond with, "That sounds great."

"See you tonight?" Gayle's hopeful smile warms me.

"See you tonight. I'm off to work with Niko after lunch, but I'll be back this evening." I reach out to place a hand on her shoulder. Instead of grabbing my other shoulder, she pulls me into a tight hug. My whole body tenses at the contact, and I can feel her pulling away. Then I relax and return her hug with a big squeeze.

She jogs back toward the training area and, with a bit more lightness in my step, I head to the kitchens to see if they need any help with lunch. I've enjoyed helping in the kitchens here. I like what they stand for.

Everyone here eats the midday meal together. I had thought that the big table under the canopy of the trees was for special events, but it turns out it is where everyone gathers each day. People in the kitchens provide the main dish. So far, I've enjoyed trying all the new dishes, especially the big bowls of spicy vegetable soup with coconut and the root vegetable tatin. Everyone else brings something to share.

The amount of vegetables is another thing I've had to get used to. But the ways they're prepared here always leave me scraping the bottom of my bowl. Almost everyone in the village is a Shifter, which means no matter where you are on the food chain, at midday meal, everyone is shown respect.

For other meals, everyone does their own thing, whether that's with their families or their packs, which aren't necessarily the same. Carnivores hunt within the forest, marine life takes to the bay, and winged animals take to the skies. But at midday, everyone eats together. I like the balance of it. At the castle, there was always more emphasis on putting distance between people because of their differences, whether that was their wealth, their skillset, or their race. Here, everything different is celebrated. It's refreshing.

It also makes me look inside myself differently. I try to pull out those differences and let them shine, rather than hide behind what makes me the same as everyone else.

Niko's more patient than I thought he'd be. He's a good teacher. As promised, he's been working with me on flying. I can almost call on my wings whenever I need them now. In the past few days, I've jumped off cliffs, landed among treetops, and fallen from the sky more times than I'd like to count. But Niko has been there every time, to encourage me or gently suggest an alternate way to try it.

This afternoon, though, he has insisted that we hike back up to his cave. The rough rock face contrasts with the warmth of the fading sun along my skin. The air hints at spring, the sweet smell of the surrounding pine trees mingling with the salty sea air.

Memories of the last time we were here, when I kept tripping and stumbling noisily through the forest, come unbidden to mind. This time, I notice my feet have learned how to deftly navigate the forest floor. I step lightly over roots and avoid uneven places as if I'm one of the forest's creatures.

"And why can't we just fly up?" I ask again, waiting for a more satisfactory answer.

"You'll see. We have to time it right. Aren't you enjoying our gentle stroll through the forest?" he asks, his deep voice as light as if he were floating on air.

I'm surprised to realize that I am enjoying myself. The way the sun plays on the lichen-covered tree bark and the long shadows cast as it sinks are beautiful to watch as they shift with the gentle, chilly breeze.

Distracted by my thoughts and the scenery, I don't even notice we've progressed up the cliff face. This side rests in the shadows of the setting sun. I look out across the village to the bay, the water glistening like a thousand sea pearls on a dress of velvet.

"It's stunning." I breathe out as we walk right up to the edge of the cliff, his cave to our backs and the sun sinking lower by the minute. Up here, the only sounds are birdsong and crickets coming out to serenade the sunset. The sky fades into a deep purple, cut by reds and oranges.

"Just you wait. It gets better." Niko's smile is bright with anticipation. His eager mood is contagious, and I find myself excited for whatever is to come next. "Okay, let's go." He strips off his shirt and hands it to me.

I've gotten used to this. These past few days, I've seen more bare Niko than I believed possible for two friends practicing their flying skills. And I'm not complaining. I've started carrying a side pack to stuff his clothing into when he shifts. That way, wherever we land, he's still got a change of clothes, and we're not stuck flying in the same circle repeatedly.

"From up here?" I look dubiously at the straight descent and unrelenting rocks below. Before I even have to think, my wings spread behind me, reflecting the purples of the sky and deep greens of the forest below.

He nods me forward, and I lean into the bay breeze, letting the soft zephyr fill my wings. I tip forward. This continues to be both my most and least favorite part. The thrill of nothing below me is what propels me forward and terrifies me at the same time. But I have learned to trust the drop in my belly as my center readjusts to being weightless.

The bay beckons me closer, and I obey. The air, hinting at spring, gently kisses my skin, from my fingertips to my toes. This feeling is better than any warm blanket wrapped around me or any bubbly bath I've slowly sunk into.

Just as my fingertips brush along the glassy bay, burning bright with the reflection of the setting sun, I feel a heavy presence behind me. The hot breath of a dragon presses along my back. It mingles with the sea air, sending playful shivers up and down my spine.

This is breathtaking. Flying across the water like two giant dragonflies, with the water below on fire and the evergreen trees stretching up to the sky to meet us. I never thought it could be like this. That *I* could be like this. I feel light and free. I feel strong. I feel connected to all those in the village below.

With his remarkable size, Niko easily overtakes me, and his pearlescent scales shimmer as he passes below. I watch as those bright white scales shine against the many colors blurring into the dusk all around us. He flaps his mighty wings hard, gaining height and speed and then looping back around in lazy circles across the bay. If I listen hard enough, I can hear the villager children whooping and hollering behind us. From what I've gathered, it's not every day Niko graces his village with the sight of a dragon.

When we've had our fill, I follow his lead back toward his cave, the darkness of night following closely on our tails. As we approach the ledge, the ground dances with shadows. At first, I see only trees and branches below us—but with a double take at the darkest copse of trees, I see two ice-cold eyes glowing back at me.

I am frozen with fear at the thought of those eyes devouring me whole, for surely that's what they would do if ever brought into the light.

Suddenly, I've completely lost myself in the darkness surrounding me, growing over me like thick, sticky tar. The air whooshes past me, tearing at my clothes as I fall. My wings—what happened to my wings?

In my stricken state, they must've disappeared. And I'm left falling fast toward the moss-covered rocks below.

Chapter Fifteen

Twisting and flipping chaotically through the air, I reach out, hoping to find purchase on any of the tree branches that blur by, but my wings are gone. I'm falling, with no hope of magic, and no chance of finding a foothold before impact with the rock-hard ground below. Inwardly, I'm screaming at myself, trying in vain to re-engage my wings or grasp some tendril of magic yet to be discovered.

Nothing. Nothing, until a white lightning streak flashes straight past me. I don't even have time to blink before I feel the solid weight of a scaly body beneath me.

I sprawl out on Niko's wide back, gasping for breath that is not there. I dig my nails deep into his scales, holding on tighter than I need to to ensure I don't fall off.

I focus on matching my heartbeat to the solid flap of his wings as we rise higher and higher into the indigo sky. The stars twinkle brightly around us as if they're completely unaware of what just unfolded on their watch.

Niko settles gently on the landing before his cave at the top of the mountain. Still too afraid to move, I wait as he shifts back and quickly gathers me in his arms. Shaking so hard my teeth are chattering, I press into his strong, bare chest. I find comfort in his heat and firm muscles.

He whispers into my hair, "I've got you. You're safe." And I believe his words with my entire heart.

The sun has fallen fully into the sea by the time I stop shaking and step out of Niko's warm embrace. He uses this time to pull his pants on and then guides me away from the cliff and back toward his cave. I let him sit me down before he breathes the fire to life in the middle of the room. Sitting beside me, he's close enough I can feel his solid warmth, but with enough space to allow me to gather my thoughts.

"What happened out there?" His question comes gently, along with his now comforting scent. He's playing it off as not a big deal, but I can tell he's spooked by the way he's checking me over for any visible signs of harm. As he frantically flips my hands back and forth, I realize we've become more to each other than the princess he wants dead and the overbearing, closed-off Ultor Regni of nightmares.

Over the weeks we've been in Sverreian, he's grown on me. I still don't know all his secrets, but maybe that's okay. At least I know he no longer wants me dead. There's a seed of something between us, and if we try, maybe something can grow from it.

I set aside my blossoming feelings and answer his question, which seems more pressing at the moment. "It was Ombretta. I can sense it somehow. She's still searching for me, and she's close."

I look back at Niko, thinking he will doubt my answer. But he's looking at me with understanding, his rich brown eyes swallowing me with their warmth.

"We'll alert the scouts, double them. You're safe here," he repeats as he stands, ready to take action.

"She's not here. Not really. It's like she has scouts too, eyes everywhere." Even as I say it, I know it sounds ridiculous, but I can sense its truth:

she wasn't here physically, but somehow projected her presence while searching for me. "She's growing stronger. Thaddeus must have reached her, empty-handed. We don't have as much time as we thought."

My thoughts are all over the place on the walk down the mountain. Of course, Ombretta weighs heavily on my mind. Despite what I've said to the group, I still think the bond between us will be stronger than the hatred she's harboring. I won't have to land that fatal blow. Not to my own blood.

Amid the drawn-out undercurrent of turmoil about Ombretta, the thought of going out with the girls tonight registers. Funnily, there's the same feeling of impending doom weighing on me about that, too. It's silly, at my age, but memories still plague me of not fitting in with visiting children at the castle, of being ostracized even in my own home. And tonight, the idea of going out with a group of girls who are all close already makes my palms sweat.

We're making impressive time heading down the mountain. My movements are sure and fluid. The weeks of training here have been well spent. Hopefully, soon I'll meet this Iolanthe and have more answers about my Fae powers as well. I'll have to show her my book. I wonder if she'll be able to decipher it.

Just as my mind wanders toward the next leg of our journey, Niko pauses ahead of me. I realize I haven't been paying attention to my surroundings, much too distracted by the different vines of thought twining through my mind. I'm instantly on high alert, and my hands hover over the short blades on my belt.

In front of me, Niko turns to see what's spooked me. After a quick scan of our surroundings, the look on his face says it all. But a gravelly laugh escapes his lips anyway.

"I was correct in assuming we could use a break." He steps to the side, and I smile at the view his huge frame was blocking.

I don't know how I missed the sound of the cascading waterfall. I'll have to work on balancing my thoughts with awareness of my surroundings. But I can worry about that later. I instantly start unlacing my boots, impatient to feel the cool water on my toes.

Surprise registers as I edge into the shallows, the rocky sand a welcome relief beneath each weary step after the long trek down the mountain. The water isn't chilly—it's unnaturally warm, like a perfectly drawn bath. I turn back to find Niko unlacing his boots as well, another soft laugh escaping him at my bewildered expression.

I want nothing more than to sink into this warmth. This is breathtaking. A deep, comforting hum seems to emanate from the water itself, or perhaps, from within me. I can't tell.

"I thought it might help." He gestures to the shimmering surface, and I finally take in the delicate steam rising from the small lake. The waterfall, a cascade of deep, clear blue, is framed by ancient conifers, some as wide around as Niko's waist. The water is so pure, so inviting, I feel I could drink straight from it.

"Can we..." I begin, the words a breathless whisper. All I want is to dive in, to float weightlessly, letting the warmth dissolve all the burdens weighing so heavily on me.

"Of course. And you have it all to yourself." He scans the treeline once more, and I wait, confused by his meaning. "Usually, there are others here. It's a well-known place. There are a few hot springs around Sverreian, but this is the only one with a waterfall."

"It's beautiful." I give what I hope is a winning smile, then shed my heavy cloak and grab the hem of my tunic, pulling it over my head in one swift movement. The cool air kisses my skin, a welcome chill after the workout we've had. I do the same with my pants, leaving just my underclothes and only pausing a moment to see if Niko is following my lead. Sure enough, he's already pulled his shirt over his head. As he adds it to my pile of clothes, I can't help but take the opportunity to look down, even though I shouldn't—the bulging outline against his pants causes the area below my belly button to tighten. Trying to ignore all the feelings swirling around, I wade out into the water.

I don't even pause when it reaches my hips; there's no need. The water is so warm and welcoming. It ripples against my skin, a soft, refreshing touch compared to the surprises of the day. If only it would wash away all the worry in my mind.

As soon as the water is almost up to my armpits, I dive toward the waterfall, loving the caress of the pool, then bracing for the pounding sensation that crosses my back as I swim under the waterfall itself. I come up for air, and the inside surprises me.

A curtain of moss hangs across the rocks, waving in the breeze coming off the waterfall. I lift myself onto the rocky platform hidden here behind the torrent, enjoying the way the constant pounding of water dampens the thoughts running through my head. I lean back, my arms holding me up, and close my eyes, letting the sounds wash over me.

"You look like a siren."

Niko's rough timbre rises over the steady beat of water. I open my eyes, smiling. He's grinning too, still hip-deep in the pool.

"This place is..." I motion to the rest of the flattened rock behind me, the greenery braving the underside of the falls, and the steam coming off the water.

"I know. I used to come here a lot. To clear my head." He tilts his head, letting the steam and spray cleanse him. As I watch him, it doesn't escape my notice that perhaps the reason he enjoys this spot so much is because the attraction of it is very much like him. Harsh and solitary on the outside, but on the inside, something of quiet beauty. I've seen both sides of him in the past weeks. And I still wonder which side is the real Niko. The Ultor Regni, the nightmare whispered on the realm's lips—sometimes a protector and sometimes a curse, the one that wants my entire family wiped from the realm. Or is he the patient teacher, the thoughtful baker of favorite treats, and the man who takes my breath away in the dark?

Could I be wrong about him? Or is he just like all the others, getting close to me only to reveal his true desires when I'm already too far in? Am I willing to risk what's left of my heart to find out?

It's like he can read my thoughts. He hesitantly approaches, perhaps weighing his own demons with each step. But whatever he decides, he reaches where I'm perched on the rock and his palms stroke the backs of my calves, the only part of me still in the pool.

His touch, even warmer than the water, lights something within me. I take it as a silent invitation and slide down off the edge of the rock, back into the depths. His hands guide me, trailing from my calves, alighting on the backs of my knees, and slowly tracing their way up my thighs.

"Datura." He exhales the nickname he gave me, although this time, it's reverent and full of desire. It's as if this feels different for him too.

He walks backward, finding a place where the water is hip-deep. He doesn't break eye contact, and the depths of warm brown swallow me whole. I move forward, matching him step for step, entranced by his smoldering gaze. Tracing his jawline, I wonder if I'm brave enough to make the first move.

But I don't have to. His fingertips dance across where my scar rests, tracing the vine-like pattern across my collarbone. "You're a siren," he says with the same reverence he spoke the name *Datura*.

I brush his hair off his shoulders so I can wrap my arms around his neck, needing him closer. That's all he needs as a sign. His lips are on mine in an instant. Soft kisses that savor the moment between us. I open to him, letting his tongue collide with mine. My legs tighten around him, and he answers by palming my ass and moving us through the water.

Niko places me on a hidden ledge just under the surface, freeing up his hands to slip under the fabric still covering my peaked breasts. He brings one hand to my face, tracing my lips with his thumb. In response, I kiss and then nip playfully at his thumb. A smirk pulls at his mouth, and his eyes go from my lips to my eyes and back.

The attention causes me to bite my lip, which has him groaning in response. He closes any remaining space between us, so from hip to chest, we're one. Another kiss, this one hungrier than the first. Kissing him is like kissing fire. And I'm ravenous for the burn. His hands trace along my ribs and cup my breasts, then he continues down, his fingertips gently grazing my stomach all the way down to my hips. I pull him closer by wrapping my legs around his hips. His rigid length presses into me, and I can't help but grind against him.

His hands move from my hips to the inside of my thighs. I loosen the grip of my legs, making space for him. Another moan escapes his lips as his fingers trace along my linen underclothes, pushing them aside to find my heat within.

Niko slips two fingers in, working them inside me until I open my legs further. The warm water lapping against my skin encourages me to relax into him. He widens his stance and pulls his fingers out, only to add another. He knows what he's doing, and it won't take me long to find release.

My hands, one in his hair at the nape of his neck and the other propping me up, clench and unclench as I ride higher on this swell of euphoria. My whole body warms as he finds that perfect spot, while his other hand comes around to work that small, powerful bundle of nerves. That's when I come undone. The pleasure I've been riding twines with the heat within, localizing in my core before spinning back out in tingles all across my body.

"Niko." A gasp escapes my lips as my body tightens around his fingers, pulsing until the ride of ecstacy softens.

Gently, he pulls his fingers from me, bringing them to his lips and sucking my wetness from each finger, one at a time. My muscles tighten at his hunger for me, and I need him inside of me.

I pull at the waistband of his drawers and breathe, "Niko, I need you. Now."

His hand reaches below the band and comes back full. He pumps his cock a few times, and watching it does something to my insides. I can't decide if I should spread my legs wider in welcome or close them to find the friction I so desperately need. He decides for me, rubbing the pre-come beading along his tip across his shaft, then fitting it to my center.

He drives straight into me in one filling motion.

He pauses, giving me time to adjust to his fullness. One of his hands is planted beside my head, holding his weight, and the other stretches along my neck, his thumb tracing downward from chin to chest as I open myself to him. His lips follow the trail his thumb has made, licking along my collarbone and pulling my earlobe into his mouth.

Even as he starts pumping inside me, I can't help but think how different this time is from the cave. Instead of the urgent motions of desire mixed with anger, we both take our time, learning each other's body, each watching the way the other responds to a touch, a lick, a movement. There's no denying there's something between us, and as he pulls me closer, grabbing my ass and lifting me back into the water, I surrender myself to him, body and heart. Because whatever is building between us is worth seeing to the end.

He wraps his arms around me, driving hard and fast. I bite my lip and then his shoulder, the surge building again, the movement of the water around us only adding to the push and pull of our need. My fingernails trail down his back as my breathing becomes uneven. His thrusts quicken once more, and the way he stretches me has me seeing stars.

I let go, surrendering to each burst of rapture as it pounds into me, reveling in where our bodies connect. His rhythm quickens, and then his whole body tightens as he drives into me one more time. We both relax into each other, not yet willing to let go. The spray of the warm falls mixing with the chill of the winter air only intensifies the last spasms.

As he slips out of me, we both sink deeper into the warmth of the spring. Neither of us is willing to leave the perfect moment we've created.

Chapter Sixteen

What in the shooting stars does one wear to a bar in the middle of the Dread Forest? Especially if my options are limited to my training gear or the too-tight, torn-to-pieces clothes in my pack. At a loss, I decide to leave clothing choices until the end.

Happily, the cool forest air agrees with my hair, especially after the afternoon I've had, leaving me with little time to get ready. My thighs press together, remembering the feel of Niko between them as I admire what all that warm water did for my hair. The loose waves that usually become a frizzy mess cascade down my back. I try to pull the front into a few high braids, like so many here wear, but that's going to be something to keep practicing. I settle on pinning the front back and keeping the rest loose.

The cosmetics here are certainly lacking compared to Marlys' stash, but as I check myself in the mirror, I realize I like what I see. Between the fresh foods and all the training sessions, even my skin has benefited.

A knock at the door startles me. "It's me, Pris. Gayle mentioned you're coming for girls' night. I thought you might need some options."

"Oh! You're star-sent!" I open the door and wave her in.

She looks beautiful as always, but her hair is softer, with only one braid crowning her head and the rest cascading down her back. I notice she's used something to make her lips stand out, but that's it. I suppose everyone here is more content with how they look naturally.

Pris gives my training gear a glance and tries not to make a face, but I see her lips harden in a tight line before she smiles wide and sashays over to the bed, her arms laden with clothing of all sorts. "So, I just grabbed a few things, but I assumed we were about the same size." She pulls out different outfits unlike any I've seen before.

The dress that catches my eye has a simple cut to it. I pull it on, and it feels like it hugs all the right places. It falls just below my knees, and then one side angles lower.

"Oh! Lilac makes your eyes stand out! I had a feeling that would be the one!" She claps her hands together while her reflection jumps in and out of sight over my shoulder.

"Pris, you're amazing!" I hadn't realized I missed looking nice. I do love how the cut-off tunics, resting just above my belly button, show off my newly forming ab muscles. And shorter, skin-tight pants make everything easier, so I most definitely haven't missed the frilly ball gowns that made it difficult to walk, let alone breathe. But this—this is perfect.

"I'll leave the rest for you to go through on your own. Hopefully, you'll need them at some point."

"Wow, thanks, Pris! It'll be so nice to have some options. Even though we're heading out in a few days." The words come out before I realize what I've said.

"You're leaving?" Her eyebrows knit together, and she looks hurt that I haven't already mentioned this.

"Oh. Yeah. We're continuing our trek north in a day or two."

"You and Baylor?" Now she looks miserable. So, she and Baylor do have something going on. I'll have to remember to give him a hard time about it later on.

"Yeah. And I think Gayle and Niko, too."

She brushes it off and composes herself. But I'm pretty sure she's trying hard to blink away tears. Stars alive, Baylor must've done a number on her.

"Well then, we must celebrate while we can." She resolutely brushes the remaining tears from her glistening eyes and grabs my hand, leading me down the staircase and toward the front door.

We stop at the sound of a throat clearing in the room by the entrance. The space glows softly with firelight. Niko is sitting in a large, pillowed chair right beside the fireplace. He looks more relaxed than I've ever seen him, his feet propped up on a small wooden stool and a thick, worn book resting on his crossed legs.

"Hi, Niko Bear." Pris reaches for the door to continue. Her casual endearment catches me off guard, leaving me once again to wonder what past these two share.

"Pris. Rowandine." I can feel his eyes trace slowly from my sandaled feet up to meet my eyes. "Pris. Rowandine," he says again.

"You said that already." Pris tilts her head, then looks at me and gives Niko a slow smile. "We're headed to Torelai's. Girls' night." Her smile gets even bigger, and with her lips painted darker, the cutest dimples stand out on her cheeks.

"Go easy on her, Pris," Niko says. His eyes never leave mine.

"Of course I will." She winks and pulls me out the door.

We walk arm in arm along a street I haven't yet ventured down. We reach the end of it, and I look at the buildings surrounding us. The lights are off inside each of them, and all is quiet. I look questioningly at Pris, but she doesn't miss a beat as she grabs the rope ladder beside her and hoists herself up toward the treetops. As she climbs, the torchlight plays on the bottom ladder rungs, goading me into motion. I swallow my reserve and remind myself I've spent tons of time in trees. When I was little. Oh, stars.

I stand with my feet firmly planted on the solid ground for just a moment longer, questioning my decision to go out tonight. But then I'm reminded of the easy way between Gayle and the rest of her training crew. With that in mind, I grab the first wooden rung and pull myself up toward where Pris continues her climb.

I try to make out where she's headed, but all I see are branches as I look up. These trees are so wide around that they could easily support an entire house. The branches are each as thick as a horse where they meet the trunk. Up here, the leaves have already started to bud, and their fresh scent laces with that of the ever-burning fires throughout the village homes.

The climb is easier than I thought it would be, but the rungs go on forever. The ladder stops swinging so much, so I stop to check my progress. It looks like Pris has cleared the ladder, and her smiling face pokes out from whatever landing she has reached.

I reach the top and pull myself up and over, then give myself a moment to recover. The branches are dense up here, but without the leaves, I can see the moon and the way the stars dance across the sky.

"There are so many more than I thought," I say, looking up at the inky black sky spotted with tiny pricks of light.

"Yeah, it's a long climb up, but it keeps out the riff-raff." She laughs as she realizes I'm talking about the stars, not the ladder rungs. "Oh, yeah—there's less light up here, so they're brighter. We like to say the stars shine brightly upon us here at Torelai's."

We follow a sturdy rope bridge toward another landing. I make the mistake of looking down. The buildings on the ground have been reduced to tiny blocks. Up here, the stars look closer than what's left of the torches lining the streets below.

"Don't do that on the way back, or you risk falling," Pris says as we reach a new landing. "Always hold on. Two hands."

I feel as if I'm a child being reprimanded for stealing too many sweet rolls from the kitchens. But up here, I realize, it's a matter of life or death. One wrong step and it would not end well.

Pris' voice softens as she says, "I haven't seen Niko look at someone like that in... a long time."

I wish I could see her face as she makes this observation. I still haven't figured out what the closeness between the two of them is, and the way she says that makes it seem... like something's there, or something's a little off. I can't decide, so while I figure out what to say, I stall with, "Oh, you mean Niko Bear?"

She snorts behind me. "Sometimes I forget we're all grown up now. That's a nickname from childhood."

"So you two grew up together?" I press, hoping to get to the bottom of it.

"You could say that, but I was asking about you."

I give in. I take a deep breath and hope whatever was between them is long over. "Yeah, we've been spending a lot of time together. He's... different than I first thought," I say, testing the waters.

"You mean an arrogant brute with a sword?"

I pause on the bridge connecting the trees we're walking between and turn to her. "That's *exactly* what I thought."

We laugh, and something shifts between us. We've found common ground, even if it is Niko's savage ways. Pris motions me forward, both to get off this bridge and continue sharing.

"He's sweet, though. And patient," I continue. "And despite the fact he wanted me dead when we first met, I think I can trust him now."

"Wait, what? He wanted you dead?" She pauses, and I can feel her trying to put the pieces together. "Oh—because he's the Ultor Regni, and you grew up an Aeronwick?"

"Exactly. There was a lot to get through."

She snorts again. "I think if he pushed through that, you must mean something to him. He used to be different, more swing-his-sword-first-and-ask-questions-later, but a lot has happened. He's been through some really hard things."

I want to ask a follow-up to this, but as we move to the front of a round wooden building constructed around the trunk of the tree, I realize we must be here. The structure is fitted with some type of rush rooftop that angles up toward the trunk all around. The building has a wide deck that sticks out far into the branches on the other side. I notice it's held in place by thick ropes on all sides to relieve some of the pressure on the tree trunk.

The wooden sign above the door reads *The Viper's Den*. The large curling letters are in direct contrast to how portentous the title is. I have the distinct feeling I'm going to love it here.

Pris pushes open the door, and we walk into a warm, candlelit room. The bar itself loops all around the trunk of the tree, and is shelved with different-colored bottles filled with amber and clear liquids. The rest of the room has plenty of tables, some low with chairs, some high with stools. The outer wall has smaller groupings of pillowed chairs. And it doesn't smell like a bar, instead it smells like cinnamon and nutmeg, with hints of citrus.

Pris moves toward one of these groupings. I recognize Saleen, Holden, and Gayle, who all wave our way. Reinette turns around and sends a scowl my way before smiling and waving at Pris. I quickly decide I won't let her ruin my evening and sit down between Pris and Saleen.

"You didn't tell me you were heading out so soon!" Pris greets Gayle, giving her a glare that would make anyone think twice before crossing her.

Gayle shoots a quick look my way, but meets Pris head-on. "I didn't think it mattered to you so much anymore."

Suddenly, the air feels heavy with a tension that is way over my head. I jump up, mumbling, "Drinks," and head toward the bar.

I recognize the barkeep—Torelai—as the warrior who invited me to the first day of training. Her long, dark hair is slicked back and runs stick-straight down her back. It moves hypnotically with her wide hips. Once again, I think back to the way these warriors have so much control over their bodies and can't help but think she's putting on something of a show.

"Fledgling." She nods to me as she dries a clean glass. "What'll it be?"

I inwardly smile at her greeting, suddenly feeling even more a part of this wonderful place. "Oh, anything, I suppose." Used to drinking whatever wine my father ordered to the table, I've never really thought about what other options there could be.

She looks disappointed. "That's a dangerous thing to say in a bar. Not much for a cold one in a tavern, huh?" She shrugs and fills a tall tankard with a pale, milky golden liquid, pushing it my way.

I sniff it hesitantly, and the scent of florals and honey wafts up toward my nose. I think back to the feast night and smile to myself. "Thanks. This is the same stuff from the midwinter celebration, right? It's amazing. What is it?" I ask, hoping to start a conversation so I don't have to get up quite yet. I want to leave Gayle and Pris plenty of time to hash out whatever is bothering them before I return. I would feel terrible if I caused a rift between the two people who have shown me nothing but kindness since I've arrived here.

"It's my special vintage. Dandelion wine. It's big in the village."

"Why dandelions?" My knowledge of drinks is limited, but I don't think I've ever tasted anything like it. She knows her stuff, that's for sure.

"So glad you asked." She leans in, as if getting ready to tell a tale. "You know, a dandelion is the only flower that represents the three celestial bodies."

"Oh? You mean the sun, moon, and stars?" I decide to humor her, but now I'm also interested in how she ties this to a flower, or what's in my cup.

"Those very ones. The yellow flower is the sun in all its glory. The puffball is as round and white as the moon. And the floating seeds are like the stars above, always shining and twirling around us. Deciding our fate." She points to a painting behind her, fluid and bright: a field of dandelions blowing in the breeze.

"Beautiful. I never thought of them like that," I respond, touched that she would share something so obviously meaningful to her with someone new to her village.

From the bar, the coziness of the round room settles over me. The small touches, like fresh flowers in vases and small picture frames on the tables, make it feel more like someone's home than a tavern. Even the musician, plucking away on her stringed instrument, has made herself at home, sitting cross-legged atop a large pillow. Her soothing notes float around the room in a slow, calming rhythm.

Torelai notices my hesitation to return to my group and comes back over. "This place..." I begin.

"Yeah, there's no place like it," she finishes for me.

"It's so..."

"Warm? High up?" she guesses.

"Well, yeah," I laugh, "but I was going to say homey."

She gives me a half-smile, and her eyes sparkle, as if I've landed on exactly what she was going for.

"And it's only for females?" I ask, noticing that Holden stands out like a sore thumb in this fairly full space.

"Not exclusively. But males tend to stay away. Females know they can come here anytime and they'll find comfort and the perfect drink." She stands a little taller as she says this, clearly proud of the space she's created.

"The perfect drink?" I ask, looking at the pewter cup in my hand. As good as it is, I'm not sure it would go well with breakfast.

"In the daylight hours, it's more of a tea shop. Same vibe, different drinks." She nods to the large mugs stacked neatly in between bottles, and what I now notice are jars of tea leaves lined up on the shelf above.

"You've thought of everything." I mean what I say. The castle kitchens are the coziest spot I can think of, and even the big burning fires and aroma of freshly baked bread can't hold a candle to all of this.

Torelai folds her arms and leans back against the bar. "I'd like to think so." She nods back to Pris and Gayle. "First pour's on me. From the looks of it, you'll need it."

I salute her with my drink and head back to meet the mess I've made head-on.

Back within the cozy confines of our pillow-filled chairs, Pris and Gayle lean toward each other, hissing short, clipped words in an attempt to keep their voices low. Their words are completely inaudible, but the incredibly quick volley between them sounds like they're weaving incantations around each other. Holden and Reinette are in danger of getting whiplash from how quickly their heads turn back and forth.

In the interest of my safety, I grab the spot next to Holden. I lean in and whisper, "Will they be okay?"

His eyes don't leave the action, but he leans my way. "Give them another minute or two. They run hot. They'll be all over each other again before the night's end."

I raise my eyebrows, remembering Pris' encounter with Baylor. Oh. Baylor. Now it all fits together. Okay, so it's not my fault. This is all Baylor's fault. And maybe a little my fault for sharing that we're leaving again.

Tiring of their back-and-forth, Holden turns to me and asks about castle life.

"It's incredibly dull compared to all this." I motion to encompass all that's transpired since I've arrived. "I mean, we're sitting on pillows having drinks in the highest branches of the trees!"

"But seriously," he presses, "tell me about the balls! Tell me about the view from the highest tower!" I can see Reinette inching closer to hear, even if her eyes remain focused on Pris and Gayle.

"The balls were extravagant, to say the very least. The king would spare no expense when entertaining the visiting nobles. But I never found much joy in them. The dances were always so stuffy, and all my partners always looked at me like I was their next meal."

He looks at me as if I've just slapped him in the face. "They couldn't all be bad."

"The dresses weren't, I suppose. Despite not letting me breathe properly for the entire night, they were always something to behold in their own right. And Marlys, my maid, always had a way with a kohl brush and a hot iron. I always looked like someone else entirely when I strode down the massive staircase. But I was always terrified I was going to land on my face at the bottom." I laugh, remembering how I gripped the banister until my knuckles went white every time I had to travel down a staircase, and the grace with which Licia floated down before me as I tried my hardest not to barrel into her.

Holden asks more about the castle and what my days there were like. While I talk, even Gayle and Pris turn our way. I tell them all about my tutors, and how Gryphon and I would sneak away any chance we got. Soon, Gayle and Pris' legs are tangled into each other while they sip their tankards of dandelion wine.

When my voice is almost hoarse with regaling them about my past, I decide to turn the questions to them. I learn more about daily life here in the Shifter village, and how, now that midwinter is over, they're all gearing up for the upcoming spring equinox. I hadn't realized we'd made it so far through the winter months already. I am sad to hear I'll miss a big holiday while we're traveling, but I suppose it's a small price to pay in the long run.

Pris tells us about how the other day, a parent stopped by her classroom to commend her on *not* teaching her son a single thing all year. Pris was instantly mortified, but the parent quickly reassured her that her child was in fact learning, but was having so much fun doing it, he had no idea! The room erupts in laughter, and Pris blushes all the way to her hairline.

Holden has us hanging on his every word as he recounts his last job out at sea. He's a crabber on a large fishing boat that travels for weeks, sometimes months at a time. A member of their crew was tossed out to sea, saved by a sea maiden. But when the crew approached her, she refused to give him back, saying she won her lover fairly. I didn't know sea maidens were so crafty, but they were able to outwit her in the end.

Even Reinette looks like she's having fun, until we make eye contact. Then she looks like someone slipped something sour into her drink.

"The way you all talk about your village is heartening," I say, completely in awe of the stories they share of their upbringing. "Everyone here is important to the success of everyone else. It's amazing."

An older woman who's been nursing a beer at the bar turns around and chimes in, pleased with my observation. "You're right. Especially among us women. Sisterhood is our lifeline. From the moment we're born, we cling to each other. No matter what animal family we are born into, other women have our hearts. We lean on our entire community. There is an unspoken connection between us all. Our mothers become our friends' mothers too. If you approach your community with a full heart and a full body, your returns will be fruitful."

The woman, as tall and broad as any warrior, says this matter-of-factly, but this is all news to me. Her words are the most beautiful thing I've ever heard.

"Oh, and I suppose you're pretty essential too." The woman comes closer, knocking Holden on the shoulder as his fake pouting begins to get out of hand. She squeezes in next to him, and he doesn't bat an eye. No one does. Am I the only one who thinks it's strange that this old woman, as wrinkled as an old tomato, has joined us mid-conversation?

"No need to prattle on about crowns and gowns. You know ol' Juniper only hauls herself up here for the *real* gossip." Pris and Gayle settle in closer to one another, their bodies melting into each other. As if the arrival of this older female has them thinking twice about their fight.

"Ah," she says when her eyes, trailing around the group, land on me. "You're the one who's got our young Nikodemus in a pother." Juniper's eyes crinkle as she looks me over.

"I'm sorry?" I say, looking to the group for some help.

"Juni, you can't dive right in on our newly winged Fae royal," Pris says, jumping in at my bewilderment.

"I suppose you're right. I wouldn't dare start another catfight." She narrows her eyes at Reinette. "Don't think I don't see you bickering over here. You two"—she points between Gayle and Pris—"have almost ruined my night. The two of you better figure out your love sandwich before he goes, or there will be several broken hearts."

My jaw hits the floor. This Juniper is relentless. She goes in for the kill. I can't decide if I want to laugh or cry at how direct she is. But I hear a sound back at the bar, where Torelai has her mouth covered with the back of her wrist. I wonder if this is a usual occurrence here at the Viper's Den, or if someone should change the subject. I look between Holden, who's the quietest I've seen him all night, and where Gayle and Pris share a cushion, but no one seems to want to make eye contact.

I ask the first question that comes to mind. The question I've been dying to ask. "So what is everyone's Shifter form?"

All eyes turn to me. I can't tell if everyone is grateful for the change of subject or if I've just committed some kind of taboo. But before I can apologize, Juniper smacks her lips and says, "Well now, I'm a black bear by day, ale hound by night—right, Tor?" She glances back to make sure everyone's eyes are still on her. There's no doubt she's captured the room. Torelai nods, but doesn't say anything, as if she knows she won't be able to get a word in edgewise while Juniper is talking. "I didn't first shift until I was eight years old. A late bloomer, some would say—"

Gayle cuts her off. "I'm a jaguar." This is followed by a deep-throated growl and a clawing hand motion.

Pris swats at her and adds, "I'm a cottontail." Her nose twitches, and Gayle lightly brushes it with a kiss.

"Reinette is a rattlesnake, and I'm a swan," Holden says, gracefully flapping his arms. "Can you guess what Torelai is?"

"A viper?" I ask, fairly confident in my answer. Everyone laughs, shaking their heads. I turn to Torelai, confused.

"My mother was the viper. This was her place before it was mine. I'm the runt of the family. A mouse." She shrugs, and her hands go wide. That gets another big laugh, but it's quickly followed by a big yawn from Pris.

"That must be the seventh time you've yawned in a minute." Gayle squeezes Pris' hand, which she's been holding for some time now. I guess whatever was between them has passed. "Maybe we should call it a night? You have to teach in the morning, after all. Or, maybe we could go see if Baylor is still up?" The heat between Gayle and Pris is suddenly palpable.

Pris turns back to everyone else. "I'll walk you home, Roe."

"Sounds good. I'm not sure I'd find my way back through the treetops." I laugh, but on the inside, I remember the rope bridge and the ladder we climbed on the way here. Suddenly, I'm glad that someone will be with me as I try to navigate everything slightly less sober and way more tired than I was before.

To keep my mind off the distance between where I currently stand and the ground, I reflect on the evening. It was so different from the stuffy dinners at the castle, where no one would say a word until the king rose and exited, and a collective exhale of tension would leave the room with him.

Never have I been so relaxed in a group of people. Never have I been able to share my true thoughts on balls and instructors. And the way women of all ages—and Holden—come together here, learning from each other, comforting each other. How exhilarating!

In sharing like this, I'm more aware of my emotions and desires. I'm lighter and more at ease with myself after one night out. And I don't think the sweet dandelion nectar can take all the credit.

"See you after training tomorrow," I say as Pris turns toward the glowing light of the stables. "Thanks for inviting me tonight." My voice is warm with dandelion wine and gratitude. She waves over her shoulder and disappears into the barn.

Chapter Seventeen

Shutting the door as quietly as possible, I turn to find Niko dozing in the same pillowed chair. The fire burns low in the hearth, as if he's been asleep for a while now. I urge my toes to be light on the cool wooden planks below. They moan under my weight, and I pause to silently curse them. There's no movement from my left, so I power on, only to startle when a deep voice laced with sleep says, "You're back."

"You were waiting for me." I had intended it to be a question, but it comes out more like a statement.

"Everything here is new." He stumbles over his words, probably because of the late hour. "I was just making sure you got back in one piece."

I move toward the warmth of the fire's glowing embers, putting my hands on my hips, my dress fluttering around my calves. "I was with Pris."

"Exactly." He stands up and mirrors me, his hands raised to his hips as well. The sleepiness quickly leaves his eyes, replaced with something more smoldering. Protectiveness? But not the stifling kind, the warm kind, full of feeling. He slowly raises his hand and gently brushes my hair away from my face. His fingers are warm, his movements precise. I hold my breath and lean into his caress. His eyes are still on me, and he's waiting for me to respond.

"I'm back now." I lick my lips, the dandelion wine making me bold.

Stepping forward, I rest my hands on his chest, the now familiar heat radiating off it.

I look up. That same smolder is still there in his eyes, and he reaches one hand around to rest on the small of my back.

"I..." he starts. I lean in, memories of this afternoon at the waterfall warming my core. We stand there, frozen in place, as a log on the fire falls, crumbling into ash. "I... can't."

The desire in his eyes fades as he moves back. There's only a step between us, but it may as well be a chasm.

He kisses my cheek. "Goodnight, Roe. Sleep well."

For a moment, I can't make sense of it. I thought something was growing between us, but his response makes me think twice. He's so hot and cold. One moment, he has me backed against a wall, or splayed out under a waterfall, and the next, he's giving me a chaste goodnight kiss and backing away.

Before he can see the hurt on my face, I turn toward the stairs. I have too many things to say in response, but all the feelings swirling around are just muddled enough by dandelion wine that I don't want to let any of them out. The stairs creak under my feet, and I no longer have any desire to be quiet.

"Roe, wait."

I pause, but don't turn around. At his silence, tears trail down my cheeks and I resume my trek upstairs.

We agree to leave in three days. I decide to use most of that time to train. Despite my worst thoughts being voiced aloud by Reinette, I enjoy the time with the others in the village. And I love how it makes me feel. Energy courses through my veins after a thorough session. The tough workouts Gayle continues to throw my way have already honed my muscles. Although each morning I wake up sore, it hurts less each day, and I know the pain is my body knitting itself into a stronger version.

Rather than standing back to watch, I now hold my head high as I walk into the training grounds. I bypass Reinette, but everyone else has kind things to say, even if just in greeting. She continues to throw glares my way, but doesn't seem to put too much more into it than that.

Today, the weather is warmer. The entire village seems lighter somehow. More people than usual are sitting around the ring this morning, mugs of steaming hot tea in their hands as they wait for the fun to begin.

Baylor, despite his size and skill, is still considered a recruit, so he and I line up along with the others. Unfortunately, all the other new warriors are much younger, and we both tower over most of them. Gayle instructs us through some quick warm-ups and what I've come to call rhythmic form, because while we practice our technique in slow motion, I've found a certain rhythm to my movement. And although it feels tedious, Gayle has drilled into me how form is much more important than speed. Speed will come later.

Next, she pairs each of us off with a seasoned warrior to spar. This gives me a chance to practice my technique, but also try out new skills. I've learned a lot by just watching the ways these more skilled fighters move.

"Good movement, Roe," Holden says as I try to stay out of his range, sliding in toward him when I choose to strike. "Try to remain level, though. Those bobs will get your head taken right off."

Instantly, I stop bobbing as I move from side to side. While keeping my knees bent, I learn I have more control of my movements and don't need to commit to a specific direction too soon. I'm doing better, but Holden keeps hitting his mark.

Someone from outside the ring offers, "Watch his hands, not his eyes. He's been goading you this whole time. The sword hand speaks the truth!" And I realize that's what my problem has been. Holden's been looking high and striking low, and vice versa. I silently applaud his crafty deception.

Watching the way Holden moves, I notice he's heavier on his feet, just like Gryphon. But Holden seems to use it to his advantage. It's distracting. And the way he plants himself allows for quick shifts or use of his weight that wouldn't work for me.

This seems to contrast with what he said last night. I would think a swan Shifter would be more graceful and light on their feet, not big and burly. I make a note to ask Gayle why the Shifters don't use their animal forms in our morning sparring sessions. I've seen many types of animals around the village. I wonder what the rules or etiquette of that are, especially since Niko gave me a hard time when I asked why he didn't just shift when fighting off the guards or Thaddeus. A grin spreads across my lips as I remember Reinette shrieking about my shift mid-fight—I know I'm missing some of the unspoken rules here.

After I've lost one too many rounds and effectively boosted Holden's ego for the day, he sends me back to the other fledglings to practice with someone on my own skill level.

"Roe, let's go!" Baylor is just finishing with his partner as well. He's big, but I'm faster, so it'll be fun to see where this goes.

I start confident that this is one round I can win. I've seen the way Baylor moves, and I'm both stealthier and more flexible. We soon find ourselves in a perfect flow, going blow for blow, attention only on one another's next moves. I lose focus on the crowd watching and throwing out pointers—until a familiar husky voice catches me off guard.

"Bend your knees. Stay on the balls of your feet. Every time, Rowandine."

Niko hasn't been to any of the morning sessions, and I glance over my shoulder to find him. The look costs me. The wooden blade of Baylor's practice sword connects with my jaw, and I'm sent reeling to the ground.

"Starballs! Roe!" Baylor is on his knees beside me before I even know what has happened. "Roe, talk to me! Are you okay? I didn't mean to..." He trails off as his hands pat along my jawline, trying to find where I'm hurt. He's in a complete frenzy.

I try to push him away—he's doing more harm than good. But all I can manage is a gentle swat as stars dance in my vision.

"Roe?" Niko's grumbling voice pulls me out of the fog. Focusing on him, I push myself up to my elbows. He comes down on one knee to push my hair away from my face. His rough fingers trail along my jawline, gentle and light.

"Niko," I breathe, waiting to see what he does.

After making sure I'm okay, he turns on Baylor. There are small tendrils of smoke trailing him. I wonder if, like with me, powerful emotions tempt a shift. If he's thinking of shifting, there are a lot of people here who might get crushed by an angry dragon's tail. I might've gotten hurt, but I don't need someone else to fight my battles for me.

"Niko, I'm fine." I try to get up, but my head is still spinning. "Niko!" I shout, and those who weren't already watching pause. Everyone goes silent around us, waiting for Niko's reaction.

He turns, looking from me to Baylor. Baylor stands frozen, holding his hands in the air, silently promising he's not a threat. Something shifts in the air. Niko's shoulders relax, and his fists open and close as if he's still deciding. His eyes fall on me, still stuck on the ground. I shake my head, just enough to get my point across.

He gives Baylor one last look and nods, making his way toward me instead.

That breaks whatever spell we were under. I may've been hit too hard, but any anger from the night before dissolves as Niko quickly picks me up by my upper arms and sets me back on my feet. I know it was just sparring, and just Baylor, but Niko chose to trust me, to put his faith in me and my decision for him not to rip Baylor's head off. A small step, but a meaningful one.

Baylor and Gayle crowd around me, and I watch Niko stride off toward the meeting hall.

"Well, you're getting there. But stars alive, Baylor! It's just sparring," Gayle scolds him while tilting my burning cheek up toward the morning sunlight. "Come on, Roe. Turn that pain into power. Up you go."

"This is on you, hon." Baylor ignores Gayle, his eyes narrowing at me. "It's not my fault you're over here taking a break to blow kisses to all your admirers." His gaze shifts to Niko in the distance. "You're alright, though? Because if you are, I'll keep going." It seems he's reined in his cosseting and is gearing up for something big. A small smile plays at the corners of his mouth, and he pounds against my back in what I've learned is his way of showing affection.

"Ouch! Baylor! Control yourself!" I push him away more forcefully this time.

∞

The next morning brings a renewed sense of purpose. But downstairs, rather than having a quiet mug of tea before setting off for training, I meet Niko, Gayle, and Lady Alasie with two others I don't recognize—but with their knotted hair and dirt-stained clothing, they look like they've been sleeping rough for at least a few days. They stand with their backs to me and are speaking low and quick to those circled close around them. Niko rubs one hand thoughtfully against his chin as his mouth quirks to the side. Gayle is hopping from foot to foot and looks worried. And Lady Alasie is pursing her lips together so tightly they've turned white.

This doesn't bode well for my newly forged positive energy.

Gayle's eyes meet mine, and she throws an elbow into Niko. He coughs loudly, and the two who were speaking turn toward me. Their eyes widen before they school their features into calm demeanors.

"Well, don't everybody speak at once. Out with it!" I prod as I reach for the teakettle. Niko hands me the mug I've favored of late, and I smile at this small gesture.

"We have word of the king's guard close by," he says. "Unfortunately, they'll certainly be within range when we begin our trek northward."

"That doesn't seem like that big of a deal, does it? Can't we just go around or evade them?" I ask. The concern on their faces doesn't match what Niko's just shared. "I mean, I know one trek through the Dread Forest doesn't make me an expert on anything, but is there something else?"

"Well, yes, a small something," Niko begins. "Killian is leading them. And he's out for your blood." His eyes do that crinkle thing where he's waiting for someone to snap, but he just ends up looking even more attractive.

"He'll have to get in line." I force a laugh, but it comes out more like I've gone hysterical. Which perhaps I have, given the circumstances. I'm on my way to find a sister I don't yet know, who wants me dead. And now I find out my brother would love to join in. Meanwhile, I'm riding away from a sister I've known all my life, even though she recently risked her own life and position to come on this small errand with me.

I keep laughing. It all sounds so absurd. And to think I woke up this morning believing I had it all figured out.

I don't even make it to my first sip of morning tea before it all comes crashing down around me. At this point, I'm gasping for breath, and tears are streaming down my face. Everyone looks from me to Lady Alasie. The two who brought the news begin to slowly back out of the room.

Gayle strides closer. Before I can take another breath, she has wrapped me tightly in her embrace and holds me close. Her body moves slowly back and forth to a rhythm I cannot hear. The gentle rocking settles me, and her body's warmth calms me.

The laughter fades, but the tears remain. They fall silently onto Gayle's soft tunic. She hums tunelessly as if she were soothing a small babe in her arms. I let her pull me in tighter for a few more moments. And then I straighten and take a step back.

Everyone's eyes have found somewhere else to look while I pull myself together. I sniff and wipe my nose on the sleeve of another of the shirts Pris has lent me. I take one more big breath to center myself, roll my shoulders back, and ask, "So, when do we leave?"

Gayle looks surprised, but Niko gives a nod of appreciation to the resilience I hope I'm projecting. "You tell us."

I beam at him. For him to acknowledge my role in our group as something of a leader shouldn't be such a big deal, but it is. To go from a father who controlled my every move, to a nightmare of a husband, then top it off with an Ancient who wants to feed me to my sister—and now to whatever this is with Niko, a partner who sees me as a leader, makes me feel like a sunflower opening its petals toward the sky.

"Plans remain the same," Gayle suggests. "Why should anything change? We can elude a few of the king's men with ease."

Her confidence further strengthens my resolve. "Yes. We leave tomorrow for Iolanthe's. We'll be ready this time."

My thoughts drift to Licia, who paid dearly in our first encounter. I've trained relentlessly since then, and hope that next time we will walk away unscathed.

My last training session goes smoothly enough. I try to ignore all the sidelong glances and stares I receive. As if I've just grown a second head. Mostly, everyone here can shift, so I don't understand what all the fuss is about a set of sparkly wings.

Reinette keeps her distance, but I catch her watching me once or twice. She even shakes her head at me at one point, letting me know she still thinks I somehow cheated her in our sparring session. As if I did that on purpose! And it was so long ago at this point.

My muscles scream at me as I work through each movement, so I move more slowly today. I try to keep some energy stored, knowing that the days on the road will be long and hard.

After training, I look for Pris. I know she helps the younger children with their studies, so I head toward the small schoolhouse. The building looks much like the others on the ground here in the village. The stone walls meet the same straw roof as the Meeting House, but the windows are large and the double doors open to a long hallway with several doors along each side.

Luckily, I spot Pris in the first room, working with several young children. "Now, you must remember, always be aware of your surroundings," she is saying. "It could make the difference between life and death, especially when you're young." As she spots me, she rises from the circle of small children on the ground. "Go ahead and talk the next scenario out with the person next to you. I'll be right back." She nods encouragingly to a few slow starters and then walks toward me. "Roe! You've never ventured to the schoolrooms. Is everything okay?"

"Oh, yes. Everything is fine. We leave tomorrow, and I just wanted to make sure I got to say goodbye to you. You've been so kind, sharing your clothes and your friends with me." The words come out jumbled, and they sound so insignificant compared to all that she's given me in this short time.

"Well, of course," she says, smiling softly. "But you must know by now, they are your friends too, Roe."

"Oh. I suppose," I say haltingly. "Yes. Thanks." I want to slap my forehead for being so awkward, while this all seems to come so easily to her.

"And it's certainly not 'goodbye,' Roe. You'll be back. Our paths will cross again," she says, with a certainty I don't have.

"So now you're a seer?" I smile at her easy confidence in herself, hoping one day to match it.

She winks. "I've been known to dabble here and there."

"I'll let you get back to your students. Thanks for everything, Pris." I wave to the children, all now watching us rather than practicing whatever task Pris asked of them.

"See you soon, friend." She waves and heads back to her waiting class. "Oh! Just remember," she calls over her shoulder, turning once more to face me. "There's only one thing stronger than magic. Sisterhood." She flicks her eyebrows and blows a kiss my way. And with that, she turns back to her students.

She's right, of course. If there's one thing I've learned here, it's that there's an unbreakable bond between women. This I will carry with me into the North, and to Ombretta, where I can hopefully melt her heart of ice.

Chapter Eighteen

It feels too soon to be back in the saddle, but the rhythmic beat of Navi's hooves on the leaf-strewn forest floor soon pulls me into a pensive state. I let my mind drift as it will. I wonder, if and when we meet with Killian, if he'll bother to fill me in on how Licia is before he attempts to silence me forever. It feels like a lifetime since I last saw her, kicking and screaming while an unlucky king's guard rode away with her—straight to the castle. Leaving many of his kinsmen to die. But it has not even been two months.

I wish I had had more time here in Sverreian. I've learned a lot from Gayle in the sparring ring. And this time, when I meet those same king's men, I'm confident I'll be able to hold my own in a fight.

The women in that village amaze me. The way Pris took me under her wing and gave me a glimpse of what friendship could be was heartwarming. The easy conversations and late nights sitting around on big fluffy pillows have been good for my soul, in a way I never even imagined. With friends like them, I feel held tight and free at the same time.

Niko catches my eye as he slows his horse to cross a small stream. He's trimmed his beard close in preparation for travel. Again, I'm caught off guard by his stubborn beauty. He can certainly take a girl's breath away, but with more than just his good looks. His very presence causes me to feel light with dizziness, especially when I'm close enough to smell his woodsmoke and leather scent, which makes my toes curl in my boots.

Navi takes the stream too quickly, and I'm jostled out of my daydream and reminded that I should pay closer attention to her footing. Baylor gives me a questioning look as he crosses, but I pretend I'm too focused on the uphill stride.

I start as Niko says my name, for what I realize must be at least the second time. In my daydreaming state, I missed him riding up next to me. "I'm sorry, what?" I ask as I try to clear my head of all the thoughts I was just having about the male now beside me.

His brows knit together, and he runs his hand along the top of his braids. Stars, the way his muscles flex when he does that.

Stop it!

To help change my train of thought, I ask him about his Warden duties. "You said previously that you haven't been home in years. Where'd you spend most of your time?"

Looking surprised by my question, he takes a moment to think. "Well, I spend most of my time on the road. Gayle and I ride around the Wastelands of Glorixia, making sure everything is as it should be." He looks at me, gauging my interest, but also something more.

"You mean empty?" I ask. My knowledge of the Wastelands isn't much, but from its name, anyone could guess that there's little left of what was once a grand city in the middle of the kingdom.

"Well, yes, empty. Especially of living things," he says cryptically.

"You mean humans and such?"

"Exactly. Humans poking around the Wastelands are the last thing we need."

"Why would it matter if the humans are poking around a big pile of rocks? Unless it's more than just a pile of rocks. And who is this 'we'?" I wonder if there's more to the Wardens than just aimlessly riding between villages.

"Nothing gets past you." His tone drips with sarcasm, but approval sparks in his eyes.

"Killian would always speak cryptically. I learned to read between the lines. At one point, it became more of a game to see how much I could glean from just one or two words from him." I remember fondly our many hours spent in the library, where he would describe past wars and the decisions made by each general. I could always tell which actions he deemed appropriate and which ones he would have steered clear of if it were him deciding. He would make a formidable opponent on the battlefield. Pity the fool who ends up on the opposite side of him. "Anyway," I continue, not letting myself get distracted, "you were saying?"

"There's a..." He looks around to see if Baylor is paying him any attention, but Baylor is enjoying Gayle's tough love at the moment. "There's a library within the Wastelands." His voice is barely more than a whisper.

I nod, as if I've heard this before, until I realize I haven't heard it, but seen it. In a book?

No. A dream. I've seen a library that is only found by those who seek it. A library that is deep within the earth. Shelves that would make my neck ache from looking up to the highest books. Doors even within the towering shelves, leading to more books. Ancient texts kept safe under the guard of those sworn to secrecy. Those who vow to lead a life underground, never to leave the confines of the books surrounding them—a life of many journeys, but none of their own.

Niko's jaw drops as I share this vision with him. He nods along as I recall even the smallest details of this most secret place. "That settles it, I suppose. It sounds like the library has requested a visit from you. You had better acquiesce. Sooner rather than later."

"Yes, let me add that right in between destroying my flesh and blood and saving the entire realm," I say acerbically. But really, when would I have time to go visit a few dusty books? What good would it do?

"It may seem inconsequential now, but perhaps we'll stop in at some point." He nods, agreeing with his own idea.

"We? You mean I'm stuck with you?" I say mockingly, but my heart flutters at the realization that he sees us still riding around together weeks, maybe months from now.

If I didn't know better, I would think I saw a slight blush creep up his lightly stubbled cheeks.

"I just mean, since I'll be headed that way, anyway."

I'm left doubting that there was any more meaning than just that.

I can tell we're approaching the edge of the forest by the way the trees thin out. There are fewer here, and they all seem like babies compared to the ones surrounding the village. Next time we stop, I'll have to ask why the biggest trees are closest to Sverreian.

The past few hours have been silent as we all keep our ears out for any twig snap that is not our own. Sure enough, as we hug the outskirts of the forest, we spot tracks. Niko and Gayle decide there must be about twenty men, all on horseback. Baylor could probably name most of the horses from just their hoof marks, and he confirms they are all from *his* stable.

Now, at least, we know where they are. Ahead of us. But Niko and Gayle keep an eye out at all times. With Killian so close, we decide to keep riding as long as we can and hope to skirt the forest for as long as possible. Out in the open, we'd be sitting ducks to be picked off at any moment by prowling wolves.

We continue as dusk fades into night. My belly rumbles, already missing the fresh rolls baked each morning in the kitchen, and the entire community gathered around that huge table for supper together. Eating jerky and cold rolls while bumping through the forest in the saddle certainly isn't the same.

Mid-chew and mid-thought, I see torches glow to life. They form a circle all around us, held by men and women, the flames dancing eerily in the night.

I instantly recognize their glinting armor. It's plated with the curling snake of Hadeon's sigil—Killian's sigil now.

Chapter Nineteen

The torches illuminate the large rock formations around us. Killian's outline is unmistakably front and center, standing tall against the rock face, triumph lighting his face.

His eyes fix on me. They are wild with animosity and dark from sleepless nights on the road. His usually perfectly styled hair is long and tangled, and his princely fashion has been replaced with battle attire. It dawns on me that this is not the same brother I left behind.

"Licia said I'd find you heading this way." His eyes flash with malice as he looks me up and down, searching for the sister he once knew. "She said a lot of things. Including that you are an imposter. Living among royalty this whole time, when you're nothing but star-charred dragon droppings. You're one of them." His eyes cut toward the tall mountain far to the southeast, where it's said the last of the Fae retreated.

Licia is alive. It sounds like she's still angry with me if she told Killian where to find us, but at least she's alive. "We can work this out, brother."

"I am *not* your brother," he spits, jumping down from his ledge. He fingers a necklace at his collar, drawing my attention. Are those teeth hanging around his neck? "I promised her I'd give you a message, though. So, as the caring *brother* I am, here it goes: 'Do not worry for me. I'll be well in due time. For with every sickness, a new life grows, and for every death, there will be a birth.'" He grins as he moves closer to me. Now within striking distance, if he so chose. "I blame her dramatics on her inability to sleep. She roams the halls at night, gripping her belly and singing odd tunes to herself. You've killed her, and now you too will die."

I slide off Navi to meet him, and I feel Gryphon and Baylor do the same, standing on either side of me. As I step closer, the malice emanating from Killian is almost tangible. I cringe as I look closer at his face. Once so beautiful and beloved by all the girls at court, now it's etched with pain and hate, marred with the desire for revenge.

"I'll always be your sister, Killian. That much is true." His words have shaken me, and I fight to sound half as bold as I now feel. Could he be right? Is Licia wasting away at the castle?

"You're *not* my sister. You're a monster," he snarls, pacing before us as if a caged monster himself. "My sister is dying because of you."

"We can fix what he destroyed. We can fix everything King Hadeon's torn apart." I search his darkened face for the brother I knew and loved, only seeing a profound loathing.

"Destroyed?" He laughs. "Father only made this kingdom stronger. We are prosperous and could not want for anything. Or have you already forgotten, *sister*?"

A shudder rolls through me at his mocking tone. "I haven't forgotten the court and all their finery. The dazzling balls, the feasts that could have fed hundreds if we allowed it." Against my better judgment, I continue. "I also cannot forget the way our servants would move in ghostly silence and then skitter from the room in fear. And what about the people of the village, who hide away in their homes on every other day, but during the celebrations, are out in the streets, coming together? Happy?"

I let my last word fall. Hopeful that he's seen this too, but knowing he's been blinded by privilege and filled with stories of contempt for those unlike him. He's been fed a steady diet of tales about Fae destruction and Shifters we should fear.

These are the same stories I grew up with. The difference is that I want to see the truth. I want to become more. For our world to become more. He wants everything to remain the same, no matter the cost.

There's a moment when a question builds in his eyes. Where the brother I knew replaces this undiluted contempt before me. But before I can blink, he rolls his shoulders back, and the brother I knew is gone.

Realizing I can't reach him, I try another tactic. "You mentioned Licia?" I ask, looking for safer ground. As I speak, I can feel Gryphon's body humming beside me, desperate for answers.

"She's ill." His tone is full of anger aimed at me and sadness for Licia. "She can't keep anything down and is wasting away before us. You've killed her as surely as if you drove a knife through her heart with your own hands."

That very same knife stabs deeply into my own heart. I picture her wandering around the castle, broken and lost without the people she holds most dear. I thought she was stronger than this, though. I thought she'd be fine without us. But she's alone, probably worried sick knowing we're out here risking our lives.

I look at Gryphon on my left and Baylor on my right for help. But I know my mistake as soon as I take my eyes off of Killian. I hear his movement as he draws his longsword, followed swiftly by all his guards.

I throw myself to the ground, rocks digging into my palms, as the glint of his blade narrowly misses me and whirs too close to my head for comfort.

I look up at him, incredulous. A dawning realization strikes deep within my heart. There will be no mercy. He's not here to return me to the castle. He is here for only one thing.

The rest of his sentinels encircle us. They're so close I can smell the steel of their armor and their days-old sweat. Many have circled behind us, unnoticed, while Killian and I spoke. Each of them is on foot now, their silver armor twinkling in the pale moonlight. Niko and Gayle have dismounted as well, creating a circle to meet Killian's soldiers, their swords held at the ready.

Killian doesn't wait for me to respond to his missed blow. With a grunt, he brings his blade down in another deadly strike.

I roll out of the way just in time and jump up into position, on the balls of my feet and just out of striking distance. But as I come up, a sharp clang of metal rings through the air. I snap my head up. Niko's sword is locked with Killian's, glinting in the moon's glow. Killian's guards step closer as one, making the circle surrounding us that much smaller.

He gets a few more swings in, and I use them to read him with my newly skilled eyes. This time, I'm watching him not as my brother, but as an opponent.

"Brother, your fight is with me," I call, sparing a glance at Niko, my eyes narrowed in disbelief. I thought he trusted me. I thought he saw my strength. When it comes down to the real fight, does he not have the faith in me I thought he did?

Niko's jaw tenses, and the inner turmoil he's facing is clear as he looks from me to Killian, his features masked in a terror that doesn't fit here. I look to Gryphon and Gayle for help. Gryphon takes a step away, showing Niko that it's space and trust I need right now. Gayle rubs Niko's shoulder, not taking her eyes off the encroaching guards, her touch allowing him to snap out of whatever scene is playing across his eyes. Finally, he takes a small step back. The message is received, I hope.

Killian thinks he has me now, that he and his men will be done and returned to the castle before daybreak. I let him keep talking, distracting himself, rather than me having to engage at all. I let his hurtful words roll off me in waves before they knock me to the ground.

He finally gives the order for his soldiers to join us, and they pounce, the sound of metal on metal ringing through the air.

"I see you've picked up a thing or two while on the road with these scoundrels." He continues his charge at me, untiring in his aggression. "Too bad all that hard work won't pay off."

His expertise wears on me. At this rate, I fear I'll fatigue before he even breaks a sweat. I'm quickly tiring from blocking blow after blow. But the surprise on Killian's face that I haven't fallen sooner keeps me going.

I know I'm no match for him. He's a trained warrior, son of a king, and now he wears the crown. He's honed both his mind and his muscles to defend and kill. And he sees me as his enemy. I can't defeat him—and I don't want to. I just hope I can hold him off so the others can take down enough of his men for him to realize he'll not win this battle.

The king's men fall, one after the other. Our circle stays intact, each of us still only a pace or two from the other. Gayle's left with three swinging at her. She moves with the speed and grace of a cat. Even if she refuses to shift, I can still see her jaguar side peeking through in her unwavering agility.

Niko takes on four guards with ease. No wonder neither of them chooses to shift—by the way they fight, they have little need. Niko holds two blades, a broadsword and a short sword, and looks as if he's dancing among the stars as each of his strikes hits its mark.

Baylor holds his own against the two guards facing him. And Gryphon stays close, attacking the ones Baylor sends his way. He's looking pretty good, and I send a silent *thank you* up to the stars that he's picked up a few things from the Shifters. That's all the attention I can spare, though, because each block of Killian's strikes quickly breaks down my remaining energy.

Niko takes notice of my slowing movements and close calls. As he glances my way, though, a sword meets his middle. His huge frame tumbles to the ground. I lunge toward him as he falls, allowing Killian to find his moment.

He stands over me, drawing out the inevitable by tossing his sword back and forth between his hands, taunting me. My hands shake as I point my sword at him, shuffling my feet against the ground, moving backward until my heels are close enough to touch Niko's shoulders.

He grunts as I scoot even closer. "I'm here. Don't worry, I'm here," I whisper, not taking my eyes off Killian for one second, but trying to give Niko as much comfort as I can—though I'm not sure what comfort I, of all people, can be as I repeat my whispered mantra.

I see Killian approach at the same time I hear the crunch of other boots nearing around us. We are as good as dead.

At that moment, a ripping sound tears through the clang of swords, followed by a high-pitched, menacing snarl that sends chills down my spine. Killian's eyes grow wide as they fall on the cause of the sound moments before a spotted blur leaps over us and knocks Killian off his feet with vicious force.

Even in the moonlight, three long claw marks stand out against his armor. Blood already pools below his unconscious body.

Gayle, now only recognizable by her cat-like eyes, stalks in front of us in her jaguar form, protecting Niko and me from the sole remaining guard. The guard's eyes go wide, and a wet mark stains the front of his pants. He stumbles toward King Killian and gathers him in his arms.

Gayle makes no move to strike as he stumbles backward, his eyes darting from her to me to Baylor, the only other left standing with a sword in his hands. Satisfied we won't harm him further, the guard turns and runs.

As I watch his retreating form, I realize there's no way I could have done that on my own. By myself, I'm nothing, but together, we are a force to be reckoned with. Absentmindedly, I register that there's a line somewhere, and maybe if we each do our part, we can both know that independence and feel supported at the same time.

A swell of emotion rises in my chest as I take in the carnage left in the wake of our victory.

"Roe." There's a hitch in Baylor's voice. "Roe, come here."

To my left, he's hunched over on the ground. I run toward him, harnessing power from the earth with each step.

As I get closer, though, I realize it's not he who is hurt.

Chapter Twenty

"Gryphon!"

My muscles scream as I skid to a stop. The reverberation of my knees crashing to the packed dirt should send pain shooting everywhere, but at this moment, I feel nothing. "Not again." I swallow the memories of Licia screaming in the distance while his blood coats my hands. The flashback brings up the terror I felt as I fought to heal him. But unlike last time time, now I have the knowledge and the strength.

His fingers trace my jawline and across my nose. His thumb brushes across the tears streaming down my cheek. "What's this?" he asks, his voice light and distant.

"Give me a minute," I say, buying time before I have to look him in the eye, as if I already know what I'll find. Instead, I search his chest, my heart screaming as a rhythmic spurt of blood leaves the area just below his collarbone.

It's different than last time.

This is happening, and there's no earth magic strong enough to bring him back to me.

I have to try anyway.

I rest my hands over the wound, careful not to put too much pressure on his body, just enough to stanch the bleeding. His hands fall to mine, but it's as if the effort to grab on to me is too much; he seems content to just have the contact.

Panic rises and I look inward, pooling magic from the earth and sending it into his body. But as soon as my skin touches his, my earth magic resists, telling me without words there's nowhere for it to go.

I draw harder, begging for it to be enough. Even the glow of my ring is a warning, warming against my finger until it burns.

And then I know.

Where I usually see the fissures mending back together and creating connections in my mind's eye, here, I only see dead ends. There's no path to connect my magic. His body is breaking down too fast, his life light extinguishing.

His unfocused eyes search for me, but instead, his gaze lands above me. Worry builds within me as the fear falls away from his face, and a still relaxation falls across his features.

"No, Gryphon, no." After all this time, I've struggled to learn how to hone my power. And just when I found a strength I didn't think I had, the realization that I can't save him is a pain that defies all comparison.

There's a gentle caress as his fingers resting atop mine flutter. I can see him trying to push past the pain to say one last thing. His mouth moves, but no sound comes out. I lean closer, so my ear is right up against his lips.

He tries again. "Licia. Save Licia." He wets his lips with his tongue. "Zeke will help."

I look at him, nodding and trying to catch his eye, but his gaze is still distant. Why would he mention his father, Zeke, along with Licia?

His hand slackens in my own.

How could I have been so naive? So blindly optimistic to think I could keep him safe? Even as his blood stained my arms up to my elbows, I still thought there was something I could do.

My best friend and cousin, who's stood by my side all my life, is leaving me. The man who's always been closer than my brother is dying in my arms.

Tears well in my eyes, refusing the truth as a sob wracks my body.

"Gryphon, I…" I'm unsure how to finish my sentence. How can I possibly tell him all the things I need to?

His eyes finally lock on mine.

Tears stream out of the corners of his eyes and down into his hairline as his pain grows.

His lips move one last time. With his final breath, he mouths, "Save us."

The life leaves his eyes, and his body relaxes.

I watch as he suddenly lets go of all the pain of this world and moves to rest among the stars.

A part of me thinks how fitting it is that he'd go on a night when the stars shine even brighter than the moon. As if he knows exactly where he's heading and the stars can't wait to have him all to themselves.

It's impossible to miss the exact moment my heart cracks. The crack widens and spreads until my heart is but a jigsaw of what it was moments before.

Without Gryphon, I'm lost.

He's the smiling sun. And now all that's left is darkness.

There's no time to mourn. Gayle stands behind me, half rubbing my back and half trying to get my attention, even before my tears can fall.

"Roe, we need you. I'm so sorry, but we need you *now*." Her voice is urgent, but I can't think of what could be more urgent than the sight in front of me.

She grabs both of my hands, slippery from the thick layers of blood, her grip gentle but firm enough to turn my body away from Gryphon. And it's like I've fallen into a repeated scene.

Now it's Niko coughing up blood.

Only he's still conscious.

The pool of blood mixing with the dirt beneath him is growing by the moment. His hands cover the wound on his side, and tears stream down his face. From the looks of it, they are more from pain than anything else.

Instinct guides me the few steps to his side. My heart is reluctant to leave Gryphon, but everything within me knows I'm the only person who can help Niko in this moment.

"No, no, no, no," I hear myself repeating as I press along his abdomen, searching for the wound. My fingers find the gash deep along his side, and it appears whoever did this missed any major organs. I apply as much pressure as I can as Baylor and Gayle kneel on the other side of him, trading looks of worry I pretend not to see. I look to them for an answer I desperately need, to a question I don't realize I am asking.

"You can do this, Roe." Baylor's voice is steady and confident. "You can heal him. Niko is hurt, and you can heal him."

I look to Niko's face. Drawing deep from the earth, I search within myself for what I need. It feels distant this time, though—too distant. My strength wavers; I can't find the energy I need to pull from the earth, even though it hums ready just below me, ready for me to make use of it. I have nothing left.

"You're leaning on me too hard, Roe. It's just a small cut." Niko's voice is breathier and raspier than usual. The sudden change shoots goosebumps along my arms.

"A cut? Just a cut? You're practically gutted from navel to neck!" I try to match his lightness, and the tension is suddenly broken.

He places his hand on my own, and his grip is strong. I find strength in it, and realize that they're right. I can do this. I have to do this.

Tears flow freely down my cheeks as I search for the warm glow deep within me, deeper than I've ever gone. It grows and builds until it is too much for me to hold on to. I send it out, placing my hands on his chest, allowing it to search for the broken parts of him. The warmth dances along my fingertips and smoothly knits across his wound. In moments, the skin has sealed back together.

Gayle and Baylor both release deep breaths as I open my eyes. I look at Niko's wound and see that only the small glint of newly healed pink flesh remains.

Niko props himself up on one elbow and then the other while Gayle launches herself at me with all the strength of the wildcat beneath her skin.

The wildcat. She shifted to finish the fight. Why didn't Niko?

"You could've shifted sooner." It comes out as a whisper, but the realization has sprouted into a full-on rage in just moments. "You could have shifted sooner, and you didn't!" My voice cracks through tears as I fling my arm toward where Gryphon still lies. "It would've changed everything."

"Roe," Gayle starts, her voice gentle with understanding and pain. "We only shift as a last resort. We can't let the humans know we're still as strong as we are. That's why I waited so long."

Too long. She eventually shifted when Gryphon fell and it was going sideways for us. But it was too late. Too little. We all did too little. If we did more, Gryphon would still be here.

"It would've changed everything," I repeat.

I fall to my knees beside my best friend. My body welcomes the pain shooting up from the earth, as if in punishment for not being able to save someone when it truly matters.

"We can't let them know, Roe." Gayle's voice is softer than the leaves of a new seedling breaking earth. "Niko is a dragon Shifter. Do you know what they'd do with that kind of information? What they would do to him if they took that information back to the castle?"

"Then scorch them all! They'd never make it back to the castle!" I hardly know what I'm saying. Through the tears, I can only see the outline of Gryphon, his beautiful auburn hair mixing with red swirls of blood. So much blood.

"I didn't think that was what you wanted." Niko's voice is low and steady, as if he's hurting this much, too.

"And you think this is what I want?" My last words are more of a sob than actual speech.

They don't understand. The only person who would lies dreaming eternally in front of me.

The still figure is wrapped tightly in roughspun and rope. The rope scratches my fingertips while I trace my way up until my hands rest once again on his heart. I try one last time to reach out to him, but of course, there's no response. His heart is still, and the air about him remains cold.

The world suddenly feels heavy. Empty. He's gone.

And Licia's gone, too.

This is not the way this was supposed to go.

Just months before, they rode romantically off into the unknown. We were creating our future and planning to save our kingdom. Together.

And now what? Where's their happy ending? Am I just supposed to keep going without them?

I'm not strong enough on my own.

Thunder rolls in the distance, and lightning blinks out the stars for a quick moment. The rich smell of rain settles around me as I spend my last moments with my friend.

I should've been able to heal him. What else have all the hours with Thaliya been for? Were they just wasted? Am I so completely useless that when my abilities are truly needed, I can't rise to the occasion?

The weight of my best friend's death presses deeply into my soul. Gryphon stood for all that was good in my life. And now I'm a dandelion without my petals. Not a single wish left to make.

"I'm so sorry he's gone," Niko says beside me.

I can't help but stiffen at his proximity. He takes a step away, as if he can feel the rage coming off of me in waves. The words dissolve on my tongue as my companions all move to where I sit beside Gryphon's body, but inside, I'm roaring at Niko for wasting his time protecting me when he should've been there for Gryphon.

My heart sinks as the dots connect. It's happened yet again. Everyone I get close to is either taken from me or finds an untimely death. Avicii was the first, and I didn't even remember it was at my hand until weeks later. Licia was abducted from us before we even got started. And now Gryphon.

It's too much. I don't think I can take even one more. Niko watches me out of the corner of his eye, and I take another step away.

I can't keep doing this, or one of them will be next.

Chapter Twenty-One

The deep hole they've dug out is right on the edge of the forest. Baylor and Niko picked a quiet alcove lined with tall, thick trees. Thunder sounds in the distance as we gather to say our goodbyes.

I stand on the soft moss alongside Baylor, beside Gryphon's resting form. Everyone else stands across the glade, giving us space.

Unsure where to begin, I clear my throat, but when I open my mouth, no words come out. I look to Baylor, and he steps forward.

He begins slowly with kind words and the recent deeds Gryphon has done for our village and court. He quickly slides into stories of all the playful tricks Gryphon would perform around the castle, breathing life and smiles into anyone who crossed his path.

"A man who could have straddled worlds, if given more time." Baylor ends by throwing a handful of rich dirt onto Gryphon's now lowered body.

The others all say something, but I am lost in thought about what this means for us now. Should I go back to the castle? Surrender to my brother and ride off into the sunset, trailing behind the one I'm promised to?

Or do I continue on into the North, to find the lost sister we set out to save? What good will I be to her if I couldn't even heal my dying friend? If I can't close a sword wound, how will I heal the lifetime of mistreatment and deep pain Ombretta has surely endured?

"... was from a good family. I fought alongside his father in the War of the Last Fae. He did everything he could to ensure the survival of the royal line."

I'm struck by Gayle's last words. She fought alongside Gryphon's father? But that would be impossible. That would make Gryphon...

My eyes rush to meet Gayle's, and she gives a small confirming nod as she finishes her goodbye.

Fae? Gryphon's father was Fae? But that would've made him a halfling. Is this why Jonaraja kept him so close? She must've known. Is that why he was so tall and gangly-looking, even as an adult? Because he was part Fae.

But he never even knew. My heart sinks even further with this knowledge.

Just before the final rock is laid on Gryphon's resting place, Gayle takes a handful of something from a pouch on her side belt, gently placing it under the last rock. I close my eyes as it all falls into place. The forest. The trees. Each tree marks the resting place of a loved one. A forest of thousands. Too many lives lost. New tears spring to my eyes, not just for Gryphon, but for all those lost, all those who still guard their village of Sverreian.

Exhausted, I lay out my bedroll beside him for the last of our morning hours, taking time to weave a crown of vines and yellow primrose around his grave. Thaliya's words run through my mind: *Know yourself, know your path.* Gryphon knew his path, and it was interwoven with mine. He never faltered, but grew and rose to the occasion. I hope I can make him proud as we continue on without him.

I lie down carefully beside my friend, watching the sunlight sparkle through the leaves as it rises. The patterns it creates as the breeze catches and releases the leaves are hypnotizing. The birds continue their early-morning song, and I realize this is the start of a new day. A day I'll begin without my best friend by my side. Another day that will pass without my sister.

My thoughts drift to Licia and the last time I saw her, kicking and screaming as if her life depended on it. And maybe it did.

Has she woven a story of lies to keep herself safe? I don't think I have to worry about her. I'll go to her as soon as I can. I trust that Thaliya and Patton will aid her until I can return.

I hear small scuffling sounds, which means everyone else is moving around and preparing for another day in the saddle. I'm not ready.

I allow myself one more moment to lie beside Gryphon, watching the sunlight dance over my skin. I remember my last moments with him, and I whisper into the morning air, "I'll save us. I'll save us all."

We ride all day and into each night, with minimal breaks. I don't think anyone knows what to do or say to me, so we just keep moving. The journey is long and hard. The cold bites at my fingertips, and my toes have lost all feeling inside my boots. My teeth ache from constantly chattering together.

We're no longer in the south, where chilly nights call for cozy fires and warm blankets. Now, it's more like wearing all your clothes and still ending up with frozen limbs.

A huge sigh of relief leaves my lips as the sun rises. The small warmth coming from the rays pushes the feeling back into my cold body—if not my heart. Ever since we left Gryphon along the treeline where the forest runs into the sand of Glorixia, the ice around my heart hasn't thawed, even on the sunniest of days.

"I think we'll arrive at Iolanthe's within a day or two." Gayle rides up next to me, and I startle back to attention.

"You don't have to keep checking on me," I say without looking up from the pommel of Navi's saddle.

"I'm not checking on you," she says carefully. "I'm having a conversation with a friend."

"Is that what you and Baylor call taking turns riding next to me? Having one-sided conversations until I demand a bathroom break just to get enough air?" The words are punctuated with the newly burning anger raging within me.

"Look, Roe, we're not watching over you, but we are here for you. We've all lost someone, and we know how painful it is." She puts her hands up in submission as I shoot a glare at her. "And I'm not saying I know what you're feeling right now, because I don't. I know you and Gryphon were close." I shrug off her kind words, knowing if I spend a moment thinking about them, I'll shatter into a million pieces.

Niko's silence and space have never been so welcome compared to Gayle and Baylor's gentle yet persistent prodding. He hasn't said one word to me in days. Which is not unlike him, but I have never appreciated this quality in him as much as I do now.

"Do you feel that?"

I turn to see that Baylor has replaced Gayle by my side. I stare at him blankly, and he realizes I'm either not answering him like usual, or I do not feel anything.

"It's getting warmer. Can you feel it?"

I turn away in an attempt not to answer, but in doing so, I take in what I've been too morose to notice. The trees along the road are no longer bare and windswept from winter. There are hints of green peeking out along the branches and small buds beginning to show.

And I'm not frozen through. I can feel the supple leather of Navi's reins in my hands once again.

"It's Iolanthe." He smiles in answer to my raised eyebrows. "She's powerful."

After several days of travel and nothing but tall, yellowing dead grass swaying in the breeze, the small road we've been following opens to a valley below, full of vibrant life. Rows upon rows of vegetables and herbs and fields of multicolored wildflowers lie before us. The air, which has sat heavy on my tongue, tasting of dust for days on end, suddenly tastes sweet and light, like fresh rain on a hot summer's day.

Amid this picturesque scene, the sun alights upon a small cabin, like a tiny beacon, with windows like bright, blinking eyes. It sits squarely, facing the road, its back pressed against the mountainside. A stone wall stands guard, gray and white against the grass, with a lichen-stained wooden barn alongside. Beyond that, I can just make out a stream—a flash of silver that licks the edge of the forest beyond, a mirror for the mountain's ivory.

We continue, slow enough to allow anyone here to notice us. And sure enough, when we arrive at the front door, a woman leans against the door frame, tranquilly awaiting our arrival.

The silver hair that curls down to her waist shifts and moves like a river in a breeze. It's the color of a slow fall of snow on a clear blue day, with a slight shimmer to it, like steam rising from a hot mug of tea. The gleam trails away from her skin as richly colored tendrils, like autumn leaves caught in the water. Her tall, lithe frame whispers of the otherworldly and the ethereal, even more so when she leaves the door frame to glide toward us in the dooryard.

Her smile is wide and kind, causing her silver eyes to crinkle at the corners. She greets Niko and Gayle as old friends, even though they embrace her with a respectful reverence. Even Baylor is greeted with an "It's been too long, friend."

She looks at me, and I get lost in the liquid silver of her gaze. Her eyes bore deeply into mine, feeling my intentions, hopes, and dreams all in one look.

Her smile grows even wider as she embraces me as well, then holds me at arm's length. Her scent is multilayered—sweet, like that of a warm summer day, walking across a field of wildflowers; like old books and wonderful exotic spices.

"I have been awaiting your arrival." Those sharp eyes take in the way I stiffen in confusion. "You have traveled long and far. Please, all of you, come in." She opens her arms and ushers us inside.

Baylor looks relieved as he moves to guide the horses into the barn, allowing himself a little extra time to soak in the familiarity of caring for them before he joins us in this next piece of our journey.

Runes and symbols cover the frame of the front door, hinting at protection wards, but I can't read them to be sure. The center topmost is a bright star, seeming to have wings. I pause for a moment to take in the beauty and then step inside.

The cabin is much larger than it seems from the outside. The entrance hall opens to a high ceiling, dancing with candlelight. The candles themselves appear to float in midair, but when the light hits just right, I see the sprawling chandelier that covers the entire tall space.

The walls are rough stone, and I realize with delight that this woman has made the inside of the mountain her home. The small cabin is merely the entryway into what seems to be an endless expanse. The large foyer makes even the royal ballroom look small and insignificant in comparison. As we move toward the middle of the open space, a beautiful fountain shoots water into the air. Its sounds are a light melody in the vast area.

This leads us off to the left, where another room opens to a blazing fire and many comfortable chairs. "Sit, friends. I will prepare some tea, and we can get to know each other. I look forward to hearing of your latest travels and what brings you my way." She floats away into yet another room.

I fall back into the luxurious cushions that smell of old books with a faint hint of sage. The space is comfortably cluttered with relics from long ago, both large and small. Shelves span to the ceiling, littered with books of all sizes. Some look as if they would fall apart with age if ever opened.

The woman glides back into the room quietly, her deep plum robes flowing behind her as if on a mysterious wind. There's something about her that feels almost familiar to me, yet she seems completely untouchable and otherworldly.

She sets down a tea tray between us and says simply, "I am Iolanthe."

Chapter Twenty-Two

After Iolanthe gracefully pours steaming tea into large mugs, she passes around plates for the food she has brought as well. Cheeses and bread, honey and small flowers. She allows us a moment to pile our plates high before she continues. Baylor finds us and doesn't miss a beat as he takes in such treats after days in the saddle. I lose myself in the fragrant steam, adding extra cream to my tea and deeply inhaling the spicy scents of cinnamon and clove.

"You have traveled far and long already," she begins. "And have many more trials and trails to cover before you find tranquility."

She speaks in such a slow, rhythmic way that, paired with the fluffy chair and cozy fire, I have to fight to stay awake.

"Your path holds many surprises and does not yet have a clear end, but through perseverance and dedication, you shall all prevail."

Baylor starts at that. "Forgive me, Iolanthe—I thought we were all here more for Roe than anything else."

"Oh?" One pristine eyebrow raises skyward. "This is as much each of your journeys as it is that of Rowandine Aeronwick, or should I say, Rowandine Agroterra of the Glen."

"Of the Glen?" At first, the surname confuses me, but then I recall what Lady Alasie said. She knew me as the same.

"But of course, Rowandine. The Glen, your homeland and the heritage you seek. Names hold power. Surely you must know your own." She folds her hands in her lap and waits expectantly.

As she says this, I feel the truth of it. Soft whispers swirl around me, still unintelligible, but the sounds grow. *"... of the Glen, Rowandine Agroterra of the Glen..."* The whispers call to me. I close my eyes and see the many who came before me, who now stand at my back, in support. The forms are out of focus, but I can feel the strength and knowledge emanating from them.

I open my eyes, expecting everyone to look as amazed as I feel, but they are all just looking between Iolanthe and me. I realize it has been silent for some time now, while Iolanthe gave me time to see.

She turns to me. "Your powers are just beginning to awaken within you. You have much to learn yet. Your power runs deep, the likes of which we have not seen in this realm in millennia."

I nod at this, once again feeling the truth in her melodic words. But on the inside, my stomach twists and turns in on itself. The expectations of me are not new, but there is a finality to them now. A weight settles, an understanding that her words hold a deeper meaning. It feels as if they are not just meant for my destiny as ruler of Everguard, but for my inner self as well.

"I've given you much to think about. Let me show you to your rooms, and you may rest until morning." Iolanthe stands, as do I. The others continue to look between us, questioning what just happened.

Iolanthe glides away, and we follow in her wake. She leads us through yet another tunneled hallway toward a wing of bedrooms. We stand in the middle of a sitting room, surrounded by four open doors. She motions for us to take our pick, and with a glance over my shoulder, I select the first room on the right.

Inside, the room has a warm, airy feeling. The bed stands against the wall on the right, and I quickly cross to the open doors that look out on the verdant fields we just crossed. I hadn't realized we were climbing inside her home, but we must be three stories up, and I can see for miles out toward the Dread Forest, with the snow-capped Periserrat Peaks far off the other way. I don't recall seeing windows, let alone balconies, on our ride in, but my thoughts were focused elsewhere. More on *who* we would find than *what*.

If the bedroom is this nice, I can't wait to see what the bathroom holds. I sniff myself, too late remembering my refusal to bathe each time we stopped. I had no energy or desire to do so.

But with the prospect of a proper bath and privacy, I grab a fluffy robe from the armoire and follow the steam wafting from the door. The torches burn low, giving a relaxing feel, while tendrils of chamomile and vanilla pull me deep into the steam toward a dark pool within.

"The water feels exquisite."

I jump at the sound of Gayle's voice from somewhere through the thick clouds of steam. As I reach the side of the pool, I see she is already lounging against the opposite side. The dark water rests just below her collarbone, and her arms move back and forth beneath the surface. Her voluminous hair is tied away from her face on top of her head.

"What are you waiting for?"

Needing no further invitation, I drop my robe to the floor and step into the steamy water. As it engulfs me, the lightness I feel is invigorating. I find another smooth rock bench across from Gayle. Making myself comfortable, I lay my head back and close my eyes.

"It's a nice change, for once, don't you think?" Gayle asks.

"Mm-hmm," I agree, unsure what she means exactly, but this is wonderful.

She notes my confusion. "I mean all of it. It's nice to be off the road for once. And all of this." She waves her hands to encompass the entire house. "Along with these hot springs we've found ourselves in."

"Mm-hmm." Fighting the thoughts of the last time I was in a hot spring—with Niko—from floating to the surface, I try to focus on Gayle's words.

"And of course, the company is top-notch." She splashes water at me to bring me back to the conversation.

"Hey!" I wipe the errant splashes away with the back of my hand. "Yes. It's all great. Wonderful. Outstanding," I say, a little harsher than I intend, trying to find the line of wanting to be left alone while also appreciating that she hasn't given up on me, yet.

"It's okay to hurt, you know." Gayle sits up straighter at my sudden attitude, but her words are gentle.

"It's just... too much." I'm not really in the mood to dive into all of it, but I'm grateful for Gayle all the same.

"Of course it is. And now you've dragged us all into it as well!" She laughs at herself and slaps a hand against the water, sending fat droplets everywhere. I use the splashes as an excuse to wipe the tears that escaped yet again. "But in all seriousness, you're right. It's an awful lot to put on one person. Which is why you're not alone. I'm sure you feel alone, but Baylor has been by your side from the very beginning. And, stars alive, do I mean the beginning. He's been watching over you since before you even knew. And Niko and I haven't gone anywhere since we saved your asses out in the Wastelands."

Nodding along with her, I realize she's right. They're all too close. They're all in danger.

"I mean, you might not even fully grasp it all yet, but you have an entire Shifter village rooting for you. There are people out there who haven't even met you yet and are rooting for you."

"That helps." I look at her with my lips pursed, sarcasm lacing my next words. "The idea of so many people depending on me calms any anxieties that were dissipating with the soothing water." But the thought looms over me just as heavily as the jasmine-scented steam: *They're all in danger.*

"We could start some breathing exercises?" Gayle says, rolling her eyes. "Or we could picture the alternative. Can you imagine what will happen if our realm continues down this path? King Killian will destroy everything. Hadeon's already done as much to his previous lands. Killian will do the same here and then continue to the next realm, like a plague ravaging the lands. Unless he's stopped. Unless we teach those humans who care how to create a life rather than destroy all they come in contact with." Her face reddens, more from her words than the rising steam.

"But what happens to everyone if I fail my destiny? If we can't save our realm from my brother?"

"If we fail? Then we try something else." She looks at me as if I should know better. "Destiny is just a pretty word. What matters are the choices you make. And then what you do with the results."

I sit up a little taller at that. "You're right. If we fail, we'll just come back stronger." We haven't solved anything while sitting here in these deep, dark pools, but just talking it through makes me feel better. I settle back into the soothing water.

"What about Ombretta? Have you decided what to do when we meet her?" Her expression tells me she knows what I have to do, but she's wondering if *I* know it.

"I know, I know. There's no hope for her. A lifetime of being slowly sucked dry by the Ancients would twist even the brightest of hearts. But what if we just talked with her for a moment? Maybe she'll see the truth of it." Secretly, I hope with all my heart that there's a small part of her still wanting to be saved.

"She hopes to drain you dry for the sake of the Ancients. To save herself from the pain. Revenge has already swallowed up any sister you had. She's probably more Ancient than Fae now. You're not in any position to talk her down." The tilt of her eyebrows drives home her point.

"Really? Could she be one of the Ancients now?" My eyebrows knit together as I try to picture what that would be like. Is she weak and haggard? Is she all skin and bones, hanging on to life by a tiny thread? Bile rises at the thought of having to live on the blood of others, of *desiring* the blood of others. But tears sting the corners of my eyes at the idea of anyone being so trapped.

"Niko and I have discussed it. It's a possibility. They've been draining her dry her whole life. How has she stayed alive this long? The only answer we could come up with is that she's been given blood from the Ancients. And who knows what side effects that would produce?" Gayle wrinkles her nose and shrugs, raising her toes out of the water and wriggling them.

My mind flashes back to when Baylor was imprisoned by Hadeon and the way Thaddeus let him drink his blood, even though Thaliya was against it. What power does an Ancient's blood hold?

"Stars, I've turned into an absolute prune! Maybe we should check to see how Niko and Baylor are faring." Gayle rises out of the water and wraps her robe around her. "See you in a few." She disappears into the curtains of steam.

I float for a moment, trying to find a spark of the tranquility Iolanthe spoke of earlier, but I suppose she's right: it'll be some time before I find that peace, especially knowing everyone who gets close to me is in danger—and we're walking right into it.

Dressed in loose-fitting pants and a short top I found in the wardrobe, with my wet hair left to dry in wild waves down my back, I set out to find the others. Niko is lounging alone in the sitting room. I sink into the spot next to him. "Baylor and Gayle?" I ask.

"Just left to find some food."

I can feel the vibrations of his deep voice through the couch, and even those few words cause me to melt a little inside. Knowing that melting is not something I should do, I stiffen and try to think of other things.

"You alright?" he asks, sitting up a bit to get a better look at me.

"Fine," I grumble. I'm anything but fine.

"Suit yourself." He rests his arms along the back of the couch and props his feet up on the table in front of us, taking up entirely too much space. "You did well out there. With Killian, I mean. I know how hard it is, taking blow after blow, trying not to harm the one you're up against."

"You seem to always strike hard and fast. What would you know of waiting anything out?" I ask, thinking back to all the times I've watched him fight. His movements are always precise and calculated, anticipating his opponent's next move.

"Oh, I know a thing or two," is all he says in response, looking at me with eyebrows raised.

Suddenly, I'm not so sure we're still talking about the fighting.

Chapter Twenty-Three

I'm saved from having to respond to Niko when Gayle and Baylor arrive with their arms full of snacks. Baylor sets his down and plops himself in the chair opposite me, grabbing a handful of food and sitting back, apparently having no desire to bother with a plate.

Gayle sets her load down, but then looks between Niko and me, her cat-like eyes narrowing slightly, as if she can taste the slight tension in the air. "It went south too fast with Killian and his guard. What's the plan? How do we work moving forward?" She leans in, ready to dive into strategy and planning.

Baylor talks around his mouthful. "Why does anything have to change? We stay the course. I don't see why—" He pauses, unable to meet my gaze. The ghost of Gryphon is still too close. "We should stay the course," he repeats.

"You're quiet." Gayle throws a chunk of bread at Niko. He catches it and pops it into his mouth. "What do you think our next move should be?"

He takes his time chewing, thinking, or maybe stalling. Before he starts, he looks at me, as if he's weighing his options. I glare at him, still blaming him for Gryphon's death. It's easier to blame him than myself.

Niko shrugs. "What if..." He puts his hands up, showing he means no harm. "What if Roe goes back with her brother? Says she has a change of—"

There's a resounding "No" from all three of us. No further words come, because I'm paralyzed by shock. That he would even consider it, say it out loud, crushes any lingering hope that he believes in me.

"Niko, have you lost your mind?" Gayle jumps up, pacing the room like a caged animal. "Why would we just hand her over? You realize he would kill her on the spot."

Niko winces, but continues. "Hear me out. We get him to see the benefit of returning to the castle to make some sort of deal. Make him think he's got us spooked, and that we'd like to join forces. That way, Roe is on the inside, and we can continue up and deal with Ombretta. It's not pretty, but it'll get the job done. And before you say it again, Roe, I don't think your brother will kill you. I think by being with him, you're safer than trekking up to Ombretta."

"What in all the realms would make you think that was a good plan?" Gayle says mid-pace, and the look on her face could make even the biggest beast heel at her side. "I see what you're saying. And it would be helpful to have someone on the inside. But I don't know if Roe is the person for that. We're headed to see Ombretta, for stars' sake. Roe deserves to at least meet her. Make the judgment call there."

They all look at me, but I don't think I can say a single thing at the moment. I'm completely gobsmacked by Niko's suggestion. He still doesn't think I can do this. He wants to keep me safe—and he thinks my brother, molded by Hadeon's megalomaniacal ways, would be the best option. And the way he said he would *deal* with Ombretta... It's like the Ultor Regni is making these calls, not Niko.

But he *is* the Ultor Regni. A part of him will always seek justice for the realm. He doesn't see me. He sees a piece he can move around on a map—just like Killian.

The others are leaning back, making space between us. It seems they think I'm about to lose it. Which is how I feel. But I don't give them the satisfaction. Before I stand, I look straight at Niko, hoping he sees the hurt he's caused, the walls he's created between us. I shake my head in disbelief and head back to my room, shutting out any further discussion about what's next.

I rise early in the morning despite the immensely comfortable bed, finally deciding to give up on sleep. It completely eluded me, and I tossed and turned all night. The uneasy feeling that Ombretta is close makes it impossible to rest. I find no comfort in replaying the evening, revisiting Niko's solution to offer me up to my brother while he goes to kill Ombretta. There's no discussion in that scenario, no room for understanding.

I know the optimism I lean toward can often get me in trouble, because I only think of the one, best possible solution. But now, if I use a little strategic thinking to temper that optimism, I feel like I'll land in a better spot. I just need to figure out what that strategy is. But it's impossible to do that when all I can think about is the hole in my heart that is my best friend gone.

In between restless sleep and sobbing for Gryphon last night, Niko faded in and out of focus too—first his silent and patient strength, and then him as the protective brute who won't allow my wings to unfurl to their full potential. Even last night, he began by alluding that he was waiting for me and giving me time to come to my conclusions about him. Which seems impossible. He's tangled up with Pris, who's tangled up with both Baylor *and* Gayle. I shouldn't even spend a moment thinking about him.

In the same breath, he told me I'd be safer with Killian than trying to work something out with Ombretta. There's no trust there, even though I thought we were getting there with his gentle nudges and soft glimpses into himself.

The sun peeks through the windows, and I take it as an invitation to begin my day. I start by splashing some cold water on my tear-streaked face, hoping it helps. After dressing again in loose-fitting clothing, I strike out on my own, looking for something to occupy my mind.

I find Iolanthe in a room off the grand foyer. I wonder if she can tell me more about being Fae, or even about my parents. She's too busy mixing small amounts of herbs to notice me at first. The table she's working at is a long slab of white marble, littered with bowls and small glass containers of liquids. Herbs hang from the lower rafters of the high ceiling, drying in bunches. Behind her, glass-fronted cabinets are stacked with many of the same ingredients that are strewn out along the table, many of them wide open as if she keeps going back and forth, not bothering to close them.

"You're up early," she says when the sound of my footfalls grows louder.

"I was looking forward to starting my day." A half-truth.

Seeing through it, she comforts me by saying, "The first night in a new place is always the hardest. Especially after being on the road for so long, and certainly after the loss of a loved one. Tonight will be better, I'm sure."

Her easygoing nature and honest sympathy draw me closer to her counter. I watch closely as she mixes a few more herbs into a bowl. Recognizing the combination, I ask, "A planting charm?"

"I make one every spring as I plant new crops. It's more of a habit at this point than anything else, I suppose. I've been doing it ever since I made my home here." She gives a small smile. "I had a feeling Thaliya taught you well. This'll make things easier." She glances at me sideways, her childlike grin belying her wisdom. "And one could use a little ease every once in a while."

I smile at her light words and the realization that of course she knows of Thaliya. "Is there anything you don't know?"

She tilts her head toward me and quirks a thin silver eyebrow my way. "Very little."

I'm not sure what I was expecting, but it was not this airy, affable manner. I enjoy her soothing presence very much. But her inscrutable ways make her fascinating and frustrating in equal measure.

"I noticed your fields were already well in bloom at this time of year," I say, recalling the rows of colorful wildflowers and budding vegetables upon our entry into her valley.

"Hmm. Yes. I may use my general seclusion here to my advantage now and then." Her answer, once again, throws a thin veil across her meaning. Can she control the growth in her fields, the climate here in her valley? If so, she must be beyond powerful, just as Baylor mentioned. And why is she so secluded out here at the base of this mountain? I fear my time spent with Iolanthe will be both exhausting and enlightening.

"You know my real name. My heritage. Did you know my parents?" I prompt, hoping she'll be more forthcoming with this information than she is about the magic she weaves in her fields.

"Ah, yes!" Her face instantly brightens and her cheeks rise, the corners of her eyes crinkling. "I knew King Azulian and Queen Bronwinn before they wore their crowns. The Agroterra family, of course, has a long lineage of leadership, and their blood is rich with royalty."

She says my surname just as Alasie said it, and I lean in, hungry for information. "What were they like? I grew up learning about how feral the Fae were, and that the king and queen were more ruthless than anyone."

"Ah, dear." She gives me a sympathetic look. "Neither you nor your twin, Ombretta, received the childhood Bronwinn had hoped for you. Of course, there weren't many options at the time." She shrugs, reaching for another empty jar and emptying her mixture into it. "But I see both of them in you. You get your curls and defined cheekbones from your father, while your upturned nose and smattering of freckles come from your mother. Bronwinn also had an affinity for earth magic, like you. And if I'm not mistaken, she was gifted twice by the stars."

"You mean, she could wield other elements than earth?" I ask. That can't be a typical quality of the Fae.

"She had earth magic, but she was also gifted with air magic. She could conjure a storm on the sunniest of days."

"It sounds like you were close," I say with a sigh. It would've been so different growing up with my parents. It's strange to think that I grew up in their castle, surrounded by their ghosts.

"Your mother and I grew up together, and we were in the same calling circle."

I nod. "But I thought that was something Conjours did?"

"We learn from the best. The Conjours, of course, are where the tradition comes from. But we found that casting a magic circle enhanced and wove our powers together, making us stronger when we needed to be. We wore rings like this." She holds out a hand with her fingers splayed out.

A ring similar to my own coils up her pointer finger. But where mine has a turquoise stone in the middle with a white pearl both above and below it, hers is a deep hunter green with black pearls stacked around it. I hold out my own, and she smiles. "I knew Bronwinn would find a way to get that to you."

As she says this, that feeling of knowing tickles my shoulders. I know my mother intended for me to find it that day at the statue.

"It helps me to focus, and maybe even strengthen my magic," I offer.

"It should. Centuries of magic wielder use flow through it. It's honed and shaped through time and love." Her words remind me of the sisterhood I found within the Shifter village. My heart soars, knowing my mother had this as well. I hope to one day be as lucky.

The morning passes quickly with Iolanthe quizzing me about her mixtures. Some are salves and some are remedies to drink, most of which I can easily identify.

Suddenly, she claps her hands together. "Well done. Tomorrow, we'll begin. Let's eat—I'm famished!" Her cheeks are rosy, her eyes alight with a morning well spent. Without waiting for my response, she floats out of the room, back toward where we gathered upon our arrival.

I follow her through the sitting room and into a vast, warm kitchen. Large fires burn on both walls with pots hanging over them. There's a long preparation area in the very middle of the room, where Iolanthe begins mixing once again, but this time with eggs, cream, and a few vegetables.

"Is this all from here in your valley?" I ask, incredulous that she would have enough time in the day to tend to vegetables, chickens, and goats, and practice her skills on top of it.

"The land provides well in these parts" is her enigmatic reply.

Realizing I won't get a straight answer from her unless I ask a straight question, I try again. "If you spend your day tending to the land and your animals, how do you have the time and energy to continue practicing your magic?"

She nods, acknowledging that I'm onto her. "Oh, I make the time." She gives me a half-smile and moves toward the fire, grabbing a smaller pot along the way.

"Do you ever get lonely here?" I sweep my hand out to encompass this huge kitchen, made for many more than just one.

"I find myself rather captivating, don't you?" She releases a small laugh through her nose. "But there are travelers from time to time. Some are more welcome than others." Her eyes find mine, and I see joy, then anger, and even lust swirling around in them.

Suddenly positive she'd make a formidable opponent for anyone in the realm, especially a malicious thief attempting a quick victory in one way or another, I shudder at the thought of what the thief would find instead.

With that, she places a beautifully plated scramble in front of me, complete with berries along the side. "This is a piece of art," I say between bites of fluffy egg. "Thank you."

"Cooking is like love—it should be entered into with abandon, or not at all. Don't you agree?" Her voice lilts as she carries everything over to the wide sink, the dishes doing themselves.

I hum in response, not because my mouth is full, but because she just voiced what I always hoped. But now, I'm not so sure. Instead, I ask, "Do you think the others have eaten?"

"I am sure they've managed. By the sound of it, they're already training out in the yard."

I listen for a moment, realizing her hearing, or some other sense, is indeed stronger than any of my own.

"What do you want, Rowandine of the Glen?" she asks casually, as if the answer will be something easy, like "cake" or "a good night's sleep."

"What do I want?" I echo. No one has asked me this since the start of my journey, probably even longer than that.

Of course, I want my realm returned to its glory. And for all the terrible things to fade away. If there were some easy solution that would allow the realm to rebuild in the wake of all Hadeon's destruction, that would be ideal. If my sister hadn't suffered alone, instead of me, for so many years, maybe she would be more willing to become that solution, not contribute to the problem. But I feel like I've made a rather large mess of all of it already. It seems as if everyone connected with me meets a terrible fate, whether that be death, or kidnapping, or being filled to the brim with hateful thoughts—enough to want me dead.

"What do I want? My family back, for one." I'm unsure if I mean Gryphon and Licia, or Ombretta and my parents, who I never really had to begin with.

Iolanthe nods slowly. "Despite your many losses, you've surrounded yourself with quite the competent bunch." One perfectly curved eyebrow rises to drive her point home.

At first I'm confused, because the people I surround myself with seem to be pulled instantly from me, but then I see her meaning. Baylor, who's been with me from the start, no questions asked, has been a brother, or maybe more of a mother hen, to me. And Gayle, who jumped into my life with swords flashing, hasn't stopped swinging for me since. And then there's Niko, whose quiet ways no longer come across as cold or standoffish—just heavily guarded. Although he keeps mostly to himself, he's always been there when I've needed him. He's always been what I need him to be.

I tilt my head, considering all of this. My family's been with me this whole time.

Chapter Twenty-Four

I meet Baylor, Gayle, and Niko out at our makeshift training ring, a field recently burned in preparation for the spring growing season. I feel light after identifying salves and potions all morning with Iolanthe. It's been too long since I worked with my hands in this way.

And I realize now why I've been avoiding it. The last time I tried, it didn't go how I envisioned it. Once again, my heart snags on the fact that my best friend died because of me. Even acting on instinct wasn't enough to save him.

But between my hand being forced to save Niko and then Iolanthe's more subtle approach, I'm beginning to feel a little like myself again. Like there's a power coursing through me, even richer than my blood.

None of the trio miss a beat when I join them. Gayle throws me two of her wooden swords, and Baylor pairs off against Niko. I find my stance, making sure my feet are balanced. I point my swords toward Gayle, one elbow bent, showing I'm ready for whatever comes my way.

She attacks immediately, hoping to catch me off guard. But I meet her sword with my own and spin in the opposite direction. "I thought you'd be rusty." Gayle swings as I swing. I feel the vibration of our swords meeting down to my elbows. She smiles slyly. "But you're not."

Inwardly, I'm beaming. While Gayle is always generous with her praise, this time, she seems pleasantly surprised.

"I have a decent instructor." I bring my blade down fast in a way I've watched Niko do. It's effective; Gayle was expecting my swing to come from the side. With my other arm, I strike right along her collarbone.

"I sure didn't teach you that! That's going to bruise!" Gayle rubs her shoulder and sets her sword up. "Your balance is off, though—can you feel it?"

She goads me into tripping over myself and I roll my eyes at her, throwing my arms wide. "Well, of course it is—you're poking and prodding me and I can't keep my feet on the ground!" I yell, making sure to plant my feet before she thrusts again.

She nods and smiles, and I know she's going to strike hard. "Notice your balance." She mimics my stance. "No one always has balance; you have to work for it." Instead of attacking, she steps back, away from our training area. Her words, as they always do, feel like they have an extra weight to them, and even though my pride is wounded by her throwing me off my feet so easily, an unfamiliar warmth settles deep in my chest, as if what she said resonated with a truth I haven't yet grasped.

"Mind if I cut in?"

That deep grumble gets me every time. And now that there's more to him than just some big silent warrior, I soften even more when those notes sink all the way into my core. Inside, I'm melting. But outwardly, I set up again, invigorated by my small win with Gayle.

"I see you've picked up on a thing or two." Niko holds his stance and watches for my first move.

I oblige by slicing fast and spinning left. I'm ready when his sword hits my own as I come out of the spin. Moving quickly, I try to get behind him, but he's too fast. Nothing will surprise him. He's been going at this for too long.

I realize I have to go big, try something I've never done before. I could try to call on my wings again, but he's seen that already; it has to be something more.

"What are you smiling about? You haven't gotten one past me yet," Niko taunts as he comes down again.

"Yet," I confirm as I begin moving more quickly. My strikes are fast and true. They become even faster, almost to the point where Niko can't keep up.

This is my moment. I cut low and then drop my sword. He's distracted, watching it fall to the ground for just a moment, and then I catch it with my foot, and at the same moment, deliver several quick lunges right to his middle with my other sword. Then, before he's any the wiser, I kick the first sword back into my hands for the final blow. He's momentarily stunned, and my thrust forces him backward.

Baylor and Gayle clap slowly, completely stunned.

Baylor jumps on my back in excitement. "That was epic! Where'd you learn a move like that?" He swings me around playfully, and I see Niko coming around behind him.

"Impressive, Rowandine." He tongues his cheek as if he's not sure if he should give me the benefit of a smile.

"I've been paying attention" is all I reply. But really, I'm dancing along the clouds. Keeping up with Niko and even getting one past him! I'm not sure where that extra burst of energy came from, or what that fancy move was. But I must have seen it from one of the elite Shifters. Or could it have been that Warrior's Peace Patton talked about, settling in again?

Later, after spending some time in the cozy library, I find Niko heading back toward our rooms, too. He's lost in thought, so he doesn't hear me approaching. But when I'm just about to catch up to him, I abruptly find myself pinned against the wall with his forearm across my neck, blocking my airway.

Panic surges through me when recognition doesn't register in his eyes, just the promise of violence. I'm frozen in place, but my lips move, trying to find the words that'll snap him out of it. Nothing comes.

I struggle hopelessly against him. Pushing and scratching his arms, his face, anything I can reach. Gasping for air, I kick his shins and repeatedly try to call his name. Still, nothing.

Seconds pass. Almost out of air, I knock him across the temple. He blinks once. Then again. And I see him come back to the moment.

He sets me down immediately, grabbing both my shoulders to steady me until I find my footing. Hands on my knees, I take in huge gulps of air until my breathing returns to normal. Somewhere close but also far in the distance, his familiar scent washes waves of comfort over me, even through the panic.

"Where. Did. You. Go?" I wheeze.

Ignoring my question, he puts his hand on my back, moving it in slow circles until my breath steadies. "Are you okay? Shit, I'm sorry. You surprised me."

"Remind me never to throw you a surprise party," I say, rubbing my neck while heading off toward our rooms before he can say anything else.

"Rowandine, wait. I'm sorry. It's…" I turn back toward him. He's running his hands over his braids. "It's not something I want to get into with you. But I'm sorry."

His hands stop on the rope necklace tied around his neck. I had noticed some small beadwork tied together at the bottom, but assumed it had something to do with him being a dragon. Now I realize it may hold a greater sentiment.

"Then don't worry about it." I turn around, hurt, and disappear into my room.

There's no hope for whatever sparked between us. There's no trust here, and his true colors showed when he asked me to return to Killian.

Minutes later, there's a distant roar that must be Niko. For him to blow off steam by shifting, I must've struck a nerve.

Another sleepless night drags along until I can't take it any longer. I dress while it is still dark and head toward Iolanthe's apothecary. She's not awake yet, so first I walk the perimeter of the room, trailing my fingers across the worn leather of her myriad books. After I'm satisfied that I'd hardly make it a page into any of these books before having to look up most of the terms, I move to the shelves covered with glass and clay jars of all sizes. Organized chaos, if I ever saw it. She has a method to her madness, but it's not clear to me yet.

Most of the jars' contents I can identify by looking at them, but some I lift the lids from and sniff. With each scent, a memory of when Thaliya first showed me what to do with the substance surfaces, wrapping itself around me like a warm hug.

Each container is familiar until I come to a small, darker jar that has a faint golden glow to it. I lift the lid, only to be swallowed by images.

A woman with silver hair just like Iolanthe's, but with even more liquidity to it. Her eyes are shaped just like my own. "Too big for your head" is what Gryphon always said. But hers swim with knowledge, the color of the moon. Over her left shoulder, a blinding light shines, but along her other shoulder, darkness throws her into shadows. Unaware of the warring opposites behind her, she looks pleadingly at me. Then, her expression becomes stronger, filled with surety and confidence. The crown atop her head shines with light as bright as the stars above. She smiles. Her wings spread wide behind her, swirling with shadows and shimmering with light, blocking out both light and dark.

She points to me.

The clatter of the jar on the stone floor brings me back to Iolanthe's apothecary. I look around and find that nothing has changed, except now the small golden petals from the jar are scattered across the floor. Oddly enough, it seems like they've dried out completely, so they look like black and purple bruises. But as I shift to pick them up, the petals catch the torchlight and give off a faint shimmer, reminding me of the woman in my vision, and her wings.

My thoughts scatter like the broken glass before me when Iolanthe floats in, her deep purple robes drifting behind her. "Ah. You've come across the Glorixia petals," she says. "What did you see?"

Chapter Twenty-Five

Iolanthe's voice is soothing after such an unsettling experience. She gathers my hands in her own and guides me toward the fireplace, setting me in one of the high-backed chairs. The cushions are firm and suggest a stability I don't currently feel.

Iolanthe perches herself on the arm of the chair beside me and looks down at me patiently. "Glorixia petals show a person a piece of themselves. However, most don't go near them. Only the very strong can handle such visions of truth." As she explains this, her eyes trail along my face, looking for any hint of what I saw.

"I saw a woman. A Fae woman. Her hair was liquid silver, and she had eyes to match. A bright crown sat atop her head. But there was something wrong with the light surrounding her. It was almost perfectly half light and half darkness." My head tilts to one side as I try to recall any other details. "She had wings like my own." I'm not sure why, but I leave out that the vision ended with her pointing at me.

"Interesting. Fitting, but interesting." She settles herself on the chair and begins telling me more about the Fae people than I could ever have imagined knowing. "Those of the royal line, your own family, have ruled over Everguard since the beginning of time. The lines have ebbed and flowed, but most recently, the rulers, your parents, brought our land peace and prosperity. After hundreds of years of tirelessly working to find this peace, they gave themselves a family and their beloved people an heir."

Iolanthe nestles more comfortably into her chair, as if just beginning a long tale.

"That's when it became apparent to your parents, as well as the council, that some of the mortals among us had been feeding information across the Caldertasi Sea to King Hadeon in hopes of gaining a seat at his court, if and when he was successful."

I knew King Hadeon, the man I had grown up believing was my father until I gladly realized otherwise, was selfish and greedy. But as Iolanthe continues, even the picture I painted of him oozes red with deceit and greed.

"His lands in Nefaria were infertile, and his people were starving. His solution was to cross the sea to new, more profitable lands." I shudder as I try to match the bits and pieces from Avicii's version of history to this one. "Hadeon's spies began in the castle kitchens, lacing all the food that went out with ironwood. Ever so slowly, the whole court fell ill, quickly followed by the village. The queen, who was pregnant, was one of the last to fall, as she had little desire to eat. Being so close to her due date, everything made her ill. It was said that Hadeon's people—for they were not warriors in the least, just starved people swinging swords in hopes of their next meal—crossed into the village with little resistance."

I shudder to think of an entire village being cut down in moments, unable to defend themselves because of a sickness caused by a wormy, star-shamed villain.

"Hadeon found the king, your father, who had been guarding his wife while she gave birth. The babes had already been carried away, for there were two. I assume you already know that tale, though." I nod in sad confirmation. "He struck down your father, who, with one hand, held on to the love of his life, trying to give her some comfort at the very end. Your mother faded from life before Hadeon could strike at her."

Her voice drops to a low whisper, as if the next words are too hard to say aloud.

"It is said that before the sun set that day, the entire castle was painted red with the blood of the dying Fae. Hadeon's people pillaged and plundered the town in celebration. Huge parts of the castle and most of its surrounding village were destroyed or burned to the ground by these mortals, only for them to realize the Fae bodies remained, as they are immune to fire. So before they could settle their newly acquired lands, they had to dispose of all those they cut down.

"Some believe the last of the Fae carried off their dead beneath the cover of night, while the new king drunkenly fought with his people over how best to dispose of the dead Fae creatures. The last of the Fae carried them up and over the Periserrat Peaks, so in their death they would be reunited with their homelands. It is also said that this is why Hadeon, until his death, wouldn't go near those mountains. He believed them to be cursed or haunted, or both. Which, in all honesty, they may well be. All those souls so brutally brought to their deaths on one night…"

She switches directions faster than my stomach can settle after such a horrific story.

"The woman in your vision could have been your mother. All the books note her silvery hair. Not too many Fae were as powerful as she."

"What does her hair have to do with how powerful she was?" I ask, surprised at myself that of all the information just presented to me, this is the part that I question.

"The Fae who have the deepest connection to their power source are recognized by their flowing silver hair. It's a mark they earn from years of practice. Some say it is the cost of knowledge and skill."

I now see Iolanthe in a new light. Of course the reason she's the one most able to help me is that she is of the Fae herself. And by the look of her liquid locks, she must be powerful in her own right.

"Are there many Fae with those markings?" I wonder, as I gaze upon someone I belatedly realize must be one of the most powerful Fae still alive.

"There are few Fae left. And even fewer have retained the ability to practice their skills. Many have spent a lifetime trying to reconnect with that power, but still can't. Some say the tragic end of Everguard's peace is part of the loss of power."

"So all of our power—it comes from the earth?" My mind works frantically to piece together the information Iolanthe is giving me. Either from being told or by intuition, I recognize that my power comes from the depths of the earth. Something I've felt more than once before.

"Some call on the earth. Others the water, fire, or air. Fae are of the earth, thus their power is elemental. Not unlike the Elementals so closely linked to the Conjours. They draw their powers from these sources, too. You seem to have the gift of earth, which is why you have been so successful in healing."

"And you? Do you draw power from the earth as well?"

"Yes. As you can probably imagine, living off the land as I do takes a small amount of skill." She says this modestly, but I realize the truth of it. The other day, she said it was only her here. I cannot imagine a mortal living so comfortably off the land and all alone.

I'm unsure if I say this out loud, or if the words are just written very plainly on my face, but she says, "I may be alone, but I'm not lonely. The earth herself is my companion. We grow as the seasons change. My animals keep me company, as well as the travelers. Those who know they can stop here on a long journey do so often enough. I enjoy my solitude. I've come to know myself well, and in that way, I can help others know themselves as well."

She gets up and glides over toward the large marble table. When she opens a small jar, the petals from the ground float on a phantom breeze, back up into the jar.

"Today was more of a history lesson. Tomorrow we'll feel around for hints at your other abilities. For now, think about how your heritage will benefit you, and how your connections will strengthen you."

Taking this as a dismissal, I stride out of the room and head off to fill my growling stomach.

The sounds of banging pots and slamming cupboards fill the air as I near the large kitchen. Niko is the only one in there, and he grunts a "Good morning" to me. Giving him a wide berth, I aim for the kettle by the fireplace, swiping a mug and a jar of tea along the way. Unable to help poking the dragon, I ask, "Have a good flight last night?"

Niko grunts again in response. Even though he's being short with me, he looks cleaned up and well rested, despite his late night soaring among the stars.

"Look, you don't have to tell me what got into you last night, and I understand if you need to go your own way before we get to the North. I'm sure we can find it without you, but I'm *not* changing course. We're so close." Even as the words leave my mouth, I try to call them back. If Niko leaves, where will we be? Where will I be?

He looks at me for a long moment, and then his face falls. One of his large hands scrubs down his face and back up over his braids. At first, I think he's frustrated with me, but then he looks up again, and I see the same anger from the night before in his eyes, but also something else. It's deep and immense.

He braces himself against the prep table with both hands and faces me straight on. I put the kettle back on its warmer and my freshly poured mug to the side, thinking what comes next should not be accompanied by a warm beverage in my hands. I lean against the cabinets behind me, so Niko has my full attention.

"My wife."

The words strike me as hard as if his open hand just met my cheek. Any questions I had about the feelings between us are destroyed with those two small words, but he pushes forward.

"My wife and child are gone. They were killed." He lowers his gaze to the ground. "By my own hand."

My heart hammers in my chest as I remember the look in his eyes when he pinned me against the wall.

"It was all my fault. Our village was under attack by Hadeon's men. Another one of their raids. I was defending a small group of people." His sentences come out halted, and his gaze is far, far away. "It got to be too much. There were too many of them. I could not shift with those I cared about so close by. We were trapped. They had us surrounded."

He pauses. Looks at me pleadingly. He doesn't want to keep going. I don't think I want him to keep going.

"They kept coming, one after another. I blazed through them, the floor slick with their blood. I continued, finding my stride amid the terror. As I took one down, I spun to continue my defense, but instead of my sword meeting another of the attackers, it met my wife."

My breathing stops. I have no words for him. But his story is not yet over.

"In my shock, I was not prepared for my daughter to run toward us. Her eyes were wild and glued to her mama. She crossed the room from where she was hidden in our bedroom closet, jumping through the fighting surrounding us. Only to be run through with a sword right before she reached us. I didn't even have time to shout for her to get down. I watched as the light left her eyes and her tiny body sank to the ground right beside her mother."

Tears stream down my cheeks as he finishes. He looks up with red-rimmed eyes, haunted with memories. No wonder he reacted so quickly when I startled him. I caused him to relive the most terrifying moments of his life.

I crumble to the ground beside the fire, shedding tears for Niko's wife and young child, for their horrific fate. And I sob for him. He has lived with such a dreadful weight on his shoulders all this time.

He crosses the room in two quick strides and is at my side, comforting me, of all things. He grabs me in his arms and pulls me into a strong hug. I cling to him, knowing he needs more comfort in this moment than I will ever need in my lifetime. We sit together, gripping each other tightly, as if we're each afraid the other will fade into nothingness the moment we let go.

I draw away from him. He pulls me tighter for a moment, but then lets me hold him at arm's length. "You know their deaths are not your fault," I say carefully, running my fingers through his hair and looking into his tortured eyes, trying to bite back my tears for his sake. "You were trying to keep them safe. You were there to save them."

"And look how that turned out." He runs his hands along his braids and once again clasps the small token hanging around his neck. "I was supposed to keep them safe. I am the reason they are no longer here."

"You are the reason they lived what must have been a wonderful life. Those who attacked are to blame." And now it's as clear as daylight why he became the Ultor Regni. I run my hands down his shoulders, down his arms, then down his chest, trying to soothe through my touch, knowing that my words are insufficient. "You can't live like this. You will crumble under the weight of it all."

He nods, but does not look like he's hearing me. "I'm so sorry I hurt you. I'm so, so sorry."

"I startled you. You reacted. I now know not to sneak up on a warrior unless I am looking for a fight." I try to make my voice lighter. "Lesson learned. Consider it a kindness."

We sit there, crumpled together beside the fire, comforting each other, looking into each other's eyes. I notice that his hands have drifted down my back. That my fingers are twisting the hair at the nape of his neck. His scent engulfs me, and I can't help but lean closer. His eyes lock on mine as our lips drift toward one another. His fingertips trace the tears along my cheeks and I turn into him. My hand, resting above his chest, can feel the rapid beating of his heart. His gaze moves slowly to my lips and back up, a silent question of whether consoling might arrive in a kiss.

"What the shooting stars is going on in here? Can't a guy grab a snack?" Baylor swings open the door to the kitchen, takes one look at us tangled on the floor, grabs the entire bowl of fruit on the closest counter, and leaves as quickly as he entered, slamming the door behind him.

The moment is broken. We both stand abruptly, and I step backward, trying to find something to do with my hands. Realizing how poor my timing is, and how badly I want Niko to lift me onto that huge wooden slab behind me, covered in flour, and press his lips and his body into mine.

"Roe?" he asks, watching as I'm still taking small steps backward. I bring my gaze to his, and whatever is in my eyes causes his to widen. Deep pools of molten brown melt me from the inside out. Seeing his reaction, I feel heat rising in my cheeks, and then his eyebrows rise, as he must know what just went through my head.

I turn and leave, feeling everything all at once. Embarrassed that he saw my desire so plainly, especially as he was just baring his broken heart to me. Anger at myself that at a moment when Niko needed me, I was imagining my back hitting the hard surface of the countertop, him showering me with kisses.

I'm crushed that he has such a complicated and tormenting past, but a small, light thought worms its way through all this heaviness. Here I was, worried about my new friend Pris and whatever she had with him. This new reality is something I can't even begin to contend with. But mostly, I'm still so angry.

I shake my head as he takes a step toward me again. "You may be the Ultor Regni, but it's not your job to protect everyone. It's not your job to protect me. You need to trust that I can handle myself, that my strategy is sound, and my actions are my own. But you don't. You're ruined because of something you had no control over. And now you can't stand to let anything slip through your hands. You have to let go."

"Rowandine…" His voice breaks on my name.

I turn my back on him. Too weak to face him in a moment when he needs me most. When he continues to be what I need, time and time again.

Chapter Twenty-Six

I made it back to my room before I dissolved in a fit of tears. Angry tears, sad tears, tears of frustration. Spending the rest of the day in a daze, alternating between being upset, pacing the room, and fitfully dozing.

Eventually, I find myself on the balcony, which was my safe place at the castle too, but here there's a different view. Looking over the rows of crops all managed by the power of one woman jars me from my turmoil. I'm surprised to see the hazy colors of dusk already painting the sky. Today went from morning to night in the blink of an eye. I suppose it also went from enlightenment to exasperation in the blink of an eye as well.

What just happened?

Niko, who I thought a heartless monster, is quite the opposite. He's mourning a family lost. He's just as broken as I am. All this time, instead of letting his gruff, oafish ways offend and then endear, I should've been paying attention to the way he always stepped in front of me when there was a threat. Instead of drinking up his helpful words on the practice field or the way he knew I loved sweet pastries, I should've seen his overbearing ways and need to direct our strategy talks.

The gentle caress of his hand brushing against my cheek that night after Torelai's surfaces for a moment. And the warmth I felt when he wrapped me in his arms, saying over and over again that I was safe, comforting me even now, after all that just unfolded.

But I can't have feelings for Niko. He's created an entire plan for me, just like Avicii and Hadeon did, time and time again. I'm my own person. I deserve to be the one who makes my own choices. I knew better than to believe there is something good between us, because every time I've let my guard down, an ulterior motive destroys whatever relationship we've built. Where I thought trust was growing between us, it was just a dependence or need for him to protect me. Nothing more than that.

My hand comes down hard on the balustrade, and I realize the sun has set across the mountains. Warmth radiates from the torches that light the balcony, the ones that ignite each night with the setting sun. I wrap my arms around myself and rub them to ward off the chill of the night setting in.

Turning toward the sky-high mountains, thrown into deep shadows by the setting sun, I look for even an ounce of comfort, but find little. All I can see from here are the silhouettes of those tall, dark peaks. Way in the distance, they're said to hold all the Fae who fell when Hadeon destroyed the Southern City. My people. Far beyond the range is where the last remaining Fae reside and await my return. Mine and my sister's. I hope I won't disappoint them.

I look as far north as I can from here. The mountains there are snow-capped and spear into the cloudy sky. Somewhere within them, my very flesh and blood, the *last* of my flesh and blood, remains. What brutalities has she witnessed to want me to take her place? What thrall is she under that would make that her decision?

I hope deep within my heart that will not be the case when we arrive at her doorstep. But I fear I hope against all hope.

In the darkness of the night, guided by a sliver of moonlight and a small torch in my hand, I creep back toward Iolanthe's study. Unable to get the Glorixia petals out of my mind, I wonder what else I could see if I mixed them with something to bring out their capabilities. I brought the diary, the one I'm hoping is my mother's, to strengthen what I'm about to do.

Crossing the room, I pull a small handful of petals out of the jar, careful not to inhale their magical scent, and add them to a small wooden bowl left out on the long table. I add a sprig of rosemary, a touch of ginkgo, and the petals of a periwinkle flower. There's some sage oil on the shelf, so I add several drops of that as well. With the pestle, I blend the herbs, all the while still wondering about my sister, glad to have my mind focused on something else. I gather all the ground herbs into a vial, leaving just a small amount in the wooden bowl. After last time, I want to be careful not to destroy the last of the Glorixia petals or the small amount I've altered.

I remember Iolanthe's warning as I sit down with the bowl and its remnants in one of the high-backed chairs around the last embers in the fireplace. Settling into the chair, I place the book beside me on the table, keeping it close in hopes this works.

There are very few who can look to their inner self and see the truth. Hoping I am one of those very few, because I'm desperate to see my mother once more, or perhaps my father this time, I sit back and hold the bowl up to my nose, inhaling deeply.

It is not the rosewater or lilies of my mother that I smell. Instead, the scent of the first morning frost fills my lungs. Darkness swallows me, and feelings of rage and jealousy rise within me. Spinning all around me, hope glistens like shards of glass, shattered and strewn across the dark floor. Replaced, then, with the strength of darkness, deep carmine, like Gryphon's blood all over my hands. The dark strength pulses and urgently beckons me closer.

A pale hand reaches toward me. Swathed in midnight silks, pulling me forward. I reach toward it, hesitantly at first. Reassuring tones guide me further into the cold dark. Whispers of power creep around my limbs like vines growing up toward the sun.

My bare feet touch cool liquid, and the vague idea of a calm lake surrounds me. But when I go to take another step forward, I see that the water dripping off my raised foot is thick and deepest red. Before I can question this odd observation, those same tendrils continue to tighten their grip, no longer caressing, but constricting me and pulling me further into the liquid.

Laughter. Deep, hollow laughter fills my ears. It's as if the sound is coming from nowhere and everywhere all at once. Because of the darkness, I'm unsure where to look. And not sure I want to, even if I could.

Suddenly, I'm jarred out of this unsettling vision by two strong hands shaking me. Someone is repeating my name over and over again in a beautifully melodic voice. My eyes fly open, and even the low light of the burning embers before me seems too bright compared to where I've just been.

Chapter Twenty-Seven

"Iolanthe?" Her silver eyes are the only thing I see as I slowly withdraw myself from those creeping tendrils and focus on what's in front of me. Her eyes are full of worry as she continues to lightly tap my cheeks and call my name. Her words sound sluggish and distant in my ears as the last of the darkness shakes loose, still trying to keep its talons deep within me.

Her hands tighten around my own, and I squeeze hers back to let her know I'm with her. Her worried eyes soften and warm further, and she sees that I'm back from wherever I have just gone. She holds up a cup of tea, and I struggle to clasp it and bring it to my lips. The aromatic scent of peppermint warms the deepest parts of me, allowing me a reprieve from the nightmare I've just returned from.

"You went somewhere else this time," she states matter-of-factly, as if she can taste the difference between the two visions in the very air around us.

"I was hoping to strengthen the Glorixia petals to pick a specific place to see. I wanted to ensure I could see my mother again, maybe understand more of what she wants of me." My words come out in a stumbling mess as I realize the results of my unskilled mixture could have been much worse. I am incredibly lucky Iolanthe was here in the middle of the night to pull me back from wherever I was. "How did you find me?" I ask, realizing that if she hadn't, I would've been drawn into whatever darkness beckoned me.

"I was on my way to our morning lessons, and I could feel the darkness emanating from the heart of the mountain from my study. Naturally, I was concerned. And then to find you, being sucked dry of your light, pulled into that darkness, was too much. I thought for sure I was too late." She pulls a blanket around me and tucks it in comfortingly, then turns to the fire and builds it up to double its normal height.

"What was that darkness?" I ask, still trying to recall some of the more vivid details.

"What did you see? What do you remember?" she asks, perhaps more eager than she wanted to appear, because she tucks her chin and closes her eyes, giving me time to process.

"I didn't see anything. It was too dark. I'm not sure how to describe it other than that everything felt red. The blackest red. And there was an overwhelming feeling of being pulled into something even darker than my surroundings. And laughter, but not the happy giggles of a child. It was dark and angry." I look to Iolanthe, knowing I must sound ridiculous, speaking of feeling colors and hearing disembodied laughter. The warmth from the fire has brought back the feeling in my fingers, and the flames drive off any further darkness lurking around me. I inhale the scent of old books and dried herbs, the comfort of Iolanthe's study balancing me once again.

"She knows," Iolanthe says, digging through the bottles and jars along her table, frantically searching for something. Triumphantly, she holds a chain with an elongated crystal hanging from it high above her head. She comes back toward me, hanging the chain around my neck.

I gather the chain and the crystal into my palms. The crystal looks smoky at first glance, but then I see within it a small slash of green protected by a pale pink all around. I hold it up to the firelight, trying to see it more clearly. The small green piece within pulses, and I feel the light of the earth glowing from it.

"Wear this always. To keep the darkness at bay. It's a talisman that will ward against that darkness." Iolanthe points to the small slash within, and I nod without wholly understanding. "This, along with your ring, should keep you reasonably safe."

"She knows?" I ask, still inspecting the gift.

"Ombretta. She still searches for you and seeks to pull you to her. She almost had you, by the sound of it."

My heart sinks when she speaks of my sister in such a dark way. I'm still struggling to see that someone connected to me could be so hateful.

"You must've been thinking of her as you mixed the herbs. When all those herbs for remembrance were mixed, they formed something stronger. A connection between the living. So rather than seeing any visions of your mother, you connected with your sister. Which would not have been so much an issue, except it appears she was hoping for this to happen and just waiting for the right moment to pull you under."

Iolanthe rubs her hands together, apparently trying to warm herself against such a cold, dark prospect.

"I would steer clear of the Glorixia petals if I were you, at least until we have a better hold on your powers. Especially since you appear to take so easily to them." Her lips purse together as if she's missing something, but can't put her finger on it. "What's this?" She reaches for the diary. She holds it reverently, flipping it from side to side, hesitant to open it. "I haven't seen this in years."

"I think it was my mother's diary. I can't read anything in it. Baylor has pointed out a few things, but other than that, I just keep it with me, hoping to decipher it at some point. I brought it down here as a piece of her to guide the Glorixia petals."

"That's a clever thought. Odd that you were so purposeful and yet Ombretta still plagued your thoughts." Iolanthe begins to flip through the book, mindful of the pages that have fallen out, making sure nothing gets out of order. She fingers the yellowing edges, careful not to bend or break them. "This spell here we used often. It amplified our powers as a group. It was a tricky one, but it always gave the desired results." She angles the book so I can see the page she's opened it to. On it are the Fae runes I've been trying to decipher.

"So you can read this? Have read it before?" Excitement bubbles up from deep inside of me. If Iolanthe can read this, I'll be that much closer to my mother.

"Read it? I helped write it! It wasn't Bronwinn's diary—not strictly speaking, anyway." She flips through it some more. "It was our grimoire."

I frown at the unfamiliar word. "Is that a spellbook?"

"Sort of. It has a little bit of everything in it. There are parts where we recorded spells, and it has some thoughts or reflections—life lessons, if you will. We recorded some of our rituals that we learned from the Conjours, too. All sorts of things pertinent to our circle in particular, or life in general. I'm glad it found you. In the wrong hands, it would be dangerous."

Dangerous? I lean in closer, trying to inhale the secrets of my past.

"Look! And here's your mother's favorite cinnamon pastry recipe!"

I feel tears stinging my eyes at this.

"You don't like cinnamon?" Iolanthe tries to lighten the mood, and I can't help laughing at myself.

"Cinnamon pastries are my favorite, too." I wipe the tears off with the neck of my shirt.

"What a happy connection. She made them all the time. They came in handy when we had our early-morning circles. We'll have to make them while you're here and translate the recipe for you."

We spend most of the morning looking through the grimoire, Iolanthe explaining different things and marking pages to come back to. Afterward, we mix tinctures and make poultices, and she continues to be impressed with how much Thaliya taught me over the years. It's remarkable how alike their ways are. It makes me miss Thaliya greatly, but I feel as if she's here with me, helping me along.

Just as I'm feeling satisfied with my progress, Iolanthe takes a dagger and slices a long cut across the back of her hand. She looks at me expectantly and says, "Now heal it."

I look back at her, stunned. It's been months since Thaliya did the same thing, and I start at the sight. But then a newer memory surfaces. While Iolanthe's blood drips onto the floor, spreading toward my still-bare toes, I freeze. Visions of Gryphon bleeding out beneath my blood-soaked hands blind me. I try to swallow down a sob, but Iolanthe doesn't let me wallow. Instead, she scolds me.

"I know you can do this. Ground yourself; feel the power wash over you. Reconnect to your strength." She taps my chest with two fingers. "The magic within."

But Gryphon's hands, the way they held mine in those last minutes, cause me to shake my own hands out in front of me, trying to get rid of the memory with movement since it doesn't fade on its own. Iolanthe allows me a few moments to gather my wits before wincing as the blood continues to pool between us.

I close my eyes and try to imagine her hand healed. But when I open them, there's just more blood. It looks as if we're taking a blood bath instead of working a quick healing spell.

Iolanthe continues to pale, and she bites out, "Find the connection."

I close my eyes again and try to block out thoughts of Gryphon, of blood, of the way Iolanthe keeps swaying. Instead, I picture Gayle and Baylor's reassuring murmurs and Niko's belief in me.

Knowing I have to work quickly, I imagine a spark growing from deep within my core. Growing big and bright until it insists on a way out. I draw the power from the earth into my core, and then I can feel my ring pulse with power. I channel this warmth from within me and feel it leaving my fingertips and flowing into where my hands clench around her cut to stop the bleeding.

The moment I open my eyes, I know it worked. Despite my feet being sticky with pooled blood and the way Iolanthe's skin has paled even further, I know there's no more wound. The power within tells me she is whole again, that somehow we connected, and I fixed her.

"Good." That's all Iolanthe says as she moves toward her big chair. The firelight reflects in her eyes, and they look more white than silver.

I sit on the arm of the chair beside her, catching my breath and reassuring myself that she is, in fact, fine. I feel better when she speaks again.

"You did well. I see now why those in the Southern City remain so loyal to you. Continue fighting for your cause. And continue to shape you without you being aware of it."

"You mean, it's not just my sunniest of dispositions?" I laugh, although it comes out more like a cough, as I'm too exhausted for much more than that. We are quite the pair, because Iolanthe coughs too, and I take it for a laugh as well.

"You have a strength within," she says as I hand her a cloth, and she wipes at her arm. Her pale skin doesn't even show signs of redness after she wipes the blood away. "We will hone it. You will do just fine." She pats my thigh, resting along the arm of her chair, and then rises. Without looking back, she once again floats from the room on a phantom wind, her power replenished already.

As I cross the room and head outside to practice, my stomach gives a loud protest. Unsure if I should brave the kitchen, I decide it's imperative if I plan to see straight if I finally make it out to spar. I head back to the kitchen, hoping the only things I'll find inside are two blazing fires and a cup of hot tea.

"See you for training in a few?" Gayle asks as she pushes open the kitchen door and finds me on the other side.

"I don't know. I still can't stomach it. I'd rather stay inside, working with Iolanthe. I'm sure I'm fine—that's what muscle memory is for, right?"

As I move to continue into the kitchen, Gayle moves with me, blocking the path. "It's okay to be scared." She tries to catch my eye, and reluctantly, I meet hers. "And I love that you're so full of optimism. But regarding your training, you need to practice in order to become better, especially knowing what we're up against."

My lips press together, and my nails trail the scars on my palms as I try to think of anything but what she's saying to me. It hits too close.

"Losing a friend—a best friend—is the most difficult thing. But you can't ignore training just because it scares you now. It's okay to recognize the danger, and then mix in the hope. You got past it the other day. I still can't recreate that move. You should come show us how it's done."

I nod, conceding to the sense she's making. My throat is too thick with emotion to put anything into words.

"Go grab yourself something to eat real quick, then meet me out in the fields. Maybe a roll?"

"A roll?" Some butter and bread might be just the thing to set me right again.

"Yeah—all around on the prepping table?" Gayle winks on her way outside.

I pause at her remark, but I'm already through the door before it all sinks in. She knows something happened between me and Niko. Stars. And she's implying that Niko is—

"Roe?"

His deep tenor breaks into my thoughts, and I realize I've been standing frozen at the door for some time now.

"Niko." I aim for composed, but I'm positive it comes out anything but. I cross the wide floor toward the mugs and kettle. At least I'll get the tea I hoped for. Even if it's accompanied by awkwardness. "I'm meeting Gayle outside." I look back at the door, the only way out of this room.

For a moment, I could swear Niko's shoulders fall. But then he strides toward me, and I stiffen, holding my tea with both hands, torn about how to respond to his advances.

Before I can decide, he's standing right in front of me, his eyes holding mine, and I sink into those deep pools of warmth.

In one move, he reaches around me and fills a mug with hot water from the kettle. With the other arm, he reaches around my other side for the tea leaves, once again looking down at me. And then he hands the mug to me and strides wordlessly from the room.

I'm left utterly speechless and very much in need of a cold bath. Starballs. What was I thinking?

In the silence, I realize I now have exactly what I was hoping for: the big, warm kitchen all to myself. I rustle around in the breadbasket and pull out a roll, drizzling it with honey. My shoulders sag as my eyes trail across the space. I lean against the middle of the long counter, with my back to the fires.

The quiet of the kitchen presses in on me from all sides. I stare at the door, willing Niko to come back through it. Moments ago, I was hoping he'd kiss me. He looked like he was going to kiss me. And then he just left. It's the night after the Viper's Den all over again.

Anger and disappointment rise within me, and I grip my mug tightly. I look down to see bubbles rising from the water, which has already had plenty of time to cool. Oddly, I notice my ring is faintly glowing from within. The mug burns my palms. I drop it, stunned, and watch it clatter to the floor. I stare at the mess of broken ceramic shards and small puddles of water, unable to comprehend what just happened.

The common area is quiet as I move through it, needing to return my grimoire before meeting Gayle.

On my way out, though, there are footsteps heading this way, heavy, rhythmic steps that could only be one person. In the moments before he turns the corner, I have seconds to decide—do I stay and confront him, or quickly hide in my room?

I brace myself and choose the former. But the surprise on his face makes me wish I had cowered.

Until he opens his mouth. "You were right—"

But there's nothing else I need to hear.

I stand on my toes and bring my lips to his, pulling the front of his shirt forward until our bodies press together.

In between kisses, he pulls just far enough away to continue. "You—were—right—*and*—I—trust—you."

I dissolve into him. And this time, it's not just because his touch turns me to mush. It's not just because our bodies fit together as if they were made for each other. It's because despite all the ghosts between us, he sees me—both for who I am, and who I can be.

He walks me backward until we reach my room, continuing until my thighs meet the bed. Only then do we break apart, staring at each other as if we can see into each other's souls.

I move to lift my chemise but he catches my hands, gently taking over. He takes hold of both my chemise and underclothes as his fingers trace the hollow of my waist and gently graze my breasts. I lift my arms overhead as he pulls them up and off, dropping them to the ground.

Rather than the frenzy we've shared in the past, I want to take my time with him, learn his body and what makes his toes curl. My fingertips hook into the waistband of his pants, tracing back and forth until his jaw ticks and a low, resonant hum leaves his lips. But he doesn't open his eyes. I watch the way his chest lifts and falls when I take my time lifting his shirt up over his head, drinking in the way each muscle twitches as the fabric brushes over it.

With our shirts forgotten, we stand facing each other, our heavy breaths the only sound in the room. I drink in his body, as he does mine. He has too many scars to count, some small nicks, others jagged and raised. It's at this moment I know I want to learn the story behind each scar, all his adventures and struggles—everything that has brought him to me.

He moves first, stepping forward while bringing one hand around to rest on the small of my back and the other to my hip. With one smooth movement, he guides me onto the bed, the weight of him pressing into me from our chests all the way to our intertwined toes. It centers me, a welcome, delicious warmth. Pillows fall to the ground as we settle into the center of the bed, the comforter embracing us in a soft nest of fabric.

"Datura," he breathes and his lips press gently against mine. I close my eyes, letting his scent mingle with the heady smell of desire. His length, pressing against my thigh, adjusts to fit at my entrance. My muscles clench in anticipation and my thighs tighten, pulling him closer. He enters me with ease, his eyes on me until he's deep within me. He shudders as he says, "This... My body knew yours before my heart did."

He begins moving then, but his words are my undoing. As he says them, my core tightens, and warmth flows all around me. A slow thrum begins to build with each thrust, coiling inside me until I'm ready to burst.

Bringing my hips up to meet each movement has me tipping over the edge, and I finally spiral out of control when his lips find my throat.

I completely unravel, my body tense and floating at the same time. I cry out, his name on my lips as he thrusts one last time, meeting my desire with his own.

He rests his forehead on my own as our breathing evens out. I can't imagine this moment ever ending.

It's as if he hears my thoughts as he pulls his head up to meet my gaze and

I can feel him growing hard again inside me. A satisfied hum leaves my lips as I shift my hips, welcoming him further into me. One side of his lips lift and his contented smirk has me reaching my arms above my head, bracing myself against the headboard and arching into him, silently begging for more.

He tries to hide his smile in my neck, but I can feel the pure bliss radiating off him in waves. He nibbles my neck and I buck against him playfully. He answers by rising to his knees and lifting my hips to meet him. Holding on to my hips, he enters me, not slowly this time, but in one forceful motion that has me clenching my teeth and pressing harder against the headboard at the same time. He continues at this quick speed, encouraged by the roll of my hips each time he's deep within me.

In the pale morning light, the beads on his braids glint with each movement and rays of sunlight play across his chiseled chest. Watching him enter me again and again has me biting my lip until I draw blood. But I don't even notice. I'm at the point of surrender, so I do just that—surrender myself to him completely. As the final rush hits me, he drives again and again, picking up speed until I shatter beneath him. With his final thrust, we both fall apart, together.

This time, when our breathing slows, he slides next to me, adjusting until he's on his back and I'm resting on his chest, listening to the way his heart beats in rhythm with mine. He strokes my hair, his thick fingers gently combing out the fresh knots. I want to stay in this moment forever.

Maybe we can. Maybe this is what this is supposed to feel like. I drift away into a dreamless sleep, content and satiated.

I wake still blissfully drained and completely worn out with pleasure. The way the sunlight hits the room suggests I've only been out minutes, but as I twist around, Niko is nowhere to be found.

The room is quiet and there's no sign of him. I sit up, trying to process this through my muddled senses. Where would he have gone? I'm sure he just ran out for something. He'll be back in a moment.

I wait. Seconds tick by, then minutes. My heart pounds and I tell myself I'm overreacting. But I wait, and he doesn't come back. Panic is eclipsed by an anger so bright. Anger at him for leaving, but mostly anger at myself, for opening myself up to thinking this time was different—to trust.

Chapter Twenty-Eight

I dress quickly and stride down the halls and out toward the sparring fields, bypassing Gayle altogether and heading straight into the treeline. Without losing momentum, I grab one of the longswords propped against our makeshift rack. Breaking into a run with an enormous boulder set in my sights, I throw the longsword from hand to hand as if it weighs nothing, the cold, steely weight becoming an extension of me.

I strike the boulder hard. The vibrations reverberate up my arms. I barely feel it as I bring my sword up again and again. Relentlessly striking the rock over and over. There's no form to my motions, just rage and sadness. And so much confusion.

Tears blur my vision, but I continue through the physical pain, swinging my arms. Right now, this emotional volcano is erupting, and if I don't let it out, it'll swallow me whole.

My blows slow as I run out of energy. My arms are almost numb from the weight of the sword and the assault against the unmoving rock.

There's movement behind me, but I keep swinging. Gayle wraps her arms around me from behind and waits. I drop the sword and turn. Instantly, my body relaxes into hers, tears engulf me once again, and I sink into the rhythmic way her hand smooths my hair.

"I've got you. You're not alone in this. I've got you," she whispers slowly, as if speaking to a child whose favorite toy just split into tiny pieces.

Her words restore me to myself, filling an empty space within. I realize how true they are. And I repeat Iolanthe's words to myself. Family. I have a family here. I am not alone.

I inhale these words as if they are a bright new mantra. I exhale the anger that swallowed me whole. I am stronger than this, and I can rely on those around me. I am not alone.

Even if Niko did just leave me alone. After what we shared.

Even if he took the shattered pieces of my broken heart and ground them to dust beneath his heel.

"Gayle…" I stand back a little. "Thanks for that." I straighten, suddenly aware of what a fantastic spectacle I've just made.

"For what?" She brushes me off. "Let's take a walk." She motions up the rock face, and I have a feeling this will not be a picturesque stroll beside a winding river.

I look toward the rock that took the brunt of my angry explosion, my sword strikes clear on its face.

Gayle's eyes follow mine. "Is that a…" She squints a little and tilts her head to study the slashes. "Is that a moonflower?"

"Huh. It does look like one." My thoughts flash back to the vision from this morning. To Ombretta's low, maniacal laughter surrounding me. Instantly I know this symbol has something to do with us.

I turn my back on it and wrap my fingers around the crystal hanging from my neck. Warmth pulses through my hands as if in answer to my thoughts.

The climb is arduous. Gayle sets an unmatchable pace, which, of course, I aim to match or die trying. At the top, she finally sits down to rest on a log that looks like it's meant for just that purpose, aimed perfectly to look out across the wide expanse of land before us.

I sit beside her, trying to regain my breath before I pass out. She waits patiently for me to find my strength again. As she looks serenely toward the horizon, not a hint of sweat beads her brow, and her breathing remains slow and measured.

"What do you see?" she asks, gazing out at the magnificent view.

"It's beautiful" is all I say, taking in the forest below us and a hint of the Wastelands in the far distance. I follow the horizon, my eyes catching on the stunning and deadly mountains of the Fae. Again, the peaks must be under cloud cover, because they're thrown into deep shadows. My eyes continue to the spearing mountains of the North, tipped in icy points.

"Yes, true. But what do you *see*?" she asks again.

I look at her with my face screwed up tight, still at a loss as to what she's asking me. "Trees? Mountains?"

"This is you. This is your path. Our journey."

I look again and realize she's right. I can see where Merula would be, and my eyes once again travel the horizon to the icy teeth of the North.

"We've covered some ground, huh?" I'm impressed with myself for being able to keep up, for making it as far as we've come.

"That's for sure." Gayle grins at me, tilting her head. "It's been quite a ride."

"I didn't think I'd make it even this far. I suppose I owe a lot to you and

Niko. To Baylor and everyone still in Merula."

"Not as much as you think. This is all you, girl. You've brought us this far, and you'll carry us through to the end."

She speaks with a confidence I don't yet feel in myself. But her words are a warm balm I didn't know I needed, and I know she believes them wholly.

"Why'd you come with me?" I ask suddenly.

"I don't think I had a choice in the matter."

I cut my eyes toward her, not sure where she's going with this.

"As soon as I rode up that one evening, watching you, completely outnumbered, fighting for your life against all those guards. Fighting for yourself and your friends. Watching how you didn't give up, even when you knew your sister was already long gone. I knew this was something I had to be a part of. Something bigger than myself. Even before I knew who you were and what you stood for, I knew I'd stand by you." She looks at me and grins. "That, and Baylor, sitting astride a horse, did all kinds of things to my lady parts." She winks and giggles, and I can't help but join in.

"But I thought..." Welcoming the change in focus, but unsure how to finish that statement without getting into trouble, I push through anyway. "I thought you were with—" I realize I don't know what I think at this point. "Who's with Pris?" I blurt out.

"I am," she says with a smile.

"You are? But then what about what you just said about Baylor? What about Niko?" Stumbling over my words, I'm not sure if Gayle's following. I'm not even sure *I'm* comprehending.

"Pris and I have more of an open relationship. Or at least more of an open view of the word 'relationship.'"

Maybe it's a Shifter thing. Maybe not. She squints at me, trying to decipher if I'm understanding.

I am. My shoulders slump. That means I must've been right about Niko and Pris all this time. Shooting stars. My heart sinks at this realization. "Oh."

"You okay?" she asks, and I realize she's trying to pinpoint what part of her relationship status I'm disappointed in.

"Stars alive. Yes, I'm fine. No, I wasn't hoping..." I motion between the two of us, completely at a loss for words.

Gayle barks a laugh. "Of course! No, I didn't think you were." She swats at me. "But then, why does it bother you?" I realize she's thinking the worst of me. She thinks I won't accept her because of who she spends her time with.

"Oh, Gayle! No! It's not that. Who you sleep with is none of my business. If you're happy, I'm happy." Her shoulders instantly relax. "I was just hoping... I thought there was something—between Niko and me. That was, until I woke up to an empty bed."

"Ah, I was hoping that was what took you so long. And, from what I heard that one beautiful night I took a walk up to the falls, there wasn't much at all between the two of you, and from the sound of it, it was plenty fine to you." She winks and barks a laugh again, enjoying her own joke.

"I thought it was just sex."

The words tumble out, thin and unconvincing even to me. As soon as they leave my mouth, I know with a sickening certainty it has never been just sex. Not even that first time in the cave, when all we felt was burning hate for each other. There have been sparks of something else, an undeniable current beneath the animosity. And just now... But between Pris and whatever history Niko shares with Reinette, I can't compete. I don't want to.

"And anyway," I quickly add, trying to deflect, "I feel terrible." I look up at Gayle, unsure how to articulate my discomfort, especially considering what seems like a tangle of relationships in the forest. "About doing that to Pris."

"Why would Pris care if you slept with her brother?" Gayle asks, her voice laced with an odd, knowing patience. "Goodness, Roe, it's not like you're going to break some ancient pact. Some connections just are. You'll see."

My breath hitches and I choke on the very air I'm inhaling. "What? Her brother? Niko is Pris' brother?" My mind reels, frantically sifting through every interaction I witnessed between them. From the moment she ran up to him at his return, to their brief, seemingly innocent conversation on our way out on girls' night. Could I have misinterpreted everything? "Oh, stars!" My gaze shoots to Gayle, then wildly flits between her and the path leading back down the mountain.

So he's not with anyone. Hasn't been with anyone except me. He no longer wants me dead. And the look he gave me in bed, like he wanted to swallow me whole, was just that.

The hurt from our past is a chasm between us.

What did Gayle say earlier? It's okay to acknowledge the danger *and* hold on to hope. For me, love has always been a tangled mess, but maybe, with the right person, it can be a beautiful mess.

"Then where'd he go?" I ask standing, ready to find him and cross the chasm.

"I haven't seen him, but maybe he has a tray of cinnamon cakes waiting for you." She laughs, but I don't stick around for more jabs from her. My feet move before I voice where I'm headed.

"Ha!" She laughs again as she watches my dawning realization. "I'll find my way back down. Thanks for the chat, Roe. You're always around for a good laugh. Although this one tops all the rest, for sure."

I leave her slapping her knees in a fit of laughter. Glad I could at least make someone's day, I take off down the hill in search of the man who's stolen my heart.

Chapter Twenty-Nine

Flying down the rocky path, my feet fall more surely than I would've thought. It's as if each pebble is placed to my advantage, and each rock is a stepping stone rather than something to maneuver around. I try to imagine the look on his face when I leap into his arms and shower him with kisses. I feel like my feet are barely even hitting the ground. At visions of him lifting me, twirling me in the air, and me grabbing his face in my hands to tell him how much he means to me, I press on even faster.

Everything will be easier knowing that he's by my side. Even facing a sister full of hatred will be bearable now.

I'm so distracted by my thoughts of what will ensue after I tell him how I feel that I barely register Baylor running straight at me, his face stricken with worry and an eagerness I can't place. He grabs me roughly by the forearms, and his distress causes the smile on my face to dissolve.

"We need to leave. Now. Where's Gayle?" he asks in a rush.

"Baylor, what's wrong? She's..." I point up the mountain. I can see her form, a small black dot toward the top of the rock face.

"No time to explain. Niko's already left. Horses are saddled. Go fill your pack. Iolanthe is grabbing food."

Frozen in fear, I'm not sure which to respond to first. Why would Niko leave without us? What could have Baylor wound so tightly? This isn't good. I stand there with my arms reaching out, even though Baylor's already halfway up the path to Gayle.

"Go!" he shouts over his shoulder, and I rush into action.

My feet carry me to my room, where I quickly pack a set of clothes and grab the grimoire and some extra layers as well, thinking of those icy spears we'll encounter sooner rather than later. I'm back at the stables within moments. Iolanthe's here too, securing packs of food to each horse. Even she looks worried.

"My training," I start. "I'm hardly ready. We never got to half the work you spoke of." I've wasted my time with her, working on salves and talking about dreams. This can't be what will save my sister—my people.

"Oh, but you are, child." She pats Navi and settles my pack onto my saddle. "You are more ready than you know."

Baylor and Gayle are up on their horses, and Baylor begins our pace at a gallop. I only look back once, Iolanthe's serene wave strengthening my small amount of resolve into something more tangible.

We ride as silently as the glacial cold surrounding us. My hands are numb. Tears stream across my face from the wind, and I'm worried they've frozen to my face.

I have only my thoughts to keep me going. What has Baylor and Iolanthe so spooked? It's big enough for Niko to ride on ahead. Is it Killian again? Or Ombretta? We're riding north, so I guess it has something to do with Ombretta, which doesn't do much for my morale.

And Niko. Just moments ago, I imagined us riding north together, hand in hand. Instead, he's gone off on his own, and he could be anywhere. He could be hurt. He could be dead. I hope he and Baylor worked out how we'd find each other.

I take deep, slow breaths. Right now is not the time to be taken by anxiety. I don't know how long I can continue like this.

Hours later, Baylor slows the horses. I think if he cared less for their well-being, we wouldn't have stopped. But the horses have been going for too long. They need some rest. And I need to defrost.

We find shelter between huge rock faces that block the wind. I immediately feel warmer and huddle closer to Gayle as we pull out a small snack, waiting for Baylor's explanation.

"It seems your sister is expecting us." His eyes cut toward me as he explains. "Iolanthe received word that the North is taking measures to fortify the Pass—the only way across the Black Abyss, for hundreds of miles in either direction." The importance of our haste is evident as he looks between us. I nod fervently, realizing that if we don't make it across the Pass, it could take months to arrive at Freathia Castle. Months we don't have.

"And Niko?" Gayle voices the question before I have a chance to.

"He rode ahead to block any first attempts. Just in case they've already begun." Baylor exhales, as if carrying the weight of that information all this way was too much. "We'll continue in an hour. Get some rest. I'll keep watch. No fire. We have to be more careful now."

I wake with a welcome warmth radiating from my chest and tiny, cold flecks of white landing on my skin. My hand reaches toward the warmth, and I find it's the crystal, glowing. Still unsure of its meaning, I know whatever it is, it can't be good. As I sit up, I notice there's a blanket of white all around us, but only a few flakes have made it into where we rest. Is this snow?

"Gayle, wake up." I shake her, and she mumbles something about another round. Stars, yes. Another round at the Viper's Den would be perfect right about now. "Sorry to rip you from your dream, but let's talk drinks later. I think it's snowing."

She snaps awake and is instantly wracked with shivers. At least we slept. I'm unsure of how long, but judging by the layer of snow on the ground, maybe Baylor gave us longer than he intended to.

He comes around with the horses. "Oh, good. I wasn't sure if I had the heart to wake you. I had half a mind to snuggle right in between what looked like some great cuddles." He smirks and looks between Gayle and me, as if he's trying to decide who he'd want to make the little spoon.

"Glad your sense of humor is still intact." I shake my head at him, but can't help but smile at his ability to joke at a time like this.

"Remind you of something?" Gayle asks with a glint in her eye. I'm at a loss, but as I look over my shoulder at Baylor, I realize he has the same look.

"Oh, gross!" I whisper-yell, stomping away to mount Navi and leave them to their warmer memories.

In what seems like no time, we arrive at the Black Abyss, and as we crest the rise, I understand why it earns its name. We've approached from high above, granting us a perfect, dizzying view into its vast inky depths. The crack in the earth looks like a wound, as if some forgotten god tried to cleave the North from the rest of the kingdom, only to falter at the last critical moment. On either side, the ground is a blinding expanse of white, glittering under the sun—my first true sight of snow. It makes the Abyss' dark maw stand out with even more terrifying clarity. In the distance, a wide, stable bridge with spires reaching like impossibly slender fingers toward the sky, unlike anything I've ever seen in Merula, connects the two severed sections of the Pass.

I realize Baylor is hesitant to continue, and I look around, trying to glean why. The air is so crisp it almost burns my lungs, and the cold bites at my exposed skin. The silence here is unlike any silence I've known—not the hushed quiet of Merula's mountains, but something absolute, almost deafening. And then it hits me: this is the problem. It's too quiet. Too still. There's no movement near the bridge, no sign of life on the opposite side either.

Is that a good thing? Does it mean we've made it in time? Or are we too late, and Niko is already gone? My eyes strain, scanning the blinding white, searching for even a speck of movement, anything to tell me where he could be.

There isn't a single footprint marring the snow-covered ground, so perhaps there hasn't been a battle yet. Or perhaps the snow is fresh, a pristine blanket that has swallowed every sign of struggle. Shimmering stars! I curse my past self. I wish I had listened closer when Gryphon tried to teach me about tracking. I stupidly assumed he'd always be with me to do it.

"What took you all so long? I'm freezing my balls off." Niko's deep voice, a welcome rumble, jolts me from my thoughts of Gryphon and back to the present. My heart leaps, and for a wild second, I almost launch myself from the saddle. The impulse to shout my relief, to confess every confused, exhilarating emotion into the cold air, is overwhelming. But a flicker of self-preservation warns me: this isn't the place for such an admission.

The swirling emotions must be written on my face. As soon as our eyes connect, he rests his hand on the small of my back and whispers into my ear, "Datura." With that one word, everything is right in the world, even while we're standing at the gates of Freathia, moments from battle. Despite what's happening around us, we can both feel the shift happening between us.

"You're mistaken. You never had any to begin with," comes Gayle's retort, jolting us out of our moment.

I shake my head at them. For her to so casually converse with him about the state of his balls means they've spent way too much time together out on the road.

"As much as I'd love to see where this conversation is going, I believe there are more pressing matters at hand." Baylor motions toward the bridge, where little black dots move back and forth between each side.

"Not good," Gayle helpfully chimes in.

"I suppose it would've come down to a fight eventually. Better now than halfway up to the castle gates," Niko rationalizes.

"So we'll shift? And take them out? Easy." Gayle looks to Niko for confirmation.

"That would appear to be the easiest solution." He stops for a moment to think. "But then we'd have a hard time with the rest of the trek if it all melts. It's all ice. What if I just burn it down?"

"I would've thought you'd have a bit more control after all this time," Gayle says smugly. "I could still shift. I may be more useful that way."

"Yeah, that'll give us a leg-up. Sounds good."

At Niko's confirmation, Gayle prepares to shift. Baylor's eyes light, though he turns to give her more privacy. But it seems the Shifters are more comfortable with the process than the Fae are. I quickly grab the clothes she sheds and drop them in my pack.

"We need to push through quickly before more come. Who knows what Ombretta will throw our way since she's expecting us," Niko says as he checks all the weapons across his back.

Baylor ties the horses to a tree, in a spot where he's dug a small amount of grass out through the snow. Then, he pulls his bow out and nods. "I'll pick a few off before they notice we're already in position."

A part of me registers this stable master turned warrior, and that small part has to agree with Gayle's comment from earlier.

He looks toward her. "What, no warrior's goodbye?" he scoffs, and she has to stifle a laugh. The tension broken, Baylor heads off in search of a good vantage point.

I turn to Niko, my gaze expectant, waiting for instructions while Baylor positions himself above us. But Niko's focus is absolute, his eyes locked on the movement far below—perhaps deciphering patterns, or seeing threats my untrained eye completely misses.

We wait, the silence before the storm stretching taut. I try to count the moving dots, estimating there must be about forty figures. Forty against the four of us. Not good odds.

Then, a sudden, dark hail of arrows rains down from above. Even knowing Baylor is up there, I can't spot him. We take his volley as our cue, and Niko launches himself forward. Not straight toward The Pass, but down the sheer rock face. I follow, scrambling after him, hands finding purchase in invisible crevices as we descend in a reckless, controlled fall. Gayle, in her jaguar form, is a streak of spots beside us, faster than either of us could ever hope to be. We hit the bridge in a coordinated surge, just as Baylor's second volley of arrows finds its mark.

At first, our raid feels like a swift, decisive success. My strategy is simple: dealing with an immortal creature means kicking them straight over the bridge, into the Black Abyss. In the initial confusion, I dispose of a handful of Ancients this way, sending them plummeting into the darkness below.

But it only takes them moments to grasp my tactics. Their defense shifts, changing in a sudden, brutal wave.

I quickly realize that fighting Ancients is a far different beast than battling mortals or even sparring with Shifters.

Our outlook swiftly goes from grim to outright lethal. Gayle, a blur in her jaguar form, is now backed against the rock face, fighting off four Northmen simultaneously. Baylor, having exhausted his arrows, is a whirlwind of frantic swings, bruised and battered, his exhaustion evident in every wild arc of his blade. Niko, however, is still a force of nature. He moves with brutal efficiency, cutting down Northmen as if he's merely warming up.

The heat in his eyes changes from amber into pools of fire. He's made for this, and although he must take no joy in driving through Northman after Northman, he certainly looks good doing it.

I, with my uneven breaths and heavy feet, am hanging on by a thread. The Northmen seem to be aware of who I am and are therefore not aiming to kill, just capture. Which I appreciate at the moment, but if they succeed, I worry that whatever awaits me will be infinitely worse.

Chapter Thirty

I have to admit that the prospect of being taken has begun to look inevitable. The Northmen continue to drive us apart from each other, and while Niko tries to remain close, we now have an entire line of fighters between us.

The Northmen are terrifying, their Ancient blood allowing them to flicker around us in disorienting blurs. It seems their lineage also grants them tireless endurance, unlike mortals, Fae, or even Shifters. Their constant dizzying movement makes my head spin. A thought sparks: can I turn this relentless speed to my advantage?

I drop into a low crouch, one knee scraping the snow-dusted stone. Diving deep, I pull at the furious, burning power within me, gathering every spark until it ignites. The glow pulses, not seeking to heal, but to destroy. A Warrior's Peace Patton would be proud of. It pours down my arms, prickling in my fingertips and humming in my toes. This time, as I rise onto one foot, almost leaving the ground, with my broadsword held aloft, pointing outward, I spin. Faster and faster, both hands gripping the hilt, my blade a straight, unwavering line before me.

The light pulses, growing so intense I can no longer contain it. It explodes outward from my sword in blinding arcs, striking down any Ancient it touches. Their bodies disintegrate instantly, dissolving into fine, red-tinged dust as the light consumes them.

I spin until the power within me begins to wane, slipping like sand through my fingers. My rotation slows, my other foot dropping to steady me, my eyes struggling to refocus on the chaos. The full impact of my blow hits me then.

The pristine snow is now a canvas of thick, settling crimson dust, filling the air. The crisp scent of Freathia is gone, replaced by the choking smell of an old, forgotten tomb, mixed with the sharp, metallic tang of blood in a truly sickening way.

My new skill, this devastating Warrior's Peace that engulfs me, has annihilated about half of the remaining Northmen. Yet it feels like a small dent in the horde still surrounding us. Completely drained, my limbs heavy as lead, I barely manage to raise my sword as a blurring strike appears. My reaction is sluggish. The blow connects, but not full on. A searing pain blossoms, and a hot trail of blood streaks down my left arm where the brunt of the attack landed.

I hear Niko curse as he strikes several Northmen down in quick succession to move closer to me. Baylor, who's exhausted his arrows and has joined us, looks as if he'll fall any moment now to the warriors who come at him in twos and threes. Gayle's holding her own, but barely. She's still backed against the rock face, but now she uses this to her advantage, attacking like a caged animal.

Just as panic begins to prick at my senses, whispering of impending doom and a dark future as Ombretta's blood keg, a sharp whistle pierces the chaos. I know looking toward the sound would cost me, so I continue to block strike after relentless strike. But I notice some of the Ancients *do* look, and whatever they see causes their eyes to gleam with dark victory.

Shimmering stars, what now? How could this possibly get worse?

Behind me, the heavy thud of galloping paws vibrates through the stone. I risk a quick pivot, catching a glimpse of the massive white blur hurtling toward us. An Amarok, a white wolf, but far bigger. Its colossal size towering even over our horses, with a familiar rider sitting astride its back.

At first, the rider is just a silhouette against the snow. But then recognition slams into me—*stars help me!*

Thaddeus.

He raises his sword high, and I can tell his sights are set directly on Niko. Niko, who's right in front of me, has his back still turned to the approaching danger, unaware of this new threat.

He must hear the thunderous footfalls, growing closer with every second. I pray he also hears Thaddeus' deadly approach. Would it help or harm him if I scream his name?

Another Northman blurs into my vision. I lunge out of the way of an incapacitating blow and strike back with the last desperate surge of my strength, barely managing to deflect him. More Ancients continue to press in, their numbers overwhelming.

The last thing I see is Niko's horror-stricken face before I'm completely overtaken by Ancients.

The darkness clears, and the weight upon me lightens. I squint into the sun directly overhead. A hand is outstretched before me to help me up. I reach toward it, but can't quite make out if it's Niko or Baylor; the sun is too much in my eyes. I just see the outline of a slim, broad frame. Hair sticking out in thick braids.

His cold touch gives him away.

My hand breaks from his, and I fall back onto my ass. The snow-packed stone does nothing to break my fall. I scramble back on all fours, trying in vain to get away from the outline of Thaddeus. I come up against bodies strewn in my path. In my haste, I attempt to skirt around or climb over them. Inside, I'm cringing at the proximity of so much death.

Thaddeus raises his hands in surrender. And I hear Niko over his shoulder. "It's okay, Roe, he's with us. I think." I can hear the hesitation in his voice, as if he's still trying to decide.

I look from Thaddeus to Niko and then to our surroundings. Bloodstains splatter the snow, and big, hulking bodies are strewn across the bridge. In addition, a light film of red dust covers a circle surrounding where I fell.

Baylor limps closer. Gayle has returned to her human form and found her clothes again. The area around her mouth is stained red, which makes my stomach churn, even after seeing all the carnage before me.

Thaddeus reaches out a second time, his hand hovering, waiting. This time, I allow him to pull me to my feet, the quick movement jarring my still-reeling senses. Closer to eye level, I can finally take in what has changed since our last encounter—fighting against him for my life, desperate to avoid him dragging me to this very place.

His hair is still flawlessly twirled into thick twists, held away from his striking face with a wide headband. His skin glows, bronzed gold in the sun's harsh light. And his eyes. How could I have forgotten those pale, piercing green eyes? I used to dream about them.

Stars, no! The thought is a raw, visceral protest. *He tried to kidnap you! Get a grip! You've taken too many blows to the head in too short a time.*

But then I look closer, seeing what is truly before me, rather than the ghost of my memories. There's only one eye. The other is carefully, elegantly covered with a swath of rich, dark cloth. Only on *him* could a patched eye look even more striking, an Ancient-sophisticated look that chills me.

My stomach lurches as I remember why he wears that patch. It's my fault. I plunged a blade into his eye, desperate for survival. Not knowing where else to look after that sickening realization, my gaze drops to the snow-dusted ground.

"I'd like to help. If you'll let me." Thaddeus' words, smooth as river stones, draw my gaze back up. I study his face, every line and shadow, searching for the false notes, the tremor of deceit. I find none, either in his tone or his unblemished features.

"I suppose you just did," I manage, the words a raw rasp in my throat. "So, thank you." My lips purse on one side, a bitter, involuntary twist as I quickly weigh our impossible options.

Niko, it seems, has already made his decision. Without a word, he sheathes his blades, their metallic snick loud in the sudden quiet. He turns, his broad back a silent dismissal as he strides back in the direction from which we came.

"Niko?" Gayle voices my question as well.

"The horses," he calls over his shoulder, and Baylor limps to action, Gayle grabbing him under the arm to help him follow Niko.

With the others gone, Thaddeus turns toward me, apparently unsure where to begin. One would imagine that after riding in to save the day, he'd be on higher moral ground. But not really.

"I swear I didn't want to. I thought it was the right thing to do. But it wasn't. I know that now." He's looking at me straight on, his hands coming up as if he wants to touch me, but is afraid to.

"You thought bringing me against my will to someone who wants to redirect her torture to someone else was the right thing to do?" I spit each word like venom, but I'm too tired to tell if each bite hits its mark.

"I know." He worries his jawline with his hand, and keeps looking over my shoulder to where the others went after the horses. "We can talk more after. I just wanted you to know that I regret my actions. And I'm sorry."

He turns at their reappearance and returns to his Amarok. We all get back into our saddles, Niko having to help me up after several failed attempts of my own. His hands on my hips are strong and warm. Neither of which I feel on my own at the moment, so I gladly welcome him and pause in his arms before reaching for Navi's pommel.

Thaddeus doesn't miss this. Before he mounts his Amarok, his face falls and his shoulders slump. Did he truly have feelings for me, then? After all this time, I've convinced myself it was all for show, to make it easier for him to sway me to go with him. Now, though, I'm less sure.

Once Niko has helped me into the saddle, I look back and forth between them. Thaddeus, the bright, enigmatic flirt, and Niko, the brooding, tortured soul. Both men have made me feel things I didn't think possible. Both men hold pieces of my heart. Both men, in their ways, have taught me more about loving myself and becoming who I need to be for my kingdom.

We ride across the remainder of the bridge, the great expanse spanning the Black Abyss, and straight through the towering black iron gates of Freathia. The frigid air, a physical force pushing us across the bridge and through the formidable gates, is nothing compared to the cold, sinking dread in my stomach as I contemplate what awaits us. This isn't Merula's familiar bustling warmth; this is something stark and imposing.

"So we're just going to walk straight through the gates?" Gayle's whisper, low as it is, carries as she leans from her horse, riding close behind Navi. "Seems a bit like asking for trouble, doesn't it?"

Her words aren't quiet enough for an Ancient to miss. Thaddeus chimes in from ahead, surprisingly calm. "You've made it through the gates. Those who make it across the bridge are assumed part of Freathia."

My gaze drifts to the subtle bloodstains on my cream tunic, then to Gayle's, not-so-subtly spattered. Her lips are still vibrant crimson. My eyes sweep across the figures near the gate's entrance. No one seems to look at us. They nod or bow to Thaddeus, but their gazes slide right over us, as if we are thin air.

"Thaddeus," I say, a tremor in my voice, "it's one thing to be welcomed by your people, but they're looking right *through* us. Like they don't even see us."

"I've heard of this." Baylor's voice is hushed with awed respect as he looks at Thaddeus' back. "He's cloaking us. They're acting like they don't see us because they *can't*. It's a skill few Ancients master. And even fewer speak of."

Thaddeus turns his head, a slight nod acknowledging Baylor's observation, then returns his attention ahead of us. Now that Baylor has voiced it, I notice Thaddeus' movements are subtly stiffer, the effort of concentrating on our invisibility, while maintaining his facade for his people, clearly exhausting.

We stick to the deepest shadows we can find, a monumental challenge for a group of our size. We start and stop frequently, making way for those moving through the surprisingly busy streets. Freathia is a landscape of stark beauty and chilling contrasts. Layers of snow blanket the tops of the buildings, blending seamlessly with the gleaming white stone walls, making the structures appear as if they're carved from solid snow. They glisten almost blindingly as the sun catches and dances across their surfaces. Yet anything not draped in white is black as deepest night, the sleek, elegant design of the spires extending into every surrounding structure. It's cold, clean, and utterly alien compared to Merula's organic sprawl.

Thaddeus leads us down a quieter side street, where the crowd has thinned and the shadows' reach is further. He motions for Baylor to take the horses around to the stable across the way. The majestic Amarok leads the way, while Thaddeus guides the rest of us toward a building much like the others: dark, smooth stone walls adorned with glittering snow and sharp icicles, broken only by an intimidating, battered steel door.

Inside, Thaddeus closes the curtains, muffling the sounds around us, and promptly begins opening cupboards and pulling items out. He places a stack of plates on the table before us and then turns to pull out some bread and cheese.

The rest of us are all still standing in the doorway when Baylor opens the door and looks around. Without missing a beat, he pulls a chair out and sits at the table, and with a look, asks the rest of us why we're all still standing around.

As Thaddeus sets a warmed kettle before us and motions for us to dig in, we all join Baylor at the table. I'm reminded of Alasie's healing tea. If there ever was a time when we all needed to revive quickly, this is it, so I spoon leaves into the kettle and pour everyone a steaming cup.

We all dive into the food as if we haven't eaten in days, which I suppose is mostly the truth. It gives us a moment to rejuvenate. Out of the corner of my eye, I see Thaddeus pouring himself something from a pitcher he's set to the side. Before I can control my movements, my lips turn down into a grimace as I realize he's helping himself to a mug of blood.

He notices my reaction and shrugs, taking a sip and slowly wiping his lips, smiling at me as if he finds my reaction entertaining.

"How did you know where to find us, anyway?" Baylor asks in between too-big bites of bread and cheese.

"A siege on Freathia is hard to miss." Thaddeus looks entertained at the question. "But you're easy to find no matter where you go." He winks at Baylor, who stops chewing immediately.

As one, all eyes turn to Thaddeus.

"What do you mean?" Baylor says slowly, so we can understand each word around the food in his mouth.

"Remember that time I saved your life?" Thaddeus asks, leaning in, as if this next sentence will be a revelation. "You and I are connected now, forever."

A stunned silence settles around the room.

"You mean..." Baylor looks to the ceiling as if he's still trying to formulate what to say.

"Yes." I want to punch the smug look off Thaddeus' face. "You lived, but at what cost?"

Baylor's eyes narrow and his hands brace against the table, as if he's about to leap over it.

I quickly try to come up with a way to stop this inevitable confrontation, but I'm too shocked. Memories flash of the small, burning village, and how Thaddeus found me there. And the day flying with Niko, the way Ombretta found us deep in the Dread Forest.

Thankfully, Gayle can always think fast on her feet. "Boys." She puts her hands up, both placating and warning. "We can deal with the past later. What's done is done. We have a larger issue at hand. We need to figure out how to get into the castle."

That seems to work. The tension in the air fizzles to an insignificant hum.

"We have a few options, and we must move quickly. Ombretta has eyes everywhere, and someone will surely spot us before we reach her." Thaddeus looks around the table before continuing. "You need to know that she's different from you." His eyes travel toward Baylor, who must've suspected something from his comment earlier. "She's also like us."

Chapter Thirty-One

"So you did change her." I stand, knocking my chair down in my haste to rise. Even with warnings from Gayle and Niko, I'm incredulous that this is the case, that there's no hope for her. She's an Ancient now.

"No, Roe—Rowandine." His shoulders meet his ears as he remembers we are no longer on informal terms. "I mean, not intentionally. We, the Ancients, needed to keep her alive. After so much blood was taken, it had to be replenished somehow." His tone denotes that this was a simple conclusion to a simple problem. However, this changes everything.

"A Fae is hard enough to immobilize, let alone kill. But a Fae with Ancient blood coursing through her veins? She may as well be completely untouchable." Baylor's fury is clear in the low growl of his voice. "And I'm sure she's developed at least some of her Fae abilities?"

"She seems to have an affinity for air," Thaddeus says while looking at me.

"The contrasting elemental power to earth?" I ask, thinking of my abilities.

"Or complementary." Thaddeus shrugs at the connection.

I throw my hands up in defeat. "We may as well turn back now."

"Has she learned to shift yet? Or just wield the air around her?" Baylor asks pragmatically.

"She's just started wielding the air. She's not been able to transmute into a cloud form, *yet*." Thaddeus emphasizes his last word, clearly impressed with how far she's come already.

"A challenge." Niko's comforting rumble breaks in for the first time. "That is all. A mere challenge."

"Exactly." Gayle nods in agreement. "Hard is good." I can see the glow of anticipation alight in her eyes as she warms to the idea.

Thaddeus looks grateful for Niko and Gayle's readiness. "It won't be easy, but it *can* be done. And if we play it right, you'll still have the element of surprise on your side."

"So, where will we find her?" I look toward the window. This city is much larger than Merula, which I've counted as a blessing, because so far we've stayed hidden easily enough. But as we break out in search of Ombretta, it could prove to be more of a burden.

The tea's done its job, washing away everyone's weariness like a new rain. And after a night of back and forth, we finally agreed upon the plan. Now, we prepare for battle. Between the revitalizing tea and the promise of confrontation, the energy in the room is bursting at the seams.

Thaddeus provides Baylor with extra arrows and a mace. He lays out his impressive collection of blades and swords for Gayle and Niko to choose from as well.

He then looks from Niko to me and produces an intricately worked blade that seems to shimmer in the faint candlelight. "Pattern-welded steel. Forged in the belly of the North by layering Ancient iron and silver together, heated just enough to allow the two metals to bind, but not lose their properties." He holds it out toward Niko.

"The perfect weapon against one of both Fae and Ancient blood," Baylor says, trying to adjust his arrows and bow to make room for his new weapon.

Niko shakes his head and motions toward me. "It'll have to be Roe."

I grasp the blade, not missing the way Thaddeus cringes at Niko's casual use of my name and the way Niko smirks in response, even at such a significant moment as this. The blade weighs heavily in my grip, and the steel itself looks as if it could writhe to life in my hand. I add it to my belt while attempting to ignore the two males standing over me.

"Enough, you two. This is painful to watch," Gayle chimes in, and I give her a grateful glance.

"Okay, but why?" I ask. Thaddeus has shown he can't be trusted. "Why should we trust that you want to help us now?"

He recoils at my question but when he looks at me, his eyes are screaming for a way out. "She's too powerful. She has to die."

As the promise of a new day bleeds across the horizon, painting a stark landscape in muted grays, we set off. The streets are quieter now, though figures still move, possessing that sleepy, end-of-night air. I realize that the Ancients likely prefer the cloak of darkness for their true waking hours, using daylight to rest. And if the myths are true, the sunlight could even be harmful.

A sudden surge of worry for Thaddeus propels me forward as he moves to step out, and I instinctively shift to block the doorway. He pauses, looking at me with confusion, then follows my quick gaze to the brightening sky.

"That's sweet, Rowandine. It's nice to know you still care." A faint, amused smile plays on his lips. "But that particular myth is just that—a myth. While we prefer the dark because our sight is better, daylight is not harmful in the least." He steps out, unbothered, into the rising sun.

He leads us toward what could only be the North's crowning achievement: its impossibly tall castle. It rises from the landscape like a spear of black ice, its sleek form piercing the clouds, almost mirroring the jagged spires of the surrounding mountains in both its height and its sharp, deliberate lines.

"Behold the castle of the North. In all its iciness," Baylor breathes, his gaze tracking the colossal walls skyward.

"Ombretta's castle." Her name is a chilly whisper on my lips. "I never thought I'd see the day."

Its surface of polished black marble shines with an almost liquid sheen, as if buffed nightly with glistening lacquer, reflecting the pale light. The sheer abundance of glass and razor-sharp lines would be an obscene, jarring sight in Merula's organically flowing architecture. But here, it simply mimics the spearing mountains and the gaping maw of the Black Abyss we just crossed, belonging chillingly to this harsh, unyielding land.

Once again, the people on the street don't seem to register us. With our sun-kissed skin and visible cache of weapons, I would expect at least a flicker of attention.

"Thaddeus put the glamour in place again. Can you feel it?" Gayle whispers, leaning closer, her voice barely audible. I nod, recognizing the familiar, low hum of magic that now surrounds us. "Instead of a bunch of Fae and Shifters, they must see something more mundane, and less threatening, or maybe nothing at all."

Even the armored guards stationed at the thick black doors show no sign of alarm. It's proving to be a handy trick, and I almost say as much to Thaddeus. But then I glance sidelong at him, and notice a faint sheen of sweat around his temples—something I've never witnessed before. The glamour must be taking an immense toll, demanding every ounce of his concentration to maintain for this long.

We say little, the quiet tension thick, as Thaddeus leads us inside. He stops in a small, empty room just beyond the entrance. My guard snaps up immediately. The heavy doors slam shut behind us, and I jump, my heart lurching as the room plunges into absolute darkness. When he finally lights a small, flickering candle, the space is revealed to be entirely bare, a claustrophobic box of smooth, black stone. The sharp spike of panic I feel is mirrored in the wary faces of my companions. There is only one way in and out of the room, and Thaddeus stands, blocking the door.

Niko draws his sword, sensing danger. Gayle and Baylor follow suit. I turn to Thaddeus with my hand on my blade, hopeful that this is not his endgame.

"Easy, easy. I'm on your side, remember?" His fingers spread wide, arms outstretched as he takes a step back, knocking into the door behind him.

"I must've forgotten. You seem to regularly defect," Niko grumbles as he replaces his sword in its sheath, but refuses to take his eyes off of Thaddeus.

"Well? What is it, Thaddeus? Speak quickly," Gayle demands as she looks from Thaddeus to the closed door, clearly not as easily convinced.

"This is where we go our separate ways." Thaddeus' voice is smooth. Too smooth. He gives a nonchalant shrug in my direction. "I'm afraid I can't continue with you. It would ruin my reputation, you know, just in case things go south for you all." He offers a small, apologetic smile that doesn't reach his eyes. "I'll hold the glamour as long as I can so you can travel the halls without issue. You'll find Ombretta on the topmost level. I'll see you there, I'm sure. Good luck."

His gaze sweeps the bare room, a dismissive nod his only farewell, before the heavy door clangs shut behind him, plunging us into a deeper, more profound silence.

"What now?" Baylor drawls, the words echoing in the sudden uneasy void left by Thaddeus' departure. He looks as much at a loss as I feel.

"You heard him. Find our way up, I guess. Nothing's changed. He got us this far." My voice sounds far more confident than the tremor in my stomach. The chilling thought immediately springs to mind: what if Thaddeus just sold us out? Are we walking into an ambush?

Niko answers my unspoken fear, his gaze unwavering. "We'll just have to stay on guard. Our mission remains the same. We'll continue on our way to confront Ombretta." He turns to me, his eyes searching mine. "You good, Roe?"

Completely miserable, actually. "Fine. Ready. Let's go." I keep my reply clipped, afraid that if I allow another word, I'll lose my nerve and bolt back across the Black Abyss.

Thaddeus doesn't disappoint. The glamour holds, a shimmering cloak of invisibility, up to the very top of the spire. As we ascend, the hallways grow progressively narrower, and the air grows colder and stiller. It becomes starkly apparent that few people ever travel this far up. Ombretta, it seems, values her privacy above all else. Once the staircase constricts to a single-file path, we cease seeing guards, or anyone else for that matter.

The hair on my skin prickles the instant the glamour begins to wear off, right at the top of the last winding stair. Before us looms a set of dark, double doors made of heavy, unyielding metal, looking both impenetrable and impressively grand. The glamour fizzles off with the delicate sigh of a butterfly taking flight, leaving the surrounding air exposed and sharp.

She must have stronger wards up here. My gut clenches. Which means she probably knows we've arrived. I steel myself, dragging a quick, deep breath into my lungs, and stride forward. Ready to face a sister I have just learned of, and whom I wish I had been given more time to understand.

The heavy iron doors sting my palms with an icy bite when I press against them, as if the metal itself pulses with a ward meant to repel me, to keep the other Fae out. We step through, and the polished black marble floors, streaked with crimson veins, reflect my image at me—a distorted ghost. A dim hallway stretches ahead, lined with low-glowing torches that cast dancing shadows, leading to the only set of doors on this level: another oversized, ominous iron double door. Along the deep red walls, gilt-framed portraits hang in solemn rows, drawing my gaze, almost against my will.

The first one depicts jagged rock faces, violent crashing rapids, and behind them, two figures locked in a lovers' embrace, their forms silhouetted against the turmoil. It's a scene of clear strife, yet it holds a strange, undeniable beauty.

For Baylor, it seems to be something else entirely—a vision of triumph. He walks closer to it. A wide, almost reverent smile spreads across his face, his eyes gleaming with a kind of awed recognition. He traces the rough lines of the painting as if reading a forgotten saga.

The next portrait shows three figures, purposefully blurred, shrouded in mountain shadows but radiating a faint, hopeful glow, arms outstretched together, overlooking a wide expanse of land. The colors here are softer, less violent.

Gayle turns back and forth between the two sides of the hall, her brow furrowed in confusion, a hint of unease in her features as if the disparate emotions of the art unsettle her.

Along the opposite side of the hallway, the dark series continues. The first is a massive canvas, but it's almost impossible to decipher; all the colors swirl darkly around a lone, indistinct figure in the middle. It feels like a deep, consuming sorrow rendered in paint.

And then, the last painting. It depicts a single figure, luminous amid the darkness, with vast wings outstretched behind her under a star-strewn sky. A small circlet on her head pulses with white-hot fire, yet every other detail in the picture screams icy coldness, an ancient, devastating power. It's disturbing, mesmerizing, and evokes a feeling of profound, disquieting familiarity within me.

Niko's reaction is the strangest of all. His gaze is locked on this final, unsettling image. His eyes, usually unreadable, now hold a raw, dawning comprehension. He looks from the glowing figure to me, and back to the painting; his gaze a physical weight, pressing down. He squints as if trying to reconcile the two, a silent, significant question in the depths of his eyes.

I can't fathom what he sees in such a dark, disturbing image. The strange feeling presses against me, and the intensity of his stare makes me want to flee. I turn abruptly, barreling down the hallway to the next set of iron doors. This time, though, they open of their own accord. I shake off the strange premonition those paintings left—an uneasy echo of something I don't yet understand—and brace myself for what lies beyond.

The heavy doors swing open to reveal a vast, circular chamber that swallows sound and light. Its walls, open to the frigid Freathian sky, are framed by soaring, skeletal arches that hold up a colossal domed ceiling. Below, polished black marble floors stretch into a seemingly infinite expanse, catching the distant torchlight in their slick, obsidian depths, reflecting our distorted forms.

As I step across the threshold, a wave of unnatural warmth washes over me, a shocking contrast to the biting cold that should permeate this open tower at such a height. My gaze is immediately drawn to the center of the room, where a lone figure sits on a dais, upon a towering, ornate throne. Another figure stands silently beside it, a sentinel awaiting our approach.

My steps, heavy and hesitant, carry me toward the central presence, undoubtedly Ombretta.

The reassuring rasp of my blades against my belt accompanies each deliberate footfall, their familiar weight a cold comfort. Niko moves as a shadow to my left, while Baylor and Gayle flank me on the right, all of us advancing as a single, coiled unit.

Along the pathway leading up to the dais, massive, roaring fires burn in brazier-like structures, their heat radiating outward. A warmth blossoms at my neck, and I know then: my crystal is more perceptive than I dared to hope. Its glow spreads, a subtle warmth that infuses my veins, building a quiet strength and hardening my resolve.

With every step, the details of the woman on the throne sharpen. Her hair is a cascade of shining, midnight black, so dark it seems to absorb the meager light. A circlet, lit from within by an unearthly glow, rests upon her brow. But it's her eyes that hold me—midnight pools, impossibly deep and vast, delivering an icy, ancient stare that sparks a terrifying, undeniable familiarity within my soul.

I swear I've met that gaze before, not in life, but in dreams.

Chapter Thirty-Two

"Dear sister."

Ombretta's voice, silken yet sharp, fills the vast chamber. She tilts her head, a precise, almost mechanical gesture, as if sifting through long-forgotten memories before dismissing them with a flick. Her movements have a subtle, unnerving disjointedness, making her seem less human, more predator. She wears a gown of silk, the deepest, most violent red, its neckline plunging dramatically to reveal the expanse of her shoulders before diving toward her waist, where a thick leather swordbelt rests. She makes no move to stand, instead settling deeper into the throne, crossing one thin leg over the other with a languid, unbothered air.

So engrossed am I in trying to absorb every chilling detail of the woman before me, I've completely disregarded the figure standing silently at her side. But he clears his throat, a slight sound that nevertheless jolts me, and I'm startled to my core to see Thaddeus here, positioned like a loyal guard.

His single eye narrows, just slightly. I'm at a complete loss, unsure if the movement was meant to soothe or to warn, but in this instant, rage ignites within me, hot and blinding. He's crossed me for the last time. This has been a trap all along, his "help" merely an elaborate ruse. Ombretta must've simply grown impatient. The bitter realization hits me with the force of a physical blow: I've fallen for him, for his false kindness, yet again.

I believed him, because a naive, foolish part of me so desperately *wanted* him to be good.

But he's not. He's dangerous, and there's not enough hope in the realm to make him good.

I shake my head, still in disbelief of what's before us, but it can't be any plainer at this point. Whatever Thaddeus reads in my expression causes his good eye to go wide for just a moment before he's able to school his features once more.

Until now, my need to see the good in others has been for their benefit, for them to see that I can twist and bend myself to fit whatever they need. It made me weak.

Until now.

Now, I see that it will always get me where I need to be. Even though Thaddeus is playing for the wrong team, we still got up here with only a slight effort on our part. Now, he'll see that this was *his* mistake.

I square my shoulders and return my attention to Ombretta, who's waited patiently through this silent interaction, either allowing the knowledge that Thaddeus has been hers all along to sink in deep, or allowing Thaddeus to distract us while she takes our measure. I kick myself for giving her the advantage.

Ombretta, pleased by my reaction, grins widely. Danger sparks in her eyes. "Welcome to the North. My home." Her gaze swirls with a burning rage at her last word.

She takes me in, my traveling leathers and fur-lined top layers, and must find me lacking, because she sneers before she continues.

"It's been entirely too long. I'm so grateful you've made the journey. I've been hoping you'd visit one day." Her eerie tone doesn't match the inviting smile on her lips.

"Ombretta," I begin, but I'm suddenly not sure where to start. She's already made up her mind about me. "I came as soon as I found out you were here. I... no one told me. I didn't know I had a sister—a Fae sister."

She seems taken aback by this, although only briefly.

She tilts her head to one side, as if weighing what I've just said. "You didn't know? That while you lived the life of a doted-on mortal princess, I slowly wasted away my youth until I was almost nothing?" Plucking at her dress with her long, pointed nails, she seemed dissatisfied with what she's working with. She sneers again, as if what I said is completely unbelievable, and then recovers by smiling at me once more.

The smile is more terrifying. She looks hopeful and happy to see me. Although I can tell she'd gladly throw me over the ledge if given the chance.

"Almost nothing?" I ask, then bite my tongue, realizing too late that by asking about her near-death experience, I'm doing myself much more harm than good.

"Almost nothing. Almost dead. But, luckily for me, the blood of a Fae does things to an Ancient that can only be read about in books." She lifts her thick, manicured eyebrows knowingly. "And by that point, they'd already become so enraptured by my blood that the only option they had was to turn me. To give me their blood so I could remain immortal—just. Like. Them." She says this playfully, but the simmering rage beneath each word is clear. "I suppose they thought they'd create themselves an endless supply. Little did they know that by blending their Ancient blood with my Fae blood, it would allow me to rise with more strength and power than they could ever imagine. Under the rising moon on my first night, I crowned myself queen and haven't given them a drop since." She playfully touches Thaddeus' nose, making a mockery of his need and desire. "They hunger for more. That's why I sent Thaddeus for you."

"But now that I'm here, with your knowledge and strength, you could help me understand my powers. We could grow together." I want to make every attempt to connect with her, so I must start at the beginning.

"You know nothing of your powers?" She raises an eyebrow, watching me, gauging how truthful my words are.

Shooting stars. I guess all the cards have been laid bare now. "It's the truth. I'm only just beginning to understand them. I've only just learned the depth of our shared past. And I came hoping we could share the future we were meant to." Maybe, just maybe, she'd like that as much as I would. Maybe she's interested in what I have to say.

"Hmm," she purrs, "together?" She looks to the sky and taps her talon-like nails along her chin, pondering this option as a light breeze wraps around me.

"We could restore our parents' throne. Unite Everguard once again. We could rule, you and I—together."

I speak too fast, excited that she even wants to hear me out. Excited that she might agree. And at this moment, I'm certain that we can do this together. That perhaps deep down, she hoped against hope this was an option as well. I stumble, unsure of what else to say that will convince her.

"It's Hadeon. He's the one who's done so much damage. And he's gone now. If we could just figure out a way to work together, I know we could rally the remaining Fae, the Shifters. You'd have the Ancients at your back. We could awaken the forgotten races Hadeon silenced with his tyranny, forging a new dawn beneath the Fae moon."

She pauses in thought, only now scanning Gayle, Baylor, and Niko. Her gaze lingers on Niko a moment too long, but I will myself not to react.

Turning back to me, she says, "You paint a pretty picture, sister. Almost too good to be true, one would think."

"Our parents did it. Countless Fae before them held this realm together. We could learn. Together, we could figure it out. I know it. It's written among the stars. Surely you've seen it?"

Can she see this vision too? Have her waking hours been plagued with hopes and dreams of our future together as well? Every bone in my body wants to reach forward, to touch her, embrace her, to feel another of my blood. But something stills my hand.

The breeze around us begins to rise, and I'm thankful Gayle took the time to braid my hair back in the Shifter fashion, though the loose strands whip around my face. Ombretta continues to smile, but there's something else there. I can't put my finger on it, but a part of me refuses to move any closer.

"We could," she agrees, still tapping those dark talons against her chin. "I can see it. You. Me. The entire realm behind us. It all sounds quite hopeful."

I take a hesitant step closer, ready to embrace my sister and the life we'll build together.

Too late, I hear a warning grumble from Niko behind me. "Roe."

And then I am blasted backward by an unnatural gust of wind.

Baylor and Gayle rush to my side, and as they help me up, Niko takes up a defensive stance against Ombretta, drawing each of his swords, still beside me, not blocking me. Out of the corner of my eye, I see him nod when I plant my feet, ready for what's to come.

I look at Ombretta questioningly, completely taken off guard.

"As I said before: too pretty a picture. I've planned a different approach. One I'm sure will have a similar outcome nonetheless." She stands and throws her hands wide, encircling us in a whirlwind as she steps closer.

It's fitting that her gift would be air. The opposite of earth.

I ground myself as best I can before moving forward.

As I dare a step closer, that same warning comes from inside me. Whispers of danger wrap around me, urging me elsewhere. Unfortunately, there's nowhere else to go. This is my battle.

"We'll destroy the humans. That's for certain. Hadeon…" Ombretta looks at me, eyes alight. "Although by the sound of it, you've already taken care of Hadeon, so I must thank you. Killian, his heir, will fall, as will all those he loves. He'll know what it is to lose everything. Only then will he be given to the most evil Ancients among us. They'll drain him within inches of his life, allowing him to waste away to nothingness, all the while hanging on to life by a tiny thread. He'll know what it feels like to be left to those stronger than you. His castle will crumble until there's nothing left."

Her voice rises, as does the wind around us. The fires lining the walls begin to flicker, and I pray to the stars they don't go out.

"Then, the rest of the realm will look to the North to be put back together. And I, Ombretta, Queen of the North, will be there to guide the kingdom to greatness. So, yes. I have seen it. Damn the stars and your hope. Hope makes you weak."

"You?" I pause. "Alone?" Stars, they were all right. I hoped against hope that we'd do this together, but she just wants revenge for the life she was left to. There's no hope left within her.

"I don't need you. I don't need anybody." Her voice lowers, as if the rest is just an aside to herself. "As soon as I find that Fae grimoire, I'll be completely unstoppable."

She tightens the whirls of air surrounding us, leaving Niko, Baylor, and Gayle outside the circle along with Thaddeus, while only Ombretta and I remain within. My ears prick with awareness. She wants the book I have—our mother's book. Iolanthe said that in the wrong hands, it would be dangerous.

"I've gotten this far on my own, and done quite well, wouldn't you agree?" The bursts of wind lick at my heels, throwing me off balance and pushing me toward the ledge, but I stand my ground.

Is this her idea of what *quite well* looks like? She's completely alone in this world. Thaddeus stands by her side, but even he seems hesitant.

And then it hits me. And I smile.

I'm not alone. I have people at my back. Alone, we're one thing, but together, we're something else entirely. Even now, they are fighting to help me and keep me safe. People who have been with me from the very beginning and people I've met along the way. They've taken me under their wing and shown me what it's like to be loved. To be cared for. To sit together and bounce between deep conversation and complaining with me about the morning's training session or our rocky pillows. They've seen and nurtured my hopes rather than dampening them with truths or uneasiness.

This. This is what I'm fighting for. This is what it's all about.

Out of the corner of my eye, I see Niko struggling to get through the gusts and back into the circle. Gayle and Baylor hold him back, but they look to me with fear bright in their eyes. I wish with all my heart that they stay out of this. Away from the danger. I wish it with every fiber of my body.

Thaddeus looks surprised as well, as if this isn't how he thought everything would play out. Shivers run down my spine, and I'm not sure if it's because I'm imagining what Thaddeus and his Ancients would do to me if given the chance, or because the air has lost all its warmth.

Ombretta moves closer with her unnaturally smooth movements, and I realize I haven't even drawn my sword yet. I don't want to, but now it seems I have no choice. In one quick movement, I unsheathe it from my back while pulling a small blade from my belt with my other hand.

She doesn't even reach for weapons, and that alone puts the fear of the stars in me more than anything else could. She looks entertained at the idea that I'd attempt to fight her. And a small part of me agrees, wishing I could run and hide and let someone else finish this.

But there's no one else. The realm needs a Fae of the royal line. And if she's set on darkness and vengeance, then I have to be the light. I have to do this for the sake of the realm. For the sake of my family. Any other path leads further into darkness.

Firm in the choice I must make, I stand tall and wait for her wrath to descend.

Chapter Thirty-Three

She strikes first, with a dagger she pulls too quickly from her belt. It flies across the space between us, encouraged by sharp gusts, and grazes my thigh. Her eyes blaze as the metallic scent of my blood reaches her. She throws another blade, but this time I'm ready and deflect it, knocking it to the glassy marble floor with my dagger.

She straightens and, from beside her throne, pulls out a longsword of an impossible weight, swinging it around as easily as she throws her blades.

My burst of bravado dissolves with each step she takes, closing the distance between us. This is it: my final moment. It will be spent defending myself against my own flesh and blood. Not in the arms of a lover, or with my human sister, who gave everything up for a chance to come with me and do the right thing. Not with my best friend in the entire world, who gave his life for me. But here, parrying blow after blow from a sister I'll never have the chance to know. And yet I'm still too afraid to end it.

I brace for the impact of her sword.

"Roe!" Niko's face flashes in between tornadoes of air swirling around us, and I see the confidence on his face. He no longer looks worried for me; he looks like he's cheering me on. He's the reason I've come this far. I look at Gayle and Baylor, who've stopped fighting the wind and are watching Ombretta and me through the frozen gusts.

If she ends me, then everything we've fought for so far will be for nothing. The realm will not be reunited; Ombretta will only tear it apart piece by piece until she has her revenge on all she believes have wronged her.

In between gusts, I see the look on Thaddeus' face. It appears that he's torn as well. Perhaps he's playing both sides; perhaps he's leaning to ours. Either way, he's not the same wicked Ancient who tried to carry me off for his benefit, or even the selfish fool who led us all up here straight into her grasp, giving away nothing of her power or rage.

I realize that if there's a chance he could change, then maybe even the darkest of hearts can, too.

Just as a new seed of hope blooms within me, the short blade in my hand is knocked away, and the sudden heat of metal slices through my side and fills me with pain. A strong desire to crumple to the ground overcomes me, but I stand tall, reaching deep within myself for my light, calling on my ring to sharpen my power. Even though we're far from the ground below, the marble at our feet is of the earth. And I can feel the tingle reaching out toward me, tentatively at first, then growing, but slower this time. The ring flickers and fades even as I press my hand against the wound. I must be too far from my source. But I can call on enough of it to at least stop the gash from bleeding any further.

"Well, that's a handy trick, sister." Ombretta moves closer to inspect my side, wonder lighting her face. "That will be handy indeed for the future I have in mind for you." Her voice is a malicious purr that doesn't so much hint at my impending nightmare as guarantee it.

As she moves closer, I draw another blade. This one is noticeably heavier, and I look down to see it's the blade Thaddeus gave me, silver mixed with iron. A blade that could take down a Fae with Ancient blood coursing through her veins.

I use this small moment to reset myself. I focus my mind on all the skills Gayle pumped into me. I bring my broadsword across my body, saving the smaller blade for only if I truly need it, grasping it tightly in my left hand.

Ombretta steps backward, into the whirling wind surrounding her, and comes out on the other side. A loud cackle fills the air as she watches me struggle to find where she went. Suddenly, the air is moving in too many directions at once and lightning flashes across the sky. It's so close that a metallic taste lines my mouth. Panic rises as I look back and forth, unsure how long I can keep my feet anchored to the ground before I topple from the topmost tower and plummet to my death on the rocks below. I steal a glance at the river tearing across the south side of the tower, but instead of being a potential savior, it rips and curls in on itself, promising death.

Options flit through my mind. I'm desperate for solutions to outwit the tempest that threatens to tear me from my feet.

Fly. I have wings. I can fly out.

The crushing truth, however, is that I can't feel them. My well of power is bone dry, completely used up. I focus, trying to call my wings forth the same way I summon my healing, but nothing happens.

The frantic, all-consuming whirl of air around me is a deafening distraction. The hair along my arms prickles as I feel the air gathering once more, the pressure a heavy hand, ready to unleash another lightning strike. I squeeze my eyes shut against the storm, picturing myself, iridescent wings unfurled, lifting high off the ground.

The crystal.

Quickly, I sheath a blade so I can wrap my hand around the warm, smooth crystal at my neck, clutching it like the lifeline it is. Its warmth flows into me, a grounding anchor, and power surges once more.

And suddenly, I've done it. Cool, rushing air sweeps up under my nascent wings, expanding them, dissipating Ombretta's furious whirls. I try again to call on my healing magic, but it was spent long ago, and now I must focus if I'm to finish this.

Realizing I've somehow cheated her tempest, Ombretta snaps her head around, her eyes wide as she searches the room, unable to find me. Unable to comprehend that I could have the ability to fly.

Using her confusion as my sole advantage, I land soundlessly behind her, placing her squarely between myself and her vicious whirlwind. The wind whips furiously at my back, and the faint roar of rapids crashes far below us. I know that if I dare look down, I'll see only a dizzying, fatal plunge from the cliff face straight into the icy river coursing below.

She spins on her heel, a primal instinct, feeling my presence behind her. "Wings?" she howls, her tone a mix of fury and something else—disbelief? Jealousy? I almost laugh at the bizarre, twisted emotion in her voice. "You have wings?"

"We could learn a lot from each other, I think," I offer, extending one last, desperate olive branch, hoping against hope. "If you just give us a chance."

"It will never be." Her eyes blaze, utterly devoid of warmth. "I've seen how it's supposed to be. Only one of us will rule these lands. And that one will be me."

With those last chilling words, she lunges.

Too late, I realize she hasn't pounced for my body, but has expertly swiped her blade down my right wing. The searing pain that explodes through me is absolute, crippling, and I crash, helpless, to my knees.

I lean on my broadsword to keep me upright and hold the pattern-welded dagger out in front of me. If she comes any closer, I'll have to strike. For our realm, for our people, I *will* strike.

Victory blazes in Ombretta's eyes as she closes in on me, fangs elongated in anticipation, hungry for the hard-earned reward of Fae blood. *My* Fae blood.

Her arm raises, and the huge longsword she wields with terrifying ease rises high into the air. Our eyes lock, and slowly, deliberately, I lower my blade.

I can't do this. She's my sister, the only flesh and blood I have left in this world. We should be finding a way to knit ourselves back together, not tear each other apart.

I hold her gaze, and the hate and revenge glowing in her eyes flare high and bright, like dark twin flames. The blade slices down. Not for a killing blow, I realize, but a calculated strike to wound me enough to immobilize me for whatever dark plans she harbors.

Just before contact, her smooth, predatory movement twists into a sudden stagger, the sword clattering from her fingertips. It hits the polished floor with a sharp clank, spinning back into her raging gale, which begins to sputter and die.

As she moves closer, I see the arrow embedded deeply in her left shoulder. If it hadn't been for the winds, it would've been a direct, deadly shot.

My eyes dart across the dissipating maelstrom, finding Baylor, still poised, another arrow nocked, ready to strike. I shake my head, silently begging him not to loose it.

In those short, agonizing moments, Ombretta stumbles toward me. Anger and hate still blaze in her eyes, even more intensely now, but beneath, fissures of raw pain and profound loneliness crack through her guarded facade. I make my choice. I sheath the blade that would surely bring her death, and instead reach out, desperate to finally draw her into a tight embrace.

We'll heal together.

She moves into my arms, the contact a desperate comfort. But as her arms come around me, I feel a sharp, fiery stab between my shoulder blades, followed by an instant, sickening warmth dripping down my back. My one good wing twitches violently, spasming with sudden, unbearable agony. She backs away from me, her grasp releasing, letting me fall. The sneer twisting her face slices through me with a more violent pain than any blade.

"Emotions are such beautiful little playthings, don't you think?" She licks her knife, shuddering at the taste of my blood. She's a complete monster. Is my sister even in there any longer?

Tears prick at the corners of my eyes, and I can't tell if they're from pain or shock. My knees hit the shining marble with a force that makes my teeth clatter. Already exhausted, I have nothing left to give. Her strength and will are greater than my own. With each slowing breath, my head becomes cloudier and lighter.

Another arrow flies through the air and strikes Ombretta on her other shoulder, causing her to spin off balance. She lurches to the left. Her eyes meet mine, and it dawns on us both that there's nothing there to break her fall except the serrated rocks and icy waters below.

Realizing this, I grab for her with all the remaining energy I have, thinking there's time before she topples over the deadly ledge. Our hands meet, but she slips from my grasp. I flex my wings and scream in agony, remembering too late that one wing has a jagged rip through it. I can't compensate for our weight with a broken wing and a shoulder wound that screams at me with each movement I take. Unable to find my balance fast enough, I know I'll be following her right off this edge.

This sudden discovery kills me as surely as the rocks below will. This can't be my end. I didn't tell Baylor or Gayle how much they mean to me. I didn't tell Niko how I feel about him. What about all the people counting on me? What about the fate of Everguard?

But Gayle's words echo around me: *No one always has balance. You have to work for it.* And this—the realm, my sister, all of it—is worth working for. I just have to find the right balance. My balance.

Before I can surge forward, a strong hand grips my forearm, pulling me away from the edge and hugging me close. I fight, pounding my good fist against Niko's chest, trying to catch my sister.

Niko's grip is too tight, but with all my strength, I pull free. He moves forward but stops at the shake of my head, giving me the space I need, the trust I need. With one last look back at the man who will never know how much this final gesture means to me, I twist and aim my body straight down. In one clumsy move, I pull my wings in tight and begin my dive toward the deadly rocks, hoping against hope that they have one last surge of flight left in them.

Shadow and light dance across Ombretta's alabaster skin as she continues her sickening plunge. Her crimson dress, now a cascade of fabric and blood, streaks across her chest, neck, and face, as if she were bathing in it rather than wearing it. The silk billows around her like a pillowy cloud—a cloud that holds no promise of breaking her fall.

Almost there. I stretch out my hands, desperately clawing at the air, trying to grasp at something, anything, to save her. Finally, my fingers close around hers. Her hand, surprisingly strong, grips mine.

With all that's left of my fading strength, I try to haul us upward, but the tear in my wing is too severe. It buckles under the impossible weight, and we continue our plummet toward the earth. Panic, cold and sharp, swells within me as I realize there's nothing I can do. Ombretta struggles, her free hand flailing, searching for purchase, but there's only empty air.

Suddenly, claws wrap gently but firmly around my torso, yanking me upward, away from the angry river, now close enough to spit icy spray and promise frigid death. I cling to Ombretta, my fingers locked around hers, for as long as I possibly can. But between the jarring force yanking me back into the air and the blinding, wet spray, my grip loosens, inch by agonizing inch, until I can hold on no longer. She slips right through my fingertips, and I'm left frantically grasping at nothing but her memory.

My sister is swallowed by the churning river, lost forever to the darkness.

Chapter Thirty-Four

"Niko! Let me go!" I shout over the raging river below, and as my boots skim the water, an odd, tranquil sense of calm runs through me.

I look up at him, pleading. I shove against his claws, attempting to loosen his grip enough so I can slip out. I know I can find her, and then he can pull us up. But even in his dragon form, I can read his expression.

"I can do this. Trust me."

His eyes, surrounded by bright white scales, are filled with pain and fear. But he nods, almost imperceptibly, and his talons give a quick tightening, like a hug. Then he releases me, dropping me right above the icy river.

Needles of pain engulf my body. The frigid freshwater burns my nostrils and fills my throat as I fight for control in the chaotic plunge. The only thought in my mind is to hold on long enough to find her.

The current is a monstrous force, whipping and tearing at my body and wings. I try to retract them, but they've become useless, unresponsive appendages, and with each surging swirl of water, the river rips at them, making me feel every bend and break. The agony quickly dulls, turning into a searing numbness as the cold sets in; it's such a creeping, insidious chill that I almost prefer the pain.

Above, Niko continues swooping, a magnificent white blur, but his great wingspan is too vast for the sheer, unforgiving rock face of Ombretta's castle. Even if he wanted to, I don't think he could reach me.

A flash of crimson amid the churning black waters, a desperate splash of color, rips my attention back to the present. She's close, thank the stars. I dive under, knowing the vicious current will do most of the work, pulling me in her direction. But my wings drag, and with each forward motion, they snag and tear, causing my vision to go white as a searing pain erupts. I tread water for a moment, to allow the stars dancing across my vision to fade and to gauge what meager progress I've made.

Ombretta's red dress stands out like a single defiant rose in a drowned garden. She's less than six strokes away, but she's face down, motionless. Her once-flowing gown, now saturated, balloons around her, dragging her deeper. My boots are doing the same to me. I kick them off, feeling the sudden blessed lightness, then gulp several deep breaths, bracing myself. As I tread, I feel it: an unnatural, distinct pull from the water, a gentle, guiding force drawing me closer to her. A glow catches my eye, just beneath the surface—my ring. Unsure why it would blaze at a time like this, I ignore it and press on.

With huge, desperate strokes, I close the space between us, refusing to take my eyes off her for fear of losing her. The moment I scoop my arm around her torso, her immense, waterlogged weight pulls us both under. It's mostly the dress, I know, but there's no time.

"Ombretta, I'm here! I need you to use your arms!" I yell, the words torn by the roiling waves, but it's useless; she's dead weight. Yet a fierce certainty roots itself in my bones: if I can get her to shore, we'll both live. My light and her dark, destined to return our realm to greatness.

I concentrate on each stroke, each pull, but I can barely feel my arms and legs. What I do feel is heavy with numbness, streaked with blinding pain. I let the ferocious flow do most of the work, still angling our trajectory toward the sandy bank, but my vision blurs, fading in and out of black.

I can feel Niko frantic above us, but he's had to back off—each beat of his massive wings sends me under, disorienting me every time I resurface. It breaks me to have him so close, yet so agonizingly far. But I know I can do this, and he believes in me.

Except maybe I can't.

Even though I can see the shore, it refuses to draw closer. I'm relying solely on muscle memory because I can't feel my arms or legs anymore, and even that is failing. Panic rises, swelling in longer, darker waves than before. I look for Niko, but his shape is gone, swallowed by the blurring light. The crushing weight of Ombretta, the water we've both taken on, is too much. The thought of giving up is both impossible to comprehend and the only thing my exhausted mind can conjure. Even so, I keep going.

Until the rush of water becomes absolute. Until both Ombretta and I are utterly swallowed by the river.

Underwater, the world changes. My ring doesn't just glow—it flares, a brilliant beacon that pulses with my frantic heart. The deafening roar of the water transforms, not into a mere hum, but a soothing, resonant song that fills my very bones. Words—not truly words, but understanding—wrap us in a warm, protective cocoon. A sudden, profound realization settles over me: *This is what it would be like if I were like my mother. This is the elemental power of water.*

I float, weightless, Ombretta still tight in my grasp, as we drift, seemingly in a calm, shimmering bubble. I take deep, effortless breaths, the water around us like air, enjoying the incredible warmth shielding us from the river's icy grasp.

And then I realize: something is wrong. It *wasn't* warm a moment ago; it was so cold my body was numb. And I can *breathe*—underwater. I can't be dead, can I? Death surely wouldn't feel like this, at the bottom of a relentless deluge. I always pictured something softer. I imagined Gryphon being here.

As my toes brush against the squelchy riverbed, I instinctively angle my body, guiding us. The river, which a moment ago was a tempestuous torrent, is now gently guiding us, cradling us, pushing us softly toward shore. With the last, desperate surge of what remains of my strength, I pull Ombretta up, out of the water's embrace, and then crumple to my knees beside her on the damp sand. The instant I see her chest rise with a ragged breath, the adrenaline drains, and darkness dances across my vision.

"Rowandine, wake up."

A pale green gem blinks down at me, pleading for me to come around. The faint rhythm of water lapping on the shore matches the water meeting my fingertips, waking me from this nightmare. Except as my mind clears, I can see it's not a nightmare, but reality. It hurts too much—my body, Ombretta choosing revenge. I let my eyes shut and my mind drift again.

The scent of fire-roasted meat pulls me from the sweet darkness I've enveloped myself in. My stomach grumbles; the only part of me impatient for me to wake. But this time, the pull back to reality is too strong, and I reluctantly allow my memories to drift back in.

Finally making it to Freathia. Almost losing my friends to an army of Ancients. Thaddeus aiding us, then betraying us again. The wound of Ombretta's choice, still raw on my broken heart.

But we made it out of the river. Somehow.

Those memories are a blur of pain and rushing water. But flashes of Ombretta's crimson dress, her hand slipping from mine, and my fierce, primal determination to pull us both from the icy grip of the raging river surges back into focus.

Darkness tries to claim me again, but this time the crushing hopelessness is replaced by an unshakable sense of knowing we were safe, warm, and guided by the river.

A raspy groan tears from my lips as I force my body to sit up. Every muscle screams in protest, but I *have* to see—

"Careful now," rumbles a deep voice, one I've come to know so well.

Confused, I struggle to focus on my surroundings, half expecting to see Thaddeus and Ombretta. Instead, Niko is here, and he makes his way toward me, his powerful hands rubbing warmth back into my arms—a warmth I instantly appreciate. Away from the flickering fire, facing the setting sun, Gayle stands watch, rigid with tension. Down by the river, which now looks even darker and more deadly as the last rays of sun tinge the rapids red, Baylor tends to the horses.

How did we get the horses? How far downstream and away from Freathia did we make it? My mind races, but the lingering vigilance confirms we're still on high alert. My gaze searches instinctively for Gryphon, expecting to see him too, until the familiar ache in my heart reminds me he's gone for good.

A snag of red fabric, caught on a gnarled branch wound with a vine of moonflowers, flutters in the dusk breeze. Ombretta and that pale green eye rip back into my thoughts. "Where's…" The words catch in my throat; I'm unsure if they were ever really here.

"They're long gone," Niko answers, his voice devoid of emotion. "As soon as he knew you'd make it, he lifted Ombretta into his arms and vanished into a blur of shadow and wind."

They're gone. Off then, to tear the realm apart searching for a grimoire, the powerful artifact, left by our mother. A grimoire that's safely tucked into my pack, strapped to Navi's saddle.

"She's going to destroy everything in her path to find it." Baylor's voice drifts over, the solemn observation carried by the wind as he finishes with the horses and makes his way to the fire, leaving Gayle to keep watch. His thoughts I note, mirror my own.

"It's not a matter of *if*, but *when* she finds it." After seeing that look in Ombretta's eye, the determination to destroy me and anything else in her path to get what she wants, I'm certain she'll stop at nothing to exact her revenge. "We can't let her do it," I vow, a promise to keep Everguard and its people safe.

"We'll make a Warden out of you yet, Datura." Niko's eyes, glinting across the fire, dance with amusement and something deeper, something I now recognize. This is his purpose, after all. He and Gayle are keepers of the lost city. And the "something deeper" in his eyes? It's desire. Desire to keep this realm safe, desire for adventure, and a burning, undeniable desire for *me*.

I hold his gaze over the flickering flames, matching the unspoken heat in his stare. Baylor's sharp cough beside me breaks the spell, reminding us we're not alone, and that whatever's flaring between us—he can scent it. "I'll go relieve Gayle," he mutters, his footsteps receding, leaving a sudden, potent silence between Niko and me.

The physical heat of the dancing flames is nothing compared to the blazing, untamed fire that now burns between the two of us. The crackling fire casts shifting shadows that deepen the stark planes of his face, accentuating the passionate gleam in his eyes.

What I see there mirrors the storm in my own heart—fierce determination to protect, a hunger for the unknown, and an undeniable pull toward each other. This isn't just a flicker of attraction; it's the spark of a true beginning, recognized under the vast, starlit sky of a realm we both now vow to protect.

A realization settles deep within me: this is not the end, but the very beginning of my adventure.

Want to know what happens next?
Join Scarlett M. Honey's mailing list at **scarlettmhoney.com/subscribe** *to be the first to hear details about book 3!*

If this story sparked a fire in your heart, please consider leaving a review on Amazon or Goodreads—it truly fuels my magic! Thank you.

Acknowledgments

This book was a special one to write, largely because the theme of sisterhood has become so important in my life. Support, understanding, and a generous sprinkle of fun truly make the world go 'round—and I'm thankful for all of you who prove it.

I'm so incredibly grateful to everyone who's been supportive of my Crown of Everguard series, from my friends at work who bring me copies to sign to the fans at events who peek around corners and can't wait to come chat with me at my table.

Of course, this book wouldn't be the polished gem that it is without some very important people. A HUGE thank you to Claire Bradshaw, whose eagle eye worked magic across my manuscript, and was so thorough and patient throughout the process.

The cover for *Beneath the Fae Moon's Fire* still makes me tear up every time I see it. My deepest thanks for this stunning piece of artwork go to Jemima and Louise at INK Designs.

Another big thanks to my fellow mamas in the Moms Who Write group, a true sisterhood. This group is a wealth of knowledge and full of the most amazing mamas on their own author journeys.

A big thank you to all those who supported my Kickstarter project, this was such a fun way to bring book 2 into the world! Your enthusiasm and love for *Beneath the Fae Moon's Fire* means the world! Thank you Wrightly, Joanne Almonte Mason, Carrington Beasley, Rebecca O'Neill, MaryLynne Schaefer, Valerie Perdue, Emily Yuyuenyongwatana, Patricia Reed, Kari Kilgore, Erica Rue, Carolyn McCormick, Samantha Newberry, Courtney Gittins, Terry Corle, R.S. Kellogg, Caroline Leblond, Laura Nelson, Ashley Reed, Jamie Kahler, Nikki, Bly, Chelsea Rogers, Sonya M, Sarah Maier, and Mari Ann Caudill.

A million thanks to my beta readers and my ride or dies, whose feedback made this book what it is. Thank you, Patricia Reed, Carrington Beasley, Joanne Almonte Mason, Terry Corle, Rachel Dailey, MaryLynne Schaefer, Kate Stavish, and Brooke Shetler for reading this book in its rawest form and taking time to give feedback and add your thoughts to make this book what it is today.

My parents are my biggest cheerleaders. They both instilled such a love of reading in me from the start, with memories of Little *House in the Big Woods* and *Anne of Green Gables*. They love learning about the process and have cheered me on every step of the way. My mom even volunteered to beta read this time, thoughtfully pointing out where she'd like to know more (and labeling parts "one sentence too far for your mother," which gave me a good kick!). And a big thanks to my siblings, Ashley, Wrightly, and Carrington, who from the very beginning, leaned in to all our imagination fun growing up.

My endless thanks to my fabulous husband and partner in life, Bryce. He's the one who shuffles the kids from soccer to cheer to softball while I spend a Saturday or two at a book signing. He believes in all my wild ideas—like custom blend tea we named Fae Moon & Shifter Fire—no questions asked and continues to support every step of this journey.

To my kiddos, who enjoy a good snuggle while I'm writing. And who know bringing me their latest read is a sure way to get me to put my computer down!

About the Author

Scarlett M. Honey is a dreamer, a writer, and teacher. After years of nurturing young minds, she decided to pursue her passion for storytelling. As a lifelong lover of fantasy and romance, Scarlett has always been captivated by the magic of happily ever after. After years of weaving tales in her mind amidst the chaos of diaper changes and meal planning, she finally brought her dreams to life with her debut novel, *Fae Queen Rising*.

When she's not lost in the worlds of her imagination, Scarlett enjoys embarking on adventures with her family, curling up with a good book by a crackling fire, or attempting to master the elusive yoga handstand. With a heart full of dreams and a pen in hand, she invites you to join her on a journey through enchanting realms and unforgettable love stories.

Connect with Scarlett on the web at www.scarlettmhoney.com.

www.ingramcontent.com/pod-product-compliance
Lightning Source LLC
LaVergne TN
LVHW091710070526
838199LV00050B/2341